ORBIT 5

DAMON KNIGHT'S

ORBIT 5

The Best All New
Science Fiction of the Year

G. P. Putnam's Sons   New York

PRINTED IN THE UNITED STATES OF AMERICA

CONTENTS

Somerset Dreams

by Kate Wilhelm

I am alone in my mother's house, listening to the ghosts who live here now, studying the shadowed features of the moon that is incredibly white in a milky sky. It is easier to believe that it is a face lined with care, than to accept mountains and craters. There a nose, long and beaked, there a mouth, dark, partially open. A broad creased forehead . . . They say that children believe the sun and moon follow them about. Not only children . . . Why just a face? Where is the rest of the body? Submerged in an ethereal fluid that deceives one into believing it does not exist? Only when this captive body comes into view, stirring the waters, clouding them, does one realize that space is not empty at all. When the moon passes, and the sky clears once more, the other lights are still there. Other faces at incredible distances? I wonder what the bodies of such brilliant swimmers must be like . . . But I turn my gaze from the moon, feeling now the hypnotic spell, wrenching free of it.

The yard has turned silvery and lovely although it is not a lovely place any more. Below the rustlings in the house I hear the water of Cobb's Run rippling softly, breaking on the remains of an old dam. It will be cool by the flowing water, I think, and I pull on shorts and a blouse. I wonder how many others are out in the moonlight. I know there are some. Does anyone sleep peacefully in Somerset now? I would like to wander out by the brook with nothing on, but even to think of it makes me smile. Someone would see me, and by morning there would be stories of a young naked woman, and by noon

7

the naked woman would be a ghost pointing here and there. By evening old Mr. Larson, or Miss Louise, would be dead. Each is waiting only for the sign that it is time.

I anoint myself with insect repellent. It is guaranteed to be odorless, but I can smell it anyway, and can feel it, greaseless and very wet, on my arms and legs.

I slip from the house where my mother and father are sleeping. The night is still hot, our house doesn't cool off until almost morning, and there is no wind at all, only the moon that fills the sky. Someone is giggling in the yard and I shush her, too close to the house, to Mother's windows on the second floor. We race down the path to the pool made by damming the run and we jump into the silversheened water. Someone grabs my ankle and I hold my breath and wrestle under the surface with one of the boys. I can't tell which one it is. Now and then someone lets a shriek escape and we are motionless, afraid Father will appear and order us out. We play in the water at least an hour, until the wind starts and blows the mosquitoes away, and then we stumble over the rocks and out to the grass where now the night is cool and we are pleasantly tired and ready for sleep. When I get back to the house I see the door closing and I stop, holding my breath. I listen as hard as I can, and finally hear the tread on the steps: Father, going back to bed.

I slip on sandals and pick up my cigarettes and lighter without turning on the light. The moonlight is enough. In the hall I pause outside the door of my parents' room, and then go down the stairs. I don't need a light in this house, even after a year's absence. The whole downstairs is wide open, the kitchen door, the front door, all the windows. Only the screens are between me and the world. I think of the barred windows of my 87th Street apartment and smile again, and think how good to be free and home once more. The night air is still and warm, perfumed with grass and phlox and the rambling rose on the garage trellis. I had forgotten how much stronger the fragrance is at night. The mosquitoes are whining about my face, but they don't land on me. The path has grown up now with weeds and volunteer columbines and snap-

8

dragons. By day it is an unruly strip with splashes of brilliant colors, now it is silver and grey and dark red.

At the creek I find a smooth rock and sit on it, not thinking, watching the light change on the moving water, and when the wind starts to blow, I think it must be three in the morning. I return to the unquiet house and go to bed, and this time I am able to fall asleep.

I walk to town, remembering how I used to skip, or ride my bike on the sidewalks that were large limestone slabs, as slick as polished marble when they were wet. I am bemused by the tilted slabs, thinking of the ground below shoving and trying to rid itself of their weight. I am more bemused by myself; I detest people who assign anthropomorphic concepts to nature. I don't do it anywhere but here in Somerset. I wear a shift to town, observing the customs even now. After high school, girls no longer wore shorts, or pants, in town.

I have been counting: seven closed-up houses on First Street. Our house is at the far end of First Street, one ninth of a mile from the other end of town where Magnolia Avenue starts up the mountain as Highway 590. All the side streets are named for flowers. I pass Wisteria Avenue and see that the wicker furniture is still on the porch of Sagamore House. The apple trees are still there, gnarled, like the hands of men so old that they are curling in on themselves, no longer able to reach for the world, no longer desiring the world. I come back every year, and every year I am surprised to see that some things are unchanged. The four apple trees in the yard of the Sagamore House are important to me; I am always afraid that this year they will have been cut down or felled by one of the tornadoes that now and again roar like express trains from the southwest, to die in the mountains beyond the town.

How matter-of-factly we accepted the long, hot, dry summers, the soul-killing winters, the droughts, the tornadoes, the blizzards. The worst weather in any part of the country is equalled in Somerset. We accept it as normal.

I am not certain why the apple trees are so important. In the early spring, tempted by a hot sun into folly, they bloom

9

prematurely year after year, and are like torches of white light. There is always a late frost that turns them black, and then they are just trees, growing more and more crooked, producing scant fruit, lovely to climb, however.

In Mr. Larson's store where I buy my groceries when I am home I learn from Agnes McCombs that a station wagon and two cars have arrived early this morning with students and a doctor from Harvard. Agnes leaves and I say good-by absently. I am thinking of yet another rite of passage that took place here, in old Mr. Larson's store when I was thirteen. He always handed out chunks of "homemade baloney" to the children while their mothers shopped, but that day, with the tidbit extended, he regarded me with twinkling eyes and withdrew the meat impaled on a two-pronged fork. "Mebbe you'd like a coke, Miss Janet?"

He is so old, eighty, ninety. I used to think he was a hundred then, and he changes little. His hands are like the apple trees. I ask him, "Why are they here? What are they doing?"

"Didn't say. Good to see you home again, Janet. The old house need any repairs?"

"Everything's fine. Why'd Miss Dorothea let them in?"

"Money. Been six, seven years since anyone's put up at the Sagamore. Taxes don't go down much, you know."

I can't explain the fury that is threatening to explode within me, erupting to the surface as tears, or a fishwife's scolding. Mr. Larson nods. "We figured that mebbe you could sidle up to 'em. Find out what they're up to." He rummages under the counter and brings out a letter. "From your dad," he says, peering at the return address. "He still thriving?"

"About the same. I visited him last month. I guess he thought of things he forgot to tell me and put them in a letter."

Mr. Larson shakes his head sadly. "A fine man, your dad." After a moment, he adds, "Could be for the best, I reckon."

I know what he means, that without Mother, with the town like it is, with his only child a woman nearing thirty . . . But he doesn't know what Father is like or he couldn't say that. I finish my shopping and greet Poor Haddie who is back with the truck. He's been making his delivery to the Sagamore

House. He will bring my things later. Leaving, I try to say to myself Haddie without the Poor and the word sounds naked, the name of a stranger, not of the lumbering delivery "boy" I have known all my life.

I have other visits to make. Dr. Warren's shingle needs a bit of paint, I note as I enter his house. He doesn't really practice now, although people talk to him about their sore throats and their aches and pains, and now and again he suggests that this or that might help. If they get really ill, they go to Hawley, twenty-eight miles away, over the mountain. Dr. Warren never fails to warn me that the world isn't ready for a lady doctor, and I still try to tell him that I am probably one of the highest-paid anesthesiologists in the world, but he forgets in the intervening year. I always end up listening to advice about sticking with nursing where a woman is really accepted. Dr. Warren delivered me back there at the house in the upstairs bedroom, with my father assisting gravely, although later he broke down and cried like a baby himself, or so Dr. Warren said. I suspect he did.

Dr. Warren and his wife Norma make a fuss over me and tears are standing in my eyes as they serve me coffee with cream so thick that it has to be scooped up in a spoon. They too seem to think I will find out what the flatland foreigners want with our town.

Sagamore House. I try to see it again with the eyes of my childhood: romantic, forbidding, magnificent, with heavy drapes and massive, ornately-carved furniture. I have a snapshot memory of crawling among the clawed feet, staring eye to eye at the lions and gargoyles and sticking out my tongue at them. The hotel has shrunk, the magic paled and the castle become merely a three-storied, wooden building, with cupolas and many chimneys and gables, grey, like everything else in the town. Only the apple trees on the wide velvety lawn are still magic. I enter by the back door and surprise Miss Dorothea and Miss Annie who are bustling about with an air of frantic haste.

There are cries and real tears and many pats and kisses, and the inevitable coffee, and then I am seated at the long

11

work table with a colander of unshelled peas in my lap, and a pan for them.

". . . and they said it wasn't possible to send the bus any more. Not twenty-eight miles each way twice a day. And you can't argue with that since no one's done a thing about the road in four years and it's getting so dangerous that . . ."

A cul-de-sac, I am thinking, listening first to Dorothea and then to Annie, and sometimes both together. Somerset used to be the link between Hawley and Jefferson, but a dam was built on the river and the bridge was inundated, and now Somerset lies dying in a cul-de-sac. I say the word again and again to myself, liking it very much, thinking what a wonderful word it is, so mysterious, so full of meanings, layers and layers of meanings. . . .

I know they want to hear about my father, but won't ask, so I tell them that I saw him last month and that he is about the same. And the subject changes briskly, back to the departure of the last four families with school-age children.

The door from the lobby is pushed open and the Harvard doctor steps inside the kitchen. I don't like him. I can't decide if it is actually hatred, or simple dislike, but I wish he were not here, that he had stayed at Harvard. He is fortyish, pink and paunchy, with soft pink hands, and thin brown hair. I suspect that he whines when he doesn't get his way.

"Miss Dorothea, I wonder if you can tell me where the boys can rent a boat, and buy fishing things?" It registers on him that he doesn't know me and he stares pointedly.

I say, "I'm Janet Matthews."

"Oh, do you live here, too?"

Manners of a pig, I think, and I nod. "At the end of First Street. The big white house that's afloat in a sea of weeds."

He has trouble fitting me into his list of characters. He introduces himself after a long pause while he puckers his forehead and purses his lips. I am proud of Dorothea and Annie for leaving him alone to flounder. I know it is an effort for them. He says, "I am Doctor Staunton."

"Medical doctor."

"No." He starts to turn back toward the door and I stop him again.

"What is your doctorate, Doctor Staunton?"

I can almost hear the gasp from Dorothea, although no sound issues.

"Psychology," he says, and clearly he is in a bad temper now. He doesn't wait for any more questions, or the answer to his question to Dorothea.

I go back to shelling the peas and Annie rolls out her pie-crust and Dorothea turns her attention back to the Newburg sauce that she hasn't stopped stirring once. A giggle comes from Annie, and we all ignore it. Presently the peas are finished and I leave to continue my walk through the town, gradually making my way home, stopping to visit several other people on the way. Decay and death are spreading in Somerset, like a disease that starts very slowly, in a hidden place, and emerges only when it is assured of absolute success in the destruction of the host.

The afternoon is very hot and still, and I try to sleep, but give it up after fifteen minutes. I think of the canoe that we used to keep in the garage, and I think of the lake that is a mile away, and presently I am wrestling with the car carriers, and then getting the canoe hoisted up, scratching the finish on the car.

I float down the river in silence, surprising a beaver and three or four frolicking otters; I see a covey of quail rise with an absurd noise like a herd of horses. A fish jumps, almost landing in the canoe. I have sneaked out alone, determined this time to take the rapids, with no audience, no one to applaud my success, or to stand in fearful silence and watch me fail. The current becomes swifter and I can hear the muted roar, still far ahead, but it seems that any chances to change my mind are flashing by too fast to be seized now, and I know that I am afraid, terribly afraid of the white water and the rocks and sharp pitches and deceptive pools that suck and suck in a never-ending circle of death. I want to shoot the rapids, and I am so afraid. The roar grows and it is all there is, and now the current is an express belt, carrying me along on its surface with no side eddies or curves. It goes straight to the rocks. I can't turn the canoe. At the last minute I jump out and swim desperately away from the band of swift water, and I am crying and blinded by my tears and I find my way to shore by the feel of the current. I scrape my knees on a rock and stand up and walk from the river to fall face-down in the weeds that line the banks. The canoe is lost, and I won't tell anyone what has happened. The following summer he buys another canoe, but I never try the rapids again.

And now there are no more rapids. Only a placid lake with muddy shores and thick water at this end, dark with algae and water hyacinths. I am so hot after getting the canoe on the car, and the air is so heavy that it feels ominous. A storm will come up, I decide. It excites me and I know that I want to be at home when the wind blows. I want to watch the ash tree in the wind, and following the thought, I realize that I want to see the ash tree blown down. This shocks me. It is so childish. Have I ever admitted to anyone, to myself even, why I come back each summer? I can't help myself. I am fascinated by death, I suppose. Daily at the hospital I administer death in small doses, controlled death, temporary death. I am compelled to come home because here too is death. It is like being drawn to the bedside of a loved one that you know is dying, and being at once awed and frightened, and curious about what death is like ultimately. We try so hard to hide the curiosity from the others, the strangers. And that is why I hate the Harvard doctor so much: he is intruding in a family matter. This is our death, not his, to watch and to weep over and mourn. I know that somehow he has learned of this death and it is that which has drawn him, just as it draws me, and I refuse him the right to partake of our sorrow, to test our grief, to measure our loss.

The storm hangs over the horizon out of sight. The change in air pressure depresses me, and the sullen heat, and the un-kempt yard, and the empty house that nevertheless rustles with unseen life. Finally I take the letter from Father from my pocket and open it. I don't weep over his letters any longer, but the memory of the paroxysms of the past fills me

14

with the aftertaste of tears as I stare at the childish scrawl: large, ungraceful letters, carefully traced and shaky, formed with too much pressure so that the paper is pierced here and there, the back of the sheet like Braille.

It is brief and inane, as I have known it would be; a cry for release from Them, a prayer to an unhearing child who has become a god, or at least a parent, for forgiveness. Statistics: every year fifty thousand are killed, and she was one of them, and 1.9 million are disabled, and he was one of them. Do all the disabled bear this load of guilt that consumes him daily? He is Prometheus, his bed the rock, his guilt the devouring eagles. The gods wear white coats, and carry magic wands with which they renew him nightly so that he may die by day.

Why doesn't the storm come?

I wait for the storm and don't go down to the lake after all. Another day, I tell myself, and leave the canoe on the car top. I mix a gin and tonic and wander with it to the back yard where nothing moves now. I stare up at the ash tree; it has grown so high and straight in the twenty years since we planted it. I remember the lightning that shredded the cherry tree that once stood there, the splinters of white wood that I picked up all over the yard afterward. The following week Father brought home the tiny ash stick and very solemnly we planted it in the same spot. I cried because it wasn't another cherry tree. I smile, recalling my tears and the tantrum, and the near ritual of the tree planting. At eight I was too old for the tears and the tantrum, but neither Father nor Mother objected. I sit in the yard, letting the past glide in and out of my mind without trying to stop the flow.

At six I dress for dinner with Dr. Warren and Norma. This is our new ritual. My first evening home I dine with the doctor and his wife. They are very lonely, I suspect, although neither says so. I walk through the quiet town as it dozes in the evening, the few occupied houses tightly shaded and closed against the heat. Norma has had air-conditioning installed years ago and her house chills me when I first enter. She ushers me to the far side, to a glassed porch that is walled with vines and coleus plants with yellow, red, white leaves, and a funny little fountain that has blue-tinted water splashing over large enameled clam shells. I hesitate at the doorway to the porch. Dr. Staunton is there, holding a glass of Norma's special summer drink which contains lime juice, rum, honey, soda water, and God knows what else. He is speaking very earnestly to Dr. Warren, and both rise when they see me.

"Miss Matthews, how nice to see you again." Dr. Staunton bows slightly, and Dr. Warren pulls a wicker chair closer to his own for me. He hands me a glass.

"Edgar has been telling me about the research he's doing up here with the boys," Dr. Warren says.

Edgar? I nod, and sip the drink.

"I really was asking Blair for his assistance," Edgar Staunton says, smiling, but not on the inside. I wonder if he ever smiles on the inside.

Blair. I glance at Dr. Warren, who will forever be Dr. Warren to me, and wonder at the easy familiarity. Has he been so lonesome that he succumbed to the first outsider who came in and treated him like a doctor and asked for help?

"What is your research, Dr. Staunton?" I ask.

He doesn't tell me to use his first name. He says, "I brought some of my graduate students who are interested in the study of dreams, and we are using your town as a more or less controlled environment. I was wondering if some of the local people might like to participate, also."

Vampire, I thought. Sleeping by day, manning the electroencephalograph by night, guarding the electrodes, reading the pen tracings, sucking out the inner life of the volunteers, feeding on the wishes and fears . . .

"How exactly does one go about doing dream research?" I ask.

"What we would like from your townspeople is a simple record of the dreams they recall on awakening. Before they even get up, or stir much at all, we'd like for them to jot down what they remember of the dreams they've had during the night. We don't want them to sign them, or indicate in any

16

way whose dreams they are, you understand. We aren't trying to analyze anyone, just sample the dreams."

I nod, and turn my attention to the splashing water in the fountain. "I thought they used machines, or something. . . ."

I can hear the slight edge in his voice again as he says, "On the student volunteers only, or others who volunteer for that kind of experimentation. Would you be interested in participating, Miss Matthews?"

"I don't know. I might be. Just what do you mean by controlled environment?"

"The stimuli are extremely limited by the conditions of the town, its lack of sensory variety, the absence of television or movies, its isolation from any of the influences of a metropolitan cultural center. The stimuli presented to the volunteers will be almost exactly the same as those experienced by the inhabitants of the town. . . ."

"Why, Dr. Staunton, we have television here, and there are movie houses in Hawley, and even summer concerts." Norma stands in the doorway holding a tray of thumbnail-sized biscuits filled with savory sausage, and her blue eyes snap indignantly as she turns from the psychologist to her husband who is quietly regarding the Harvard doctor.

"Yes, but I understand that the reception is very poor and you are limited to two channels, which few bother to watch."

"When there's something on worthwhile to watch, we tune in, but we haven't allowed ourselves to become addicted to it," Norma says.

I wish Norma could have waited another minute or two before stopping him, but there will be time, through dinner, after dinner. We will return to his research. I take one of the pastries and watch Staunton and Dr. Warren, and listen to the talk that has now turned to the value of the dam on the river, and the growth in tourism at the far end of the valley, and the stagnation at this end. Staunton knows about it all. I wonder if he has had a computer search out just the right spot for his studies, find just the right-sized town, with the correct number of people, and the appropriate kind of eliciting stimuli. There are only twenty-two families in the town now,

17

a total population of forty-one, counting me. Probably he can get five or six of them to help him, and with eight students, that would be a fair sample. For what, I don't know.

I listen again to the Harvard doctor. "I wasn't certain that your townspeople would even speak to us, from what I'd heard about the suspicions of rural villages and the like."

"How ridiculous," Norma says.

"Yes, so I am learning. I must say the reception we have received has heartened me tremendously."

I smile into my drink, and I know that he will find everyone very friendly, ready to say good morning, good afternoon, how're things, nice weather. Wait until he tries to draw them into reporting dreams, I tell myself. I know Dr. Warren is thinking this too, but neither of us says anything.

"I would like your help in particular, Blair," Edgar says, smiling very openly now. "And yours, Norma." I swallow some of the ice and watch Norma over the rim of the glass. She is terribly polite now, with such a sweet smile on her pretty face, and her eyes so calm and friendly.

"Really, Doctor Staunton? I can't imagine why? I mean, I never seem to recall anything I dream no matter how hard I try." Norma realizes that the tray is not being passed around, and she picks it up and invites Staunton to help himself.

"That's the beauty of this project," Staunton says, holding one of the tiny biscuits almost to his lips. "Most people say the same thing, and then they find out that they really do dream, quite a lot in fact, and that if they try to remember before they get out of bed, why, they can recapture most of it." He pops the biscuit into his mouth and touches his fingertips to the napkin spread on his knees.

"But, Doctor Staunton, I don't dream," Norma says, even more friendly than before, urging another of the biscuits on him, smiling at him. He really shouldn't have called her Norma.

"But everybody dreams. . . ."

"Oh, is that what your books teach? How strange of them." Norma notices that our glasses are almost empty, and excuses herself, to return in a moment with the pitcher.

18

Dr. Warren has said nothing during the exchange between Norma and Staunton. I can see the crinkle-lines that come and go about his eyes, but that is because I know where to look. He remains very serious when Staunton turns to him.

"You would be willing to cooperate, wouldn't you, Blair? I mean, you understand the necessity of this sort of research."

"Yes, of course, except that I'm a real ogre when I wake up. Takes an hour, two hours for me to get charged up for the day. My metabolism is so low in the hours just before and after dawn, I'm certain that I would be a washout for your purposes, and by the time I'm human again, the night has become as if it never existed for me."

Dr. Staunton is not sipping any longer. He takes a long swallow and then another. He is not scowling, but I feel that if he doesn't let it show, he will have an attack of ulcers, or at least indigestion, before the night is over. He has no more liking for me than I have for him, but he forces the smile back into place and it is my turn.

"Miss Matthews?"

"I haven't decided yet," I say. "I'm curious about it, and I do dream. I read an article somewhere, in *Life*, or *Newsweek*, or someplace, and it sounds very mysterious, but I don't like the idea of the wires in the brain, and the earphones and all."

Very patiently he explains again that only his student volunteers use the equipment, and others who specifically volunteer for that phase. I ask if I might see how they use it sometime, and he is forced to say yes. He tries to get my yes in return, but I am coy and say only that I have to think about it first. He tries to get Dr. Warren to promise to approach other people in the town, try to get their cooperation for him, and Dr. Warren sidesteps adroitly. I know the thought will occur to him to use me for that purpose, but it doesn't that evening. I decide that he isn't terribly bright. I wonder about his students, and I invite him to bring them, all of them, to my house for an outdoor barbecue the following night. That is all he gets from any of us, and dinner seems very slow, although, as usual, very good. Staunton excuses himself quickly after dinner, saying, with his off-again, on-again smile, that he must return to work, that only the fortunate are allowed their nights of rest.

No one argues with him, or urges him to linger, and when he is gone I help Norma with the dishes and Dr. Warren sits in the kitchen having black coffee, and we talk about the Harvard doctor.

"I plain don't like him," Norma says with conviction. "Slimy man."

I think of his pink face and pink hairless hands, and his cheeks that shake when he walks, and I know what she means.

"I guess his project isn't altogether bad, or a complete waste of time," Dr. Warren says. "Just got the wrong place, wrong time, wrong people."

"I want to find out exactly what he expects to prove," I say. "I wonder what sort of contrast he expects between students and our people. That might even be interesting." I wonder if the research is really his, or the idea of one of his graduate students. I try not to draw conclusions yet. I can wait until the next night when I'll meet them all. I say, "Doctor Warren, Father keeps begging me to bring him home. Do you think it would help him?"

Dr. Warren puts down his cup and studies me hard. "Bedridden still?"

"Yes, and always will be, but I could manage him in the dining room downstairs. He's so unhappy in the nursing home. I'm sure the house, the noises there would bring back other days to him, make him more cheerful."

"It's been four years now, hasn't it?" Dr. Warren knows that. I wonder why he is playing for time, what thoughts he has that he doesn't want to express. "Honey," he says, in the gentle voice that used to go with the announcement of the need for a needle, or a few stitches. I remember that he never promised that it wouldn't hurt if it would. "I think you'd be making a mistake. Is he really unhappy? Or does he just have moments when he wants the past given back to him?"

I feel angry with him suddenly for not understanding that when Father is lucid he wants to be home. I can only shrug.

"Think on it, Janet. Just don't decide too fast." His face is old suddenly, and I realize that everyone in Somerset is aged. It's like walking among the pyramids, at a distance forever changeless, but on closer inspection constant reminders of aging, of senescence, of usefulness past and nearly forgotten. I turn to stare at Norma and see her as she is, not as she was when I was a child waiting for a cookie fresh and still warm, with the middle soft and the top crackly with sugar. I feel bewildered by both of them, outraged that they should reveal themselves so to me. There is a nearby crack of thunder, sharp-edged and explosive, not the rolling kind that starts and ends with an echo of itself, but a rifle blast. I stare out the window at lightning, jagged and brilliant, as sharply delineated as the thunder.

"I should go before the downpour," I say.

"I'll drive you," Dr. Warren says, but I won't let him.

"I'll make it before the rain. Maybe it's cooler now."

Inconsequentials that fill the days and nights of our lives, non-sequiturs that pass for conversation and thought, pleasantries, promises, we rattle them off comfortingly and I am walking down the street toward my house, not on the sidewalk, but in the street, where walking is easier.

The wind starts to blow when I am halfway between Magnolia and Rose Streets. I can see the Sagamore House ahead and I decide to stop there and wait for the rain to come and go. Probably I have planned this in a dark corner of my mind, but I have not consciously decided to visit the students so soon. I hurry, and the wind now has the town astir, filled with the same rustles that fill my house; scurrying ghosts, what have they to worry about if the rain should come before they settle in for the night?

Along First Street most of the buildings are closed forever. The ten-cent store, a diner, fabric shop, all sharing a common front, all locked, with large soaped loops linking the wide windows one to one. The rain starts, enormous drops that are wind-driven and hard. I can hear them against the tin roof of Mr. Larson's store and they sound like hailstones, but then the wind drowns all noise but its own. Thunder and lightning now, and the mad wind. I run the rest of the way to Sagamore House and arrive there almost dry, but completely breathless.

"Honey, for heaven's sake, come in and get some coffee!" Dorothea starts to lead me to the kitchen, but I shake my head and incline it toward the parlor off to the left of the entrance.

"I'll go in there and wait out the storm, if you don't mind." I can hear voices from the big room with its Victorian furniture and the grandfather clock that always stutters on the second tick. I hear it now: tick–t . . . t . . . tick.

"I'll bring you a pot of coffee there, Janet," Dorothea says with a nod. When she comes back with the tray and the china cup and the silver pot, she will call me Miss Matthews.

I try to pat my hair down as I go into the parlor, and I know that I still present a picture of a girl caught in a sudden storm. I brush my arms, as if they are still wet, although they are not, and I shake my head, and at that moment there is another very close, very loud thunder crash, as if to justify my actions. The boys stop talking when I enter. They are what I have known most of my life since college: young, fresh-looking, indistinguishable from seniors and graduate students the world over.

I smile generally at them and sit down on one of the red velour couches with a coffee table before it that has a bowl of white roses, a dish of peppermints, magazines, three ashtrays, each carved and enameled and spotless. The whole room is like that: chairs and chairs, all carved, waxed, gleaming, footstools, end tables, console tables, Tiffany lampshades on cut glass lamps . . . The boys are at the other end of the room, five of them, two on the floor, the others in chairs, smoking, sipping beer or tall drinks. Dr. Staunton isn't there.

Dorothea brings my tray and does call me Miss Matthews and asks if I'd like anything else. I shake my head and she leaves me alone with the boys. There is a whispered conversation at the other end of the room, and one of the boys rises and comes to stand near me.

"Hi, I'm Roger Philpott. Are you Janet Matthews? I think you invited us all to dinner at your house tomorrow." Tall, thin, blond, very young-looking.

22

I grin back and nod. I look toward the others and say, "Maybe by meeting just a few of you now, I'll be able to keep your names straight."

Roger introduces the others, and I remember that there is a Johnny, a Victor, Doug, Sid, and Mickey. No one is grotesque, or even memorable. They regroup around me. Outside we can hear the hail, undeniably hail now, and the wind shrieking in the gables and eaves, all dwarfed by the intermittent explosions of the thunder. Several times the lights flicker, and Dorothea returns with hurricane lamps that she places in strategic places, after a glance to see if I have accomplished my goal of becoming part of the group of students.

Roger switches to coffee, but the other students reorder beer and gin and bitter lemon, and Dorothea leaves us again. Roger says, "I don't know how long some of us will be able to take life in the country. What do you do around here?"

I laugh and say, "I come here to rest each summer. I live in New York the rest of the year."

His interest quickens. "Oh, you work in the city then?"

"Yes, Columbia Medical Center. I'm an anesthesiologist."

"Dr. Staunton didn't mention that. He seems to think that all the people here are locals."

"I didn't tell him," I say. He nods and I know that he realizes that I have played the part of a local yokel with his superior. I ask, "Is this his research, or is it the theses of one of the boys?"

One of the others laughs. "It's Roger's original idea," he says. "And mine." I try to remember which one he is and I think he is Sid. Mediterranean type. I glance over the other faces, and none shows surprise. So Staunton has taken over openly, and they accept it as natural. It tells me more than they can know about Staunton.

"You see, I had this idea that the whole pattern of dream content might switch depending on the location of the dreamer. In the city we know pretty much what each of us dreams, we've been subjects and experimenters all year now, and we decided to hunt up a place where there were none of the same things at all and then run a comparison."

23

"And you'll check that against what you can find out from the people here, to see if there's a correlation?"

"We don't expect one," Sid said. "What we do expect is that our own dreams will change, but that the patterns of the dreams of the people already here will remain relatively stable."

"And what do you expect to prove?"

"I don't know that we'll prove anything, but assuming that dreams reflect the emotional states of the person, by examining them in varying circumstances we might get a clue about how to help people relax more than they do, what kind of vacation to plan for, how long to stay, things like that. If my reasoning is right, then we'll be able to predict from personality sketches whether a three-week vacation is desirable, or shorter periods more frequently. You see?"

I nod and can find no fault with the experiment. It does seem a legitimate line of research, and a useful one, perhaps. "I suppose you will have a computer run the analysis of dream content?"

Sid nods, and Roger says, "Would you like to see one of the cards we fill out? We've broken down dream content into categories . . . Like sexual with subheadings of hetero, homo, socially accepted, socially unaccepted, and so on, and a further breakdown of overt, covert; participatory, observed; satisfying, frustrating, and so on. I think we've hit everything."

"I would like to see one," I say, and he nods.

"I'll bring one out to your place with us tomorrow. Have you seen any of the sleep lab equipment?"

"Not in this context, not used in these experiments."

"Great. The first afternoon, after three or four, that you can get up here, I'll show you around."

"Perhaps tomorrow?" I say. "Will Dr. Staunton object?"

Roger and Sid exchange a hurried glance and Roger shrugs. "It's my research," he says.

"Is he setting up equipment, testing it out now?"

"No. In fact, he came home with indigestion, I think, and conked out right away."

I can't still the sudden laugh that I feel. I finish my coffee and stand up. "The storm is over, I think. At least it's catching its breath now. I'm glad I was forced to stop," I say, and hold out my hand to Roger and then Sid. "I must say, however, that I'm afraid Somerset isn't quite what you expected. I hope you won't be too disappointed in us."

"Will you help?" Roger asks.

I hesitate and then nod. "I used to keep a record for my own psychology classes. I'll start again."

"Thanks."

"If anyone in town asks my opinion," I say, standing in the open doorway now, feeling the cool wind that the storm has brought in, "I'll tell them that I'm cooperating, nothing more. They may or may not pay any attention to what I say."

"See you tomorrow afternoon," Roger says and I leave them and walk home. It is very dark now, and the rain smells fresh, the air is cool and clean. I am thinking of the two halves that make up the whole me. In the city I am brisk and efficient. I know the nurses talk about me, wondering if I am a lesbian (I'm not), if I have any sex-life at all (not now). They are afraid of me because I will not permit any sloppiness in surgery, and I am quick to report them. They don't understand that my instruments are to me what the surgeon's scalpel is to him, and they think I worship dials and stainless steel gods. I once heard myself described as more machine-like than any of the exotic equipment that I have mastered. I know that the thought of those boys staring at the charts of their alpha and beta rhythms has brought this retrospective mood but I can't break out of it. I continue to inspect my life as if from the outside. What no one understands is that it is not the machines that are deified, but the processes that the machines record, the fluctuations and the rhythms, the cyclic patterns that are beautiful when they are normal, and as hideous as a physical deformity when they are wrong. The covered mound on the hard table is meaningless when I observe it. Less than human, inert, it might be a corpse already, or a covered log, or a cache of potatoes. But the dials that I read tell me all I can know about it: male, steady heart, respiration normal . . . Body processes that add up to life, or non-life. What more is there?

My house is cool now, and rain has blown in the kitchen

and dining-room windows. I mop it up and wipe the sills carefully, and inspect the rest of the house. I can't see anything in the yard, but I stand on the back porch and feel the coolness and the mistiness of the air until I start to shiver.

I have read that dreams follow a pattern of their own. The first dreams of the night are of events nearby in time and space, and as sleep progresses and the night goes by the dreams wander farther afield, into the past, or into future fantasy, and toward morning, they return to the here and now of the dreamer. During the night I wake up three times and jot down the dreams I can recall.

Dream number one is a simple-minded wish fulfillment. I am at a party where I sparkle and dazzle everyone in the house. It is an unfamiliar house, not unlike the Sagamore House, except more elegant, simpler, with cool white marble statues replacing the clutter. I am the belle of the party and I dance with everyone there, and in the center of the room is a champagne glass that must hold gallons. Looking through the bubbling wine I see the statues shimmer and appear to come alive, but I know that it is only because of the rising bubbles, that it is an illusion. I am swept back to the dance floor and I swirl around in a delirium of joy.

Dream number two puzzles me. I am following Father, who is very small. It is not quite dark, but I don't know where the light is coming from. It is like moonlight, but without the moon, which I suspect is behind me somewhere. I am very frightened. Father starts to climb the ash tree and I retreat and watch him, growing more and more afraid but not doing anything at all, simply standing and watching as he vanishes among the leaves. I wake up in a cold sweat.

Dream number three takes place in my apartment. I am remodeling and doing the work myself. I am installing temporary wall boards, decorating them with childish pictures and pinups. I am weeping as I work. Suddenly there is a change and I am above Somerset, or in town, and I can't be certain which it is. I am calm and happy, although I see no one and hear nothing. Somerset is bathed in moonlight that is too golden to be real and the town is as I remember it from my earliest days, with striped green-and-white umbrellas in yards, and silent children playing happily in Cobb's Run.

I wake up and don't want to lose the feeling of peace and contentment. I smile as I write the dream down and when I read it over I don't know quite why it should have filled me with happiness. As I think of it more, I am saddened by it, and finally I get up wishing I had let it escape altogether. It is very early, not seven yet, but I don't want to return to bed. The morning is cool and refreshing. I decide to weed the patio out back and set up the grill before the sun heats up the valley again.

The ash tree is untouched. I work for an hour, go inside for breakfast, and return to the yard. I am thinking that if I do bring Father home, I will have to find someone who can help with the yard, and I don't know who it would be. Poor Haddie? He might, but he is so slow and unthinking. I could have a wheelchair for Father and bring him out to the patio every day and as he convalesces, we could take short trips in the car, go down to the lake maybe, or over to Hawley now and then. I am certain that he will be able to play chess by fall, and read aloud with me, as we used to do. A quiet happiness fills me as I plan and it is with surprise that I realize that I have decided about Father. I have been over the same reasoning with his doctor, and accepted his advice against this move, but here, working in the bright sunlight, the new decision seems to have been made effortlessly.

I have weeded the patio, swept up the heaps of dandelions and buckweeds and crabgrass that have pushed through the cracks in the flagstones, and set up the barbecue grill. The picnic table is in pitiful condition, but it will have to do. There are some folding canvas chairs in the garage, but I will let the boys bring them out.

It is one o'clock already. A whole morning gone so quickly. My muscles are throbbing and I am sunburned, but the feeling of peacefulness remains with me and I shower and change and then go to town to shop, have lunch with Dorothea and Annie, and then see the sleep lab equipment.

I try to explain to Dorothea the difference between living

27

in the city and living here in my own home, but she has her mouth set in a firm line and she is very disapproving of the whole idea.

Timidly Annie says, "But, honey, there's no one left your age. What will you do all the time?"

"I'll have plenty to do," I tell her. "I want to study, rest, take care of Father, the house. There will be too much to do, probably."

"That's not what she means," Dorothea says sharply. "You should get married, not tie yourself down here where everything's dying." She eyes me appraisingly. "Don't you have anyone in mind?"

I shrug it off. A young doctor, perhaps? I try to think of myself with any of the young doctors I know, and the thought is ridiculous. There are some older doctors, thoroughly married, of course, that seem less absurd, but no one my age who is unattached. I think again of the Harvard doctor's pink hands and pink cheeks, and I shudder. I say, "There's time for that, Dorothea, but right now I feel it's my duty to Father to bring him home where he will be happier."

After lunch I wander into the parlor and have Dorothea ring Roger's room and tell him I'm waiting. She is still unhappy with me, and I know that she and Annie will discuss me the rest of the afternoon.

The sleep lab is set up in the rear of the building on the second floor. There are three bedrooms in a row, the middle one the control room with the equipment in place, and the rooms on either side furnished with beds, telephones, wires with electrodes. I have seen pictures of these experiments and have read about them so that none of it comes as a surprise, but I am mildly impressed that they were able to get together so much equipment that I know to be very expensive. Harvard is feeling flush these days, I decide, or else Staunton swings more weight than I have given him credit for.

After I examine the EEGs from the night before and compare them with the reported dreams, I am introduced to the other three students that I missed before. I have already forgotten all of their names except Sid and Roger. We have a

28

drink and I learn that so far they have received no cooperation from anyone in town, with the possible exception of myself. Staunton comes in looking angry and frustrated.

"That hick doctor could do it, if he would," he says before he sees me in the room. He reddens.

"He won't, though," I say. "But I could."

"They'd tell you their dreams?"

"Some of them would, probably enough for your purposes." I stand up and start for the door. "I would have to promise not to give you their dreams, but to process them myself, however."

He starts to turn away, furious again, and I say, "I am qualified, you know." I suspect that I have more degrees than he does and I reel them off rapidly. I walk to the door before he has a chance to respond. Before leaving I say, "Think about it. You can let me know tonight when you come to the house. I will have to be briefed on your methods, of course, and have a chance to examine your cards."

I don't know why I've done it. I walk home and try to find a reason, but there is none. To puncture his smug shield? To deflate him in the presence of his students? To inflate my own importance, reassure myself that I am of both worlds? I can't select a single reason, and I decide that perhaps all of them are part of it. I know that I dislike Staunton as much as anyone I have ever met, and perhaps I hope that he will fail completely in his research, except that it isn't really his.

I make potato salad, and bake pies, and prepare the steaks that Dorothea has ordered. It crosses my mind that Mr. Larson has virtually no meat except for the special order from Sagamore House, and that I'll have to order everything in advance when I move back home for good, but I don't linger over it. The evening passes quite pleasantly and even Staunton is on his good behavior. They accept my offer and Sid goes over the cards with me, explaining what they are doing, how they are analyzing the dreams and recording them. It seems simple enough.

The days flow by now, with not quite enough time for all there is to do. The doctor in charge of the nursing home answers my letter brusquely, treating me like a child. I read it over twice before I put it on my desk to be taken care of later. I have been able to get six people to cooperate in the dream studies, and they keep me busy each day. People like to talk about their dreams, I find, and talking about them, they are able to bring back more and more details, so that each interview takes half an hour or an hour. And there are my own dreams that I am also recording.

I have found the reason for my own part in this when I first typed up my own dream to be analyzed. I found that I couldn't give it to Staunton, and the students are like children, not to be trusted with anything so intimate as the private dreams of a grown woman. So each day I record my own dreams along with the other six, type them all up, fill out the cards, and turn the cards over to Roger. By then the dreams are depersonalized data.

I finish typing the seven dreams and I am restless suddenly. There is something . . . The house is more unquiet than usual, and I am accustomed to the rustlings and creakings. I wonder if another storm is going to hit the town, but I don't think so. I wander outside where the night is very clear. The sky is brilliant and bottomless. The music of the night is all about me: the splashing water of the creek, crickets and tree frogs in arhythmic choral chants and from a distance the deeper solo bass of a bullfrog. Probably I am bored. Other people's dreams are very boring. I haven't started to categorize this latest set, and I feel reluctant to begin. I purposely don't put any names on any of the dreams I record, and I type each one on a separate card and then shuffle them about, so that by the time I have finished with them all, I have forgotten who told me which one.

I stop walking suddenly. I have come halfway down the path toward the creek without thinking where I am going or why. Now I stop and the night noises press in on me. "They are alike," I say, and I am startled by my voice. All other sounds stop with the words.

I think of the stack of file cards, and those I added tonight, and I am amazed that I didn't see it in the beginning. Roger is right, the townspeople are dreaming the same dreams. That isn't really what he said. What he said was that the dreams of the people here would remain stable, unchanged by the experiment, while those of the students would change as they adapted to this life. I haven't asked about that part of the research, but suddenly I am too curious about it to put it out of my mind.

Are they changing, and how? I start back, but pause at the door to the house, and turn instead to the street and town. I slow down when I come in sight of Sagamore House. It is very late, almost two in the morning. The second-floor light is the only light I have seen since leaving my own house. I take another step toward Sagamore House, and another. What is the matter tonight? I look about. But there is nothing. No wind, no moon, nothing. But I hear . . . life, stirrings, something. This is Somerset, I say to myself sharply, not quite aloud, but I hear the words anyway. I look quickly over my shoulder, but there is nothing. I see the apple trees, familiar yet strange, eerie shadows against the pale siding of the hotel. Across from Sagamore House on Wisteria there is the old boarded-up theater, and for a moment I think someone has opened it again. I press my hands over my ears and when I take them down the sound has stopped. I am shaking. I can't help the sudden look that I give the corner where the drugstore burned down seven or eight years ago.

We wait in the shadows of Sagamore House, under the apple trees for the movie to be over, and then Father and Mother, Susan's parents, Peter's, come out and take us along with them for an ice-cream soda in the drugstore. We know when the movie is ending because of the sounds that filter out when they open the inner doors. Faint music, laughter, a crash of cymbals, always different, but always a signal, and we come down from the trees, or from the porch and cross the street to wait for them to come out.

I stare at the theater, back to the empty corner, and slowly turn and go home again. One of the boys was playing a radio, I tell myself, and even believe it for a moment. Or I imagined it, the past intruded for a moment, somehow. An audio

31

hallucination. I stop at the gate to my yard and stare at the house, and I am desperately afraid. It is such an unfamiliar feeling, so unexpected and shattering, that I can't move until it passes. It is as if I have become someone else for a moment, someone who fears rustling in the dark, who fears the night, being alone. Not my feelings at all. I have never been afraid, never, not of anything like this.

I light a cigarette and walk around the house to enter the kitchen, where I make coffee and a sandwich. It is two-thirty, but sleep seems a long way off now, unwanted, unneeded. Toward dawn I take a sleeping pill and fall into bed.

Roger, Sid and Doug invite me to have dinner with them in Hawley on Saturday, and I accept. The mountain road is very bad and we creep along in the station wagon that they have brought with them. No one is talking, and we all glance back at Somerset at the turn that used to have a tended scenic overlook. The trees have since grown up, and bushes and vines, so that there is only a hint of the town below us. Then it is gone, and suddenly Sid starts to talk of the experiment.

"I think we should call off the rest of it," he says.

"Can't," Roger says. "Eight days isn't enough."

"We have a trend," Sid says.

Doug, sitting in the back seat, speaks up then. "You'll never keep them all here for two more weeks."

"I know that, but those who do hang on will be enough."

"What's the matter?" I ask.

"Boredom," Sid says. "Good God, what's there to do in such a place?"

"I thought that was part of the experiment. I thought you wanted a place with no external stimuli."

"Quote and unquote," Sid says. "Staunton's idea. And we did, but I don't know. The dreams are strange, and getting stranger. And we're not getting along too well in the daytime. I don't know how your people stand it."

I shrug and don't even try to answer. I know he won't understand. Traffic thickens when we leave the secondary road for the highway on the other side of the mountain. It feels

32

cooler here and I find that I am looking forward to a night out with more excitement than seems called for.

We have drinks before dinner, and wine with dinner, and more drinks afterward, and there is much laughter. Doug teaches me three new dance steps, and Roger and I dance, and I find myself thinking with incredulity of the plan I have been considering to take Father out of the nursing home where he belongs and try to care for him myself. I know that he will never recover, that he will become more and more helpless, not less. How could I have planned to do such a thing? He needs attendants to lift him, turn him in bed, and at times to restrain him. I have tried to think of other alternatives for him, but there are none, and I know that. I know that I have to write to the director of the home and apologize to him.

At eleven Roger says we have to go back. Doug passes out in the car as soon as he gets inside, and Sid groans. "There he goes," he says. "So you do me tonight."

"Where are the others?" I ask.

"On strike," Roger says. "They refused to work on Saturday and Sunday, said they needed time off. They want to forget their dreams for a couple of nights."

"I'll do it," I say.

"You're kidding."

"No. I'll do it. You can wire me up and everything tonight."

It is agreed, and we drive back over the mountain, becoming more and more quiet as we get to the old road and start to pick our way down again. By the time we get back to Somerset, and I am feeling soberer, I regret my impulsive promise, but can think of no way to back out now. I watch Sid and Roger half carry, half drag Doug from the station wagon, and I see the flutter of his eyelids and know that he is not as drunk as he would have us believe. I start to walk to my house, but Roger says for me to wait, that they will drive me and bring me back with my pajamas and things, so I stand on the porch and wait for them, and I stare across the street at the vacant theater. I know that three nights ago I imagined the past, but since then I have been taking sleeping pills, and my nights have been quiet, with no more hallucinations or dreams.

33

My house is noisier than usual. I glance at the two boys, but neither of them seems to notice. They sit in the living room and wait, and ahead of me on the dark stairs the rustlings hurry along; they pause outside my parents' room, scurry down the hallway and precede me into my room, where, when I turn on the light, there is nothing to see. I know it is the settling of floorboards untrodden for eleven months; and rushing air; and imagination. Memories that have become tangible? I don't believe that, but it has a strangely comforting sound, and I like the idea of memories lingering in the house, assuming a life of their own, reliving the past.

I fold pajamas and my housecoat, and grope under the bed for my slippers, and the thought comes that people are going to know that I spent the night at Sagamore House. I sit on the bed with my slippers in my hand and stare straight ahead at nothing in particular. How can I get out of this? I realize that Somerset and New York are arguing through me, and I can almost smile at the dialogue that I am carrying out silently. It seems that my strongest Somerset argument is that if I am going to live here with my invalid father, I can't return with a reputation completely ruined. I know what Somerset can do to a woman like that. But I'm not going to come back with him, I answer. Or am I?

It is getting very late and I have to go through with it; I have promised. Reluctantly I take my things downstairs, hoping that they have left, but of course they are still sitting there, talking quietly. About me? I suspect so. Probably I puzzle them. I regard them as little more than children, boys with school problems to solve. Yet we are all in our twenties. I suppose that because I have my degrees and a position of responsibility, my experience seems to add years to my age, and even as I think this, I reject it. Sid has told me that he spent three years in the army, served in Vietnam, so what is my experience to his? Sid has tried to draw me out, has visited twice, and has even gone canoeing with me, but standing in the doorway looking at them I think of them as so very young, prying into things they can't understand, trying to find answers that, if found, will make them question all of reality.

34

I shake my head hard. I don't know what I've been thinking about, but I feel afraid suddenly, and I suspect that I have drunk too much earlier, and I am so very . . . weary. Sleeping pills leave me more tired than the insomnia they alleviate.

They make small talk that I recognize, the same sort of small talk that a good doctor uses for a nervous patient before measuring his blood pressure. I am churlish with them in return and we go to the sleep lab silently. I understand all of their equipment and I have even had electroencephalograms made when I was studying, so nothing is new to me and the demonstration is short. Then I am alone in the darkened room, conscious of the wires, of the tiny patches of skin with adhesive gel tape that holds the electrodes in place. I don't think I'll be able to go to sleep here wired up like this, at least not into the deep sleep that should come in an hour or so. I deliberately close my eyes and try to picture a flame above my eyes, over the bridge of my nose. I know that I can interrupt my alpha waves at will with this exercise. I imagine Roger's surprise. But suddenly I am thinking of S.L. and I blink rapidly, wondering what kinds of waves I am producing now for them to study. S.L. won't go away. I ask, what does the S. stand for, and he smiles broadly and says Silas. Does anyone name children Silas anymore? So I ask about the L. and he says Lerner, which is perfectly all right, his mother's maiden name, but he doesn't like the idea of going around as S. Lerner Wright. It is a farcical name. He is S.L. Lying in the dark room of the almost empty hotel, I can think of S.L. without pain, without recriminations and regrets and bitterness. I remember it as it was then. I loved him so very much, but he said not enough, or I would go with him to Cal Tech and become Mrs. S.L. Wright, and forever and ever remain Mrs. S.L. Wright. I realize that I no longer love him, and that probably I didn't even then, but it felt like love and I ached as if it were love, and afterward I cut my hair very short and stopped using makeup and took several courses in night school and finished the next three years in under two and received degrees and a job . . .

I am awakened by the telephone and I lift it and mumble

into it. "My car isn't working right, trying to back up on the road into Somerset and can't make it go. I keep slipping downward and there is a cliff in front of me, but I can't back up."

I dream of the telephone ringing, and it rings, and I speak, less coherently, and forget immediately what I have said and sleep again. In the morning I have memories of having spoken into the telephone several times, but no memories of what I said. Sid enters and helps me out of the bird's nest of wires. I wave him away and stumble into the bathroom where I wash my face and come really awake.

Sid? I thought Roger was the meter man of the night before. I dress and brush my hair and put on lipstick, and then find them both waiting for me to have breakfast with them. Sid has deep blue circles under his eyes. At a sunlit table with a bowl of yellow roses and a few deep green ferns, I wait for them to break the silence that has enveloped the three of us. There is a sound of activity in town that morning, people getting ready to go to church in Hawley, cars being brought out of garages where they stay six days of the week, several people in the hotel dining room having an early breakfast before leaving for the day. Many of them stay away all day on Sunday, visiting friends or relatives, and I know that later the town will be deserted.

"So they talked you into letting them wire you up like a condemned man?" Dorothea stands over the table accusingly. "Are you all right?"

"Of course. It's nothing, Dorothea, really nothing."

She snorts. "Up all night, people coming and going all night, talking in the halls, meetings here and there. I never should have let them in." She is addressing me still, but the hostility in her voice is aimed at the boys, at Staunton who has just entered the dining room. He joins us, and there are dark hollows under his eyes. He doesn't meet my gaze.

We have coffee in silence and wait for our orders. I finger a sensitive spot on my left eyelid and Sid says quickly, "One of the wires came off during the night, I had to replace it. Is it sore?"

"No. It's all right." I am upset suddenly by the idea of his

36

being there in the night, replacing a wire on my eye without my knowing. I think of the similar role that I play in my daily life and I know how I regard the bodies that I treat. Irritated at the arm that has managed to pull loose a needle that now must be replaced in the vein. Never a person, just an arm, and a needle. And the quiet satisfaction when the dials are registering correctly once more. I feel the frown on my face and try to smooth it out again.

Staunton has ordered only toast, juice and coffee, and he is yawning. He finishes his last crumb of toast and says, "I'm going to bed. Miss Matthews, will you join us here for dinner tonight?"

The sudden question catches me off guard, and I look at him. He is regarding me steadily and very soberly, and I realize that something has happened, that I am part of it, and that he is very much concerned. I am uneasy and only nod yes.

When he is gone I ask, "What happened? What's wrong?"

"We don't know yet," Roger says.

Sid pours more coffee and drinks it black. He is looking more awake, as if he has taken a bennie or something. "We have to talk with you, Janet. I'd like you to hear some of our tapes, including your own, if you will."

"You should get some sleep," I say irrelevantly.

"This afternoon? Can you come here, or should we bring the stuff to your place?"

"You got him up last night?"

Sid nods. "I felt I should."

I watched Myra and Al Newton leave their table, stop at Dorothea's counter to pay the bill and leave, and I am struck by their frailty. They both seem wraithlike. Is anyone in Somerset under sixty? I suppose the Newtons must be closer to seventy-five. I ask, "Where are the other boys this morning?" The dining room is empty except for the three of us.

"A couple of them are out fishing already, and the rest are probably still sleeping. I'm taking Victor and Mickey to Hawley to catch the bus back to Boston later today," Roger says, and then adds, "Probably Doug will be the next to go."

"Doug? I thought he was one of the more interested ones in this whole thing?"

"Too interested, maybe," Roger says.

Sid is watching both of us and now he leans forward, resting his chin on his hands, looking beyond me out the window at the quiet street. "Janet, do you remember any of your dreams from last night?"

I think of what I said over the telephone. Scraps here and there. Something about putting flowers on graves in one of them. I shake my head: nothing that I can really remember.

"Okay. You'll hear them later. Meanwhile, take my word for it that some of the guys have to leave, whether they want to or not." He looks at me for another moment and then asks, in a different voice altogether, "Are you all right, Janet? Will you be okay until this afternoon? We do have to process the tapes and record the data, and I want to sort through all of them and pull out those that seem pertinent."

It is the voice of a man concerned for a woman, not of a graduate student concerned for his project, and this annoys me.

"Of course I'm all right," I say, and stand up. "For heaven's sake, those are dreams, the dreams of someone who had too much to drink, at that." I know I am flushed and I turn to leave. Have I embarrassed them with erotic dreams, concerning one of them perhaps? I am very angry when I leave Sagamore House, and I wish I could go up to the sleep room and destroy the tapes, all of them. I wish Dorothea had shown just an ounce of sense when they approached her for the rooms. She had no business allowing them to come into our town, upset our people with their damned research. I am furious with Sid for showing concern for me. He has no right. In the middle of these thoughts, I see my father and me, walking hand in hand in the afternoon, heading for the drugstore and an ice-cream cone. He is very tall and blond, with broad shoulders and a massive chest. He keeps his hair so short that he seems bald from a distance. He is an ophthalmologist with his office in Jefferson, and after they dam the river he has to drive sixty-three miles each way. Mother worries about his being out so

38

much, but they don't move, don't even consider moving. On Sunday afternoon he always takes me to the drugstore for an ice-cream cone. I blink hard and the image fades, leaving the street bare and empty.

I am too restless to remain in my house. It is a hot still day and the heat is curling the petals of the roses, and drying out the grass, and wilting the phlox leaves. It is a relentless sun, burning, broiling, sucking the water up from the creek, leaving it smaller each day. Without the dam the creek probably would dry up completely within another week or two. I decide to cut a basket of flowers and take them to the cemetery, and I know the idea comes from the fragmentary dream that I recalled earlier. I haven't been to the cemetery since my mother's funeral. It has always seemed such a meaningless gesture, to return to a grave and mourn there. It is no less meaningless now, but it is something to do.

The cemetery is behind the small white church that has not been used for six years, since Brother MacCombs died. No one tried to replace him; they seemed tacitly to agree that the church should be closed and the membership transferred to Hawley.

It is a walk of nearly two miles, past the Greening farm where the weeds have become master again, past the dirt road to the old mill, a tumbling ruin even in my childhood where snakes curled in the shadows and slept, past the turnoff to Eldridge's fishing camp. I see no one and the sounds of the hot summer day are loud about me: whirring grasshoppers, birds, the scuttling of a squirrel who chatters at me once he is safely hidden.

The cemetery is tended in spots only, the graves of those whose relatives are still in Somerset have cut grass and a sprinkling of flowers. My mother's grave is completely grown over and shame fills me. What would Father say? I don't try to weed it then, but sit down under a wide oak tree.

I look at the narrow road that leads back to Somerset. Father and I will come here often, after I have made the grave neat and pretty again. It will be slow, but we'll take our time, walking hand in hand up the dirt road, carrying flowers, and

39

maybe a sandwich and a thermos of lemonade, or apples. Probably if I start the proceedings during the coming week, I can have everything arranged by next weekend, hire an ambulance and a driver . . .

I am awakened by rough hands shaking my shoulders. I blink rapidly, trying to focus my eyes, trying to find myself. I am being led away, and I squirm to turn around because I feel so certain that I am still back there somehow. I almost catch a glimpse of a girl in a yellow dress, sitting with her back to the oak tree, but it shimmers and I am yanked hard, and stumble, and hands catch me and steady me.

"What are you kids doing?" I ask, and the sound of the voice, deep, unfamiliar, shocks me and only then do I really wake up. I am being taken to the station wagon that is parked at the entrance to the lane.

"I'm all right," I say, not struggling now. "You woke me up."

Sid is on my right and Roger on my left. I see that Dr. Staunton is in the wagon. He looks pale and worried.

I remember the basket of flowers that I never did put on the grave and I look back once more to see it standing by the tree. Sid's hand tightens on my arm, but I don't try to pull away. Inside the wagon I say, "Will one of you tell me what that was all about?"

"Janet, do you know how long you've been there at the cemetery?"

"Half an hour, an hour."

"It's almost six now. I . . . we got to your house at three and waited awhile for you, and then went back to the hotel. An old man with a white goatee said he saw you before noon heading this way with flowers. So we came after you." Sid is sitting beside me in the back seat of the wagon, and I stare at him in disbelief. I look at my watch, and it is five minutes to six. I shake it and listen to it.

"I must have been sound asleep."

"Sitting straight up, with your legs stretched out in front of you?"

We drive to my house and I go upstairs to wash my face

and comb my hair. I study my face carefully, looking for something, anything, but it is the same. I hear voices from below; the sound diminishes and I know they are playing the tapes, so I hurry down.

I see that Sid has found my dream cards, the typed reports, and I am angry with him for prying. He says, "I had to know. I found them earlier while we were waiting for you."

Roger has the tape ready, so I sit down and we listen for the next two hours. Staunton is making notes, scowling hard at the pad on his knee. I feel myself growing tenser, and when the first tape comes to an end, I go to make coffee. We all sip it through the playing of the second tape.

The dreaming students' voices sound disjointed, hesitant, unguarded, and the dreams they relate are all alike. I feel cold in the hot room, and I dread hearing my own voice, my own dreams played by the machine.

All the early dreams are of attempts to leave Somerset. They speak of trying to fly out, to climb out, to swim out, to drive out, and only one is successful. As the night progresses, the dreams change, some faster than others. Slowly a pattern of acceptance enters the dreams, and quite often the acceptance is followed swiftly by a nightmare-like desire to run.

One of the dreamers, Victor, I think it is, has a brief anxiety dream, an incomplete dream, and then nothing but the wish-fulfillment acceptance dreams, not even changing again when morning has him in a lighter stage of sleep.

Sid motions for Roger to stop the tape and says, "That was three days ago. Since then Victor has been visiting people here, talking with them, fishing, hiking. He has been looking over some of the abandoned houses in town, with the idea of coming here to do a book."

"Has he . . ." I am amazed at how dry my mouth has become and I have to sip cold coffee before I can ask the question. "Has he recorded dreams since then?"

"No. Before this, he was having dreams of his parents, caring for them, watching over them." Sid looks at me and says deliberately, "Just like your dreams."

I shake my head and turn from him to look at Roger. He

41

starts the machine again. There are hours and hours of the tapes to hear, and after another fifteen minutes of them I am ravenous. It is almost nine. I signal Roger to stop, and suggest that we all have scrambled eggs here, but Staunton vetoes this.

"I promised Miss Dorothea that we would return to the hotel. I warned her that it might be late. She said that was all right."

So we go back to Sagamore House and wait for the special of the day. On Sunday night there is no menu. I find myself shying away from the implications of the dream analysis again and again, and try to concentrate instead on my schedule for the next several months. I know that I have agreed to work with Dr. Waldbaum on at least six operations, and probably there are others that I agreed to and have forgotten. He is a thoracic surgeon and his operations take from four to eight or even ten hours, and for that long I control death, keep life in abeyance. I pay no attention to the talk that is going on between Roger and Sid, and I wonder about getting an ambulance driver to bring Father in during the winter. If only our weather were more predictable; there might be snowdrifts six feet high on the road, or it might be balmy.

"I said, why do you think you should bring your father home, here to Somerset?" I find that my eyes are on Staunton, and obviously he thinks I have been listening to him, but the question takes me by surprise.

"He's my father. He needs me."

Sid asks, "Has anyone in town encouraged you in this idea?"

Somehow, although I have tried to withdraw from them, I am again the center of their attention, and I feel uncomfortable and annoyed. "Of course not. This is my decision alone. Dr. Warren tried to discourage it, in fact, as Dorothea did, and Mr. Larson."

"Same thing," Sid says to Roger, who nods. Staunton looks at them and turns to me.

"Miss Matthews, do you mean to say that everyone you've talked to about this has really tried to discourage it? These people are your father's friends. Why would they do that?"

My face feels stiff and I am thinking that this is too much, but I say, "They all seem to think he's better off in the nursing home."

"And isn't he?"

"In certain respects, yes. But I am qualified to handle him, you know. No one here seems to realize just how well qualified I really am. They think of me as the girl they used to know playing jump-rope in the back yard."

Dorothea brings icy cucumber soup and we are silent until she leaves again. The grandfather clock chimes ten, and I am amazed at how swiftly the day has gone. By now most of the townspeople are either in bed, or getting ready. Sunday is a hard day, with the trip to church, visits, activities that they don't have often enough to become accustomed to. They will sleep well tonight, I think. I look at Sid and think that he should sleep well too tonight. His eyes are sunken-looking, and I suppose he has lost weight; he looks older, more mature than he did the first time I met him.

"Are you going to set up your equipment tonight?" I ask. "Any of the other boys volunteer?"

"No," Roger says shortly. He looks at Sid and says, "As a matter of fact, we decided today not to put any of them in it again here."

"You're leaving, then?"

"Sending all the kids back, but Sid and I'll be staying for awhile. And Dr. Staunton."

I put down my spoon and lean back, waiting for something that is implicit in the way Roger stops and Sid looks murderously at him. I watch Sid now.

"We think you should leave, too," he says.

I look to Roger, who nods, and then at Staunton. He is so petulant-looking, even pursing his lips. He fidgets and says, "Miss Matthews, may I suggest something? You won't take it amiss?" I simply wait. He goes on, "I think you should return to the city and make an appointment with the psychiatrist at Columbia."

"And the others you are sending out? Should they also see doctors?"

"As a matter of fact, I do think so."

Sid is examining his bowl of soup with great care, and Roger is having trouble with his cigarette lighter. "But not them?" I ask Staunton, pointing at Roger and Sid.

"Them too," he says reluctantly. Sid looks amused now and Roger manages to light his cigarette.

"Is this your opinion too?" I ask Sid. "That I should see Dr. Calridge?"

"No. Just go away from here, and stay away."

Dorothea is bringing in a cart now and I wonder how much she has heard. I see her lined face and the pain in her eyes and I know that she has heard a lot of it, if not all. She catches my gaze and nods firmly. Then she serves us: sizzling ham steaks, french fried fruits, pineapple, apple rings, bananas, sweet potato soufflé.

It is after eleven when we are finished with dinner, and by now Sid is almost asleep. He says, "I've got to go. Will you set things up, Rog?"

"Sure. Damn shame that Doug pooped out on us. We need all the data we can get now."

"I can do the recording," I say.

At almost the same instant Staunton says, "I thought I was going to record both of you tonight."

Roger and Sid look embarrassed, and Sid says after a pause, "Doctor Staunton, if it's all the same with you, we'll let Janet do it."

"You really think I'm that biased? That I can't get objective data?"

Sid stands up and steadies himself with one hand on the table. "I'm too tired to be polite," he says, "and too tired to argue. So, yes I think you're too biased to record the dreams. Roger, will you show Janet what we're doing?"

Roger stays with me until the eye-movement trace shows that Sid is having his first dream, and he watches as I call Sid on the phone and turn on the recorder, and then switch it off again. Then Roger goes to bed in the second room and I see that his electrodes are all working, and I am alone watching the two sets of moving lines. The mountains and valleys

44

of life, I think, watching them peak and level out, and peak again.

There is no mistaking the start of REM sleep; the rapid eye-movements cause a sharp change in the pattern of the peaks and valleys that is more nearly like a waking EEG than that of a sleeping person. I call Sid again, and listen to him describe climbing a mountain, only to slip back down again and again. Roger is on a raft that keeps getting caught up on a tide and brought back to a shore that he is desperately trying to escape.

The same dream, different only in details. Like the dreams I heard earlier on the tape recorder. Like my own.

At three in the morning Staunton joins me. I can tell that he hasn't been asleep, but I wish he had kept his insomnia to himself. He says, "You might need help. I won't bother you. I'll just sit over here and read." He looks haggard, and like Sid, he seems to have aged since coming to Somerset. I turn my attention to the EEGs again. Roger is dreaming.

"Peaceful now, watching a ball game from a great distance, very silent everywhere." I bite my lips as I listen to this strange voice that seems to have a different accent, a different intonation; flatter and slower, of course, but apart from that, it is a changed voice. It is the dream of contentment, wanting nothing, needing nothing. This is the dream that my six people keep reporting to me, modified from person to person, but the same. Suddenly Roger's voice sharpens as he recalls the rest of the dream, and now there is a sense of urgency in his reporting. "And I had to get out of it, but couldn't move. I was frozen there, watching the game, afraid of something I couldn't see, but knew was right behind me. Couldn't move."

I glance at Staunton and he is staring at the moving pens. Roger has become silent once more, so I turn off the tape recorder and look also at the continuing record. Typical nightmare pattern.

Staunton yawns and I turn to him and say, "Why don't you try to get some sleep? Really, I'm fine. I slept almost all day, remember?"

He yawns again, then says, "If . . . if I seem to be dreaming, will you waken me?" I nod and he stretches out on the couch and is asleep almost instantly.

There is a coffee maker with strong coffee hot in it, and I pour myself a cup, and try to read the book that Roger provided, a spy thriller. I can't keep my mind on it. The hotel is no more noisy at night than my own house, but the noises are not the same, and I find myself listening to them, rustlings in the halls, distant doors opening and closing, the occasional squeak of the porch swing. I sit up straighter. A woman's laugh? Not at three-fifteen in the morning, surely. I have more coffee and wander to the window. A light on in the Sayer house? I blink and when I look again, I know that it was my imagination. I remember how their baby used to keep night hours, and smile. The baby would be fifteen or sixteen now, at least. I used to babysit for them now and then, and the child never slept.

I return to my chair by the electroencephalograph and see that Sid has started a new dream. I reach for the phone, waiting for the peak to level off again, and slowly withdraw my hand. He is dreaming a long one this time. After five minutes I begin to feel uneasy, but still I wait. Roger has said to rouse the sleeper after ten minutes of dreaming, if he hasn't shown any sign of being through by then. I wait, and suddenly jerk awake and stab my finger at the phone button. He doesn't answer.

I forget to turn on the recorder, but rush into the next room to bring him out of this dream turned into nightmare, and when I touch his shoulder, I am in it too.

Somerset is gay and alive with playing children, and sun umbrellas everywhere. There are tables on the lawn of Sagamore House, and ladies in long white skirts moving among them, laughing happily. The Governor is due and Dorothea and Annie are bustling about, ordering the girls in black aprons this way and that, and everywhere there is laughter. A small boy approaches the punch bowl with a wriggling frog held tightly in one hand, and he is caught and his knickers are pulled down summarily and the sounds of hand on bottom are plainly heard, followed by wails. I am so busy, and someone

46

keeps trying to pull me away and talk to me. I shake him off and run to the table where Father and Mother are sitting, and see to it that they have punch, and then swirl back to the kitchen where Dorothea is waiting for me to help her with the ice sculpture that is the centerpiece. It is a tall boy with curly hair rising up from a block of ice, the most beautiful thing I've ever seen, and I want to weep for him because in a few hours he will be gone. I slip on a piece of ice and fall, fall . . . fall . . .

I catch the wires attached to Sid and pull them loose, half pull him from the bed, and we end up in a heap. He holds me tightly for a long time, until we are both breathing normally again, and my shaking has stopped, and his too.

There is pale dawnlight in the room. Enough to see that his dark hair is damp with sweat, and curly on his forehead. He pushes it back and very gently moves me aside and disentangles himself from the wires.

"We have to get out of here," he says.

Staunton is sound asleep on the couch, breathing deeply but normally, and Roger is also sleeping. His graph shows that he has had nightmares several times.

We take our coffee into the room where Sid slept, and sit at the window drinking it, watching morning come to Somerset. I say, "They don't know, do they?"

"Of course not."

Poor Haddie appears at the far end of the street, walking toward Mr. Larson's store. He shuffles his feet as he moves, never lifting them more than an inch. I shudder and turn away.

"Isn't there something that we should do? Report this, or something?"

"Who would believe it? Staunton doesn't, and he has seen it over and over this week."

A door closes below us and I know Dorothea is up now, in the kitchen starting coffee. "I was in her dream, I think," I say.

I look down into my cup and think of the retirement villages all over the south, and again I shiver. "They seem so accepting, so at peace with themselves, just waiting for the end." I shake the last half inch of coffee back and forth. I ask, "Is that what happened with me? Did I not want to wake up?"

Sid nods. "I was taking the electrodes off your eyes when you snapped out of it, but yours wasn't a nightmare. It just wouldn't end. That's what frightened me, that it wasn't a nightmare. You didn't seem to be struggling against it at all. I wonder what brought you out of it this time."

I remember the gleaming ice sculpture, the boy with curly hair who will be gone so soon, and I know why I fought to get away. Someday I think probably I'll tell him, but not now, not so soon. The sun is high and the streets are bright now. I stand up. "I'm sorry that I forgot to turn on the tape recorder and ask you right away what the dream was. Do you remember it now?"

He hesitates only a moment and then shakes his head. Maybe someday he'll tell me, but not now, not so soon.

I leave him and find Dorothea waiting for me in the parlor. She draws me inside and shuts the door and takes a deep breath. "Janet, I am telling you that you must not bring your father back here to stay. It would be the worst possible thing for you to do."

I can't speak for a moment, but I hug her, and try not to see her etched face and the white hair, but to see her as she was when she was still in long skirts, with pretty pink cheeks and sparkling eyes. I can't manage it. "I know," I say finally. "I know."

Walking home again, hot in the sunlight, listening to the rustlings of Somerset, imagining the unseen life that flits here and there out of my line of vision, wondering if memories can become tangible, live a life of their own. I will pack, I think, and later in the day drive back up the mountain, back to the city, but not back to my job. Not back to administering death, even temporary death. Perhaps I shall go into psychiatry, or research psychology. As I begin to pack, my house stirs with movement.

The Roads, The Roads, The Beautiful Roads

by Avram Davidson

The rumor that the already controversial new double-speed thruway would be closed to motorcycles was just that: a rumor: and it had already been officially denied—twice. Craig Burns thought now that perhaps it had been a mistake to deny it at all. Gave the rumor dignity . . . his mind absently sought a better word as he slipped through the milling crowd (*crowd?* almost a mob) on the steps and in the corridors of the new State Capital Building. Currency! That was the word.

. . . gave the rumor currency . . .

Because, besides the usual knots of little old ladies with their *Trees, Yes! Thruway, No!* buttons, besides the inevitable delegations of hayseeds from Nowhere Flats who were either complaining that the thruway was scheduled to go too near their town or complaining that it wasn't scheduled to go near enough, besides the representatives of the rival guild—the urban planners—with their other ideas and their briefcases and their indoor-pale skins (so different from the ruddy glow or tan of a real out-in-all-weather man); besides all these (and including as always some Hire More Minority protesters), today it seemed as though all the motorcycle freaks in the state were on hand. On hand, and out for blood. Well, well, what the hell. It added a little color to the scene. And wouldn't make any difference at all, in the end: Gypsy Jokers with long hair, Hell's Angels who were merely shaggy, Brave Bulls in their Viking-horned crash helmets, and the Gentlemen of the Road, so super-groomed and—

With the blank face and absent-minded slouch he had learned to be the best thing for slipping through angry crowds, Craig managed to get almost to the door of the Committee Room without being recognized. And even then, with a pleasant smile, he succeeded in getting inside before the reporters and cameramen got to him. With an apologetic gesture. No point in antagonizing Media, generally so helpful in picking out and publicizing the more outstanding of the anti-highways people and thus showing them up for the nuts and oddballs that they really were. But it made little sense to stop in the middle of them just to grant an on-the-spot interview.

In fact, Burns thought, taking one last look, head half-turned, it made no sense at all.

Horns on their crash helmets, for God's sake!

Just as some composers never tire of playing their own music, so Craig Burns never tired of driving over the beautiful highways he . . . well . . . he and his Department . . . had created. It had been a labor of love building them, seeing each one through from the preliminary survey through actual construction to the time he liked best of all. When the roads were ready to go but not yet open to the public. When he could drive along and drive alone for miles . . . and miles . . . sometimes for hundreds of miles. Just Highway Chief Craig Burns and his car and his beautiful roads, with their lovely and intricate bypasses and cloverleafs and underpasses, slow and steady when he felt like it, revving it up and gauging the niceties of the straight stretches or the delightfully calculated curves when he felt like it. Over and under and around and across and back and under and—

—nobody on the whole highway but *him*.

It was better than a woman. It was better even than the power of office. It was just about the best thing there was.

Sometimes, smiling to himself, he wondered if he really didn't sometimes push through new road plans just for the sheer pleasure of this, even if the new roads weren't really needed. But the smile was for the joke, the secret, private little joke, for there was really no such thing as a new road which wasn't needed. And as for the things which weren't so nice . . . the stupid, stupid, jackass things which people did with the beautiful roads . . . crowding and packing and jamming them with their cars and trucks and motorcycles and station wagons . . . stupid people, stupid jerks, jackasses!— so that all kinds of things had to be done, afterwards, to the sweet and clean and lovely new roads—

As for that, Craig didn't care to think about that, much. It made him get that hot feeling in the skin of his face, that surging, raging feeling around his heart. That sort of thing, he left mostly to the others in the Department. And everybody else in the Department was the others. He'd created. Let them mar it, since it had to be marred. Changing routes, adding, subtracting, closing down, chopping and changing—let *them* do it. It wasn't his fault.

Probably the hearing had taken more out of him than he'd realized. And so damned unnecessary. Legislative hearings! After all, what did the legislature have to do with it? The very state constitution granted the Highways Department all the authority it needed. It could condemn property and pay what it knew to be right and reasonable. It could say where the roads would go and where they wouldn't go. What shape they'd take. How to design and how to build. The roads, the roads were engineered beautifully. It was the stupid bastard *people* who were engineered wrong. Tiring him out and confusing him with their hearings and demonstrations. No wonder he'd missed the Hadley turnoff. That is, well, yeah, sure, he must have missed it. This cloverleaf was *after* the Hadley turnoff. Well, nothing to do but turn around and go back. The afternoon had yeah, you bet, upset him. But what in hell did the rest of the people have to be upset about? All that crap about highways de*hu*manizing, for Christ's sake.— Take this next turn.

No!

Well, had no choice, stupid jerk back there zooming along

51

and forcing him— All that crap about highways exhausting, hypnotizing, confusing . . . All that crap. Look at this lovely cloverleaf. And this neat tunnel, here. No, but it wasn't the *highway*, for God's sake, it was just that stupid—

Okay, then, he just couldn't remember this tunnel. So what? All the highways in the state— *Okay,* that was that, *out* of the tunnel! Nothing hard about that! And back on the cloverleaf again.

*Clo*verleaf? There wasn't supposed to be— And hadn't he had a clear glimpse, in the shadows and the blinking lights (make mental note: report defective lights) of another tunnel branching off back— Hadley turnoff. Great. Just tired out after that damned hearing, crowd, mob, reporters, motorcycle gangs, what the hell. What the *hell!* Cloverleaf! Tunnel! Tunnel branching off, no he didn't want it, well for God's *sake!* Here he *was.* Lights bad, lights very bad, lights worse. No lights. No traffic, either, for that matter. Must be, yes, certainly: *was*: a discontinued branch tunnel. Vague recollection. Bad drainage. Turned out not to fit in with new, unforeseen traffic pattern subsequently developed. Bad air. Bad smell. Car gone dead! Flip on the radio, signal for the Department's very own high-speed tow-car and ever-ready private Departmental emergency limousine. Radio dead. Of course. Tunnel. Okay. Okay. Okay. Get out, walk.

Seemed, it seemed to Craig that it was, must, had to be shorter going ahead than going back. A car. Stopped. He waited for the head to be stuck out of the window, the smashed and dusty window. Motorcycle on its side. Station wagon almost a third of the way up the ramp. What crazy— Of course. Word had gotten around, sure. And those in the know had taken their old hulks and abandoned them here. Oh boy. Thought they'd save money, avoid tickets, ah. Another think coming. *Look* at them all! And what a stink, what—

Definitely, someone, something, was moving up ahead there. Half in the shadows cast by strange, dim light. A man, sure enough. Black leather jacket, filthy jeans, obscene feet, and—

52

Craig Burns turned and fled, his screams echoing, echoing.

Behind him, unhurried, assured, horns jutting from the helmet on his head, the newest minotaur followed upon his newest victim.

Look, You Think You've Got Troubles

by Carol Carr

To tell you the truth, in the old days we would have sat shivah for the whole week. My so-called daughter gets married, my own flesh and blood, and not only he doesn't look Jewish, he's not even human.

"Papa," she says to me, two seconds after I refuse to speak to her again in my entire life, "if you know him you'll love him, I promise." So what can I answer—the truth, like I always tell her: "If I know him I'll vomit, that's how he affects me. I can help it? He makes me want to throw up on him."

With silk gloves you have to handle the girl, just like her mother. I tell her what I feel, from the heart, and right away her face collapses into a hundred cracks and water from the Atlantic Ocean makes a soggy mess out of her paper sheath. And that's how I remember her after six months—standing in front of me, sopping wet from the tears and making me feel like a monster—me—when all the time it's her you-should-excuse-the-expression husband who's the monster.

After she's gone to live with him (New Horizon Pillage, Crag City, Mars), I try to tell myself it's not me who has to—how can I put it?—deal with him intimately; if she can stand it, why should I complain? It's not like I need somebody to carry on the business; my business is to enjoy myself in my retirement. But who can enjoy? Sadie doesn't leave me alone for a minute. She calls me a criminal, a worthless no-good with gallstones for a heart.

"Hector, where's your brains?" she says, having finally given up on my emotions. I can't answer her. I just lost my daughter, I should worry about my brains too? I'm silent as the grave. I can't eat a thing. I'm empty—drained. It's as though I'm waiting for something to happen but I don't know what. I sit in a chair that folds me up like a bee in a flower and rocks me to sleep with electronic rhythms when I feel like sleeping, but who can sleep? I look at my wife and I see Lady Macbeth. Once I caught her whistling as she pushed the button for her bath. I fixed her with a look like an icicle tipped with arsenic.

"What are you so happy about? Thinking of your grandchildren with the twelve toes?"

She doesn't flinch. An iron woman.

When I close my eyes, which is rarely, I see our daughter when she was fourteen years old, with skin just beginning to go pimply and no expression yet on her face. I see her walking up to Sadie and asking her what she should do with her life now she's filling out, and my darling Sadie, my life's mate, telling her why not marry a freak; you got to be a beauty to find a man here, but on Mars you shouldn't know from so many fish. "I knew I could count on you, Mama," she says, and goes ahead and marries a plant with legs.

Things go on like this—impossible—for months. I lose twenty pounds, my nerves, three teeth and I'm on the verge of losing Sadie, when one day the mailchute goes ding-dong and it's a letter from my late daughter. I take it by the tips of two fingers and bring it in to where my wife is punching ingredients for the gravy I won't eat tonight.

"It's a communication from one of your relatives."

"Oh-oh-oh." My wife makes a grab for it, meanwhile punching CREAM-TOMATO-SAUCE-BEEF DRIPPINGS. No wonder I have no appetite.

"I'll give it to you on one condition only," I tell her, holding it out of her trembling reach. "Take it into the bedroom and read it to yourself. Don't even move your lips for once; I don't want to know. If she's God forbid dead, I'll send him a sympathy card."

Sadie has a variety of expressions but the one thing they

have in common is they all wish me misfortune in my present and future life.

While she's reading the letter I find suddenly I have nothing to do. The magazines I read already. Breakfast I ate (like a bird). I'm all dressed to go out if I felt like, but there's nothing outside I don't have inside. Frankly, I don't feel like myself—I'm nervous. I say a lot of things I don't really intend and now maybe this letter comes to tell me I've got to pay for my meanness. Maybe she got sick up there; God knows what they eat, the kind of water they drink, the creatures they run around with. Not wanting to think about it too much, I go over to my chair and turn it on to brisk massage. It doesn't take long till I'm dreaming (fitfully).

I'm someplace surrounded by sand, sitting in a baby's crib and bouncing a diapered kangaroo on my knee. It gurgles up at me and calls me grandpa and I don't know what I should do. I don't want to hurt its feelings, but if I'm a grandpa to a kangaroo, I want no part of it; I only want it should go away. I pull out a dime from my pocket and put it into its pouch. The pouch is full of tiny insects which bite my fingers. I wake up in a sweat.

"Sadie! Are you reading, or rearranging the sentences? Bring it in here and I'll see what she wants. If it's a divorce, I know a lawyer."

Sadie comes into the room with her I-told-you-so waddle and gives me a small wet kiss on the cheek—a gold star for acting like a mensch. So I start to read it, in a loud monotone so she shouldn't get the impression I give a damn:

"Dear Daddy, I'm sorry for not writing sooner. I suppose I wanted to give you a chance to simmer down first." (Ingrate! Does the sun simmer down?) "I know it would have been inconvenient for you to come to the wedding, but Mor and I hoped you would maybe send us a letter just to let us know you're okay and still love me, in spite of everything."

Right at this point I feel a hot sigh followed by a short but wrenching moan.

"Sadie, get away from my neck. I'm warning you . . ."

Her eyes are going flick-a-fleck over my shoulder, from the

56

piece of paper I'm holding to my face, back to the page, flick-a-fleck, flick-a-fleck.

"All right, already," she shoo-shoos me. "I read it, I know what's in it. Now it's your turn to see what kind of a lousy father you turned out to be." And she waddles back into the bedroom, shutting the door extra careful, like she's handling a piece of snow-white velvet.

When I'm certain she's gone, I sit myself down on the slab of woven dental floss my wife calls a couch and press a button on the arm that reads SEMI-CL.: FELDMAN TO FRIML. The music starts to slither out from the speaker under my left armpit. The right speaker is dead and buried and the long narrow one at the base years ago got drowned from the dog, who to this day hasn't learned to control himself when he hears "Desert Song."

This time I'm lucky; it's a piece by Feldman that comes on. I continue to read, calmed by the music.

"I might as well get to the point, Papa, because for all I know you're so mad you tore up this letter without even reading it. The point is that Mor and I are going to have a baby. Please, please don't throw this into the disintegrator. It's due in July, which gives you over three months to plan the trip up here. We have a lovely house, with a guest room that you and Mama can stay in for as long as you want."

I have to stop here to interject a couple of questions, since my daughter never had a head for logic and it's my strong point.

First of all, if she were in front of me in person right now I would ask right off what means "Mor and I are going to have a baby." Which? Or both? The second thing is, when she refers to it as "it" is she being literal or just uncertain? And just one more thing and then I'm through for good: Just how lovely can a guest room be that has all the air piped in and you can't even see the sky or take a walk on the grass because there is no grass, only simulated this and substituted that?

All the above notwithstanding, I continue to read:

"By the way, Papa, there's something I'm not sure you understand. Mor, you may or may not know, is as human as you

57

and me, in all the important ways—and frankly a bit more intelligent."

I put down the letter for a minute just to give the goose-bumps a chance to fly out of my stomach ulcers before I go on with her love and best and kisses and hopes for seeing us soon, Lorinda.

I don't know how she manages it, but the second I'm finished, Sadie is out of the bedroom and breathing hard.

"Well, do I start packing or do I start packing? And when I start packing, do I pack for us or do I pack for me?"

"Never. I should die three thousand deaths, each one with a worse prognosis."

It's a shame a company like Interplanetary Aviation can't afford, with the fares they charge, to give you a comfortable seat. Don't ask how I ever got there in the first place. Ask my wife—she's the one with the mouth. First of all, they only allow you three pounds of luggage, which if you're only bringing clothes is plenty, but we had a few gifts with us. We were only planning to stay a few days and to sublet the house was Sadie's idea, not mine.

The whole trip was supposed to take a month, each way. This is one reason Sadie thought it was impractical to stay for the weekend and then go home, which was the condition on which I'd agreed to go.

But now that we're on our way, I decide I might as well relax. I close my eyes and try to think of what the first meeting will be like.

"How." I put up my right hand in a gesture of friendship and trust. I reach into my pocket and offer him beads.

But even in my mind he looks at me blank, his naked pink antennas waving in the breeze like a worm's underwear. Then I realize there isn't any breeze where we're going. So they stop waving and wilt.

I look around in my mind. We're alone, the two of us, in the middle of a vast plain, me in my business suit and him in his green skin. The scene looks familiar, like something I had

58

experienced, or read about. . . . "We'll meet at Philippi," I think, and stab him with my sword.

Only then am I able to catch a few winks.

The month goes by. When I begin to think I'll never remember how to use a fork, the loudspeaker is turned on and I hear this very smooth, modulated voice, the tranquilized tones of a psychiatrist sucking glycerine, telling us it's just about over, and we should expect a slight jolt upon landing.

That slight jolt starts my life going by so fast I'm missing all the good parts. But finally the ship is still and all you can hear are the wheezes and sighs of the engines—the sounds remind me of Sadie when she's winding down from a good argument. I look around. Everybody is very white. Sadie's five fingers are around my upper arm like a tourniquet.

"We're here," I tell her. "Do I get a hacksaw or can you manage it yourself?"

"Oh, my goodness." She loosens her grip. She really looks a mess—completely pale, not blinking, not even nagging.

I take her by the arm and steer her into customs. All the time I feel that she's a big piece of unwilling luggage I'm smuggling in. There's no cooperation at all in her feet and her eyes are going every which way.

"Sadie, shape up!"

"If you had a little more curiosity about the world you'd be a better person," she says tolerantly.

While we're waiting to be processed by a creature in a suit like ours who surprises me by talking English, I sneak a quick look around.

It's funny. If I didn't know where we are I'd think we're in the back yard. The ground stretches out pure green, and it's only from the leaflet they give you in the ship to keep your mind off the panic that I know it's 100% Acrispan we're looking at, not grass. The air we're getting smells good, too, like fresh-cut flowers, but not too sweet.

By the time I've had a good look and a breathe, what's-its-name is handing us back our passports with a button that says to keep Mars beautiful don't litter.

I won't tell you about the troubles we had getting to the

59

house, or the misunderstanding about the tip, because to be honest I wasn't paying attention. But we do manage to make it to the right door, and considering that the visit was a surprise, I didn't really expect they would meet us at the airport. My daughter must have been peeking, though, because she's in front of us even before we have a chance to knock.

"Mother!" she says, looking very round in the stomach. She hugs and kisses Sadie, who starts bawling. Five minutes later, when they're out of the clinch, Lorinda turns to me, a little nervous.

You can say a lot of things about me, but basically I'm a warm person, and we're about to be guests in this house, even if she is a stranger to me. I shake her hand.

"Is he home, or is he out in the back yard, growing new leaves?"

Her face (or what I can see of it through the climate adapter) crumbles a little at the chin line, but she straightens it out and puts her hand on my shoulder.

"Mor had to go out, Daddy—something important came up—but he should be back in an hour or so. Come on, let's go inside."

Actually there's nothing too crazy about the house, or even interesting. It has walls, a floor and a roof, I'm glad to see, even a few relaxer chairs, and after the trip we just had, I sit down and relax. I notice my daughter is having a little trouble looking me straight in the face, which is only as it should be, and it isn't long before she and Sadie are discussing pregnancy, gravitational exercise, labor, hospitals, formulas and sleep-taught toilet training. When I'm starting to feel that I'm getting over-educated, I decide to go into the kitchen and make myself a bite to eat. I could have asked them for a little something but I don't want to interfere with their first conversation. Sadie has all engines going and is interrupting four times a sentence, which is exactly the kind of game they always had back home—my daughter's goal is to say one complete thought out loud. If Sadie doesn't spring back with a non sequitur, Lorinda wins that round. A full-fledged knockout with Sadie still champion is when my daughter can't get a sentence in for a week. Sometimes I can understand why she went to Mars.

Anyway, while they're at the height of their simultaneous monologues, I go quietly off to the kitchen to see what I can dig up. (Ripe parts of Mor, wrapped in plastic? Does he really regenerate, I wonder. Does Lorinda fully understand how he works, or one day will she make an asparagus omelet out of one of his appendages, only to learn that's the part that doesn't grow back? "Oh, I'm so *sorry*," she says. "Can you ever forgive me?")

The refrigerator, though obsolete on Earth, is well stocked —fruits of a sort, steaks, it seems, small chicken-type things that might be stunted pigeons. There's a bowl of a brownish, creamy mess—I can't even bring myself to smell it. Who's hungry, anyway, I think. The rumbling in my stomach is the symptom of a father's love turning sour.

I wander into the bedroom. There's a large portrait of Mor hanging on the wall—or maybe his ancestor. Is it true that instead of hearts, Martians have a large avocado pit? There's a rumor on Earth that when Martians get old they start to turn brown at the edges, like lettuce.

There's an object on the floor and I bend down and pick it up. A piece of material—at home I would have thought it was a man's handkerchief. Maybe it is a handkerchief. Maybe they have colds like us. They catch a germ, the sap rises to combat the infection, and they have to blow their stamens. I open up a drawer to put the piece of material in (I like to be neat), but when I close it, something gets stuck. Another thing I can't recognize. It's small, round and either concave or convex, depending on how you look at it. It's made of something black and shiny. A cloth bowl? What would a vegetable be doing with a cloth bowl? Some questions are too deep for me, but what I don't know I eventually find out— and not by asking, either.

I go back to the living room.

"Did you find anything to eat?" Lorinda asks. "Or would you like me to fix—"

"Don't even get up," Sadie says quickly. "I can find my way around any kitchen, I don't care whose."

"I'm not hungry. It was a terrible trip. I thought I'd never wake up from it in one piece. By the way, I heard a good riddle on the ship. What's round and black, either concave or convex, depending on how you look at it, and made out of a shiny material?"

Lorinda blushed. "A skullcap? But that's not funny."

"So who needs funny? Riddles have to be a laugh a minute all of a sudden? You think Oedipus giggled all the way home from seeing the Sphinx?"

"Look, Daddy, I think there's something I should tell you."

"I think there are all sorts of things you should tell me."

"No, I mean about Mor."

"Who do you think *I* mean, the grocery boy? You elope with a cucumber from outer space and you want I should be satisfied because he's human in all the important ways? What's important—that he sneezes and hiccups? If you tell me he snores, I should be ecstatic? Maybe he sneezes when he's happy and hiccups when he's making love and snores because it helps him think better. Does that make him human?"

"Daddy, *please*."

"Okay, not another word." Actually I'm starting to feel quite guilty. What if she has a miscarriage right on the spot? A man like me doesn't blithely torture a pregnant woman, even if she does happen to be his daughter. "What's so important it can't wait till later?"

"Nothing, I guess. Would you like some chopped liver? I just made some fresh."

"What?"

"Chopped liver—you know, chopped liver."

Oh yes, the ugly mess in the refrigerator. "You made it, that stuff in the bowl?"

"Sure. Daddy, there's something I really have to tell you."

She never does get to tell me, though, because her husband walks in, bold as brass.

I won't even begin to tell you what he looks like. Let me just say he's a good dream cooked up by Mary Shelley. I won't go into it, but if it gives you a small idea, I'll say that his head is shaped like an acorn on top of a stalk of broccoli. Enormous blue eyes, green skin and no hair at all except for a small blue round area on top of his head. His ears are adorable. Remember Dumbo the Elephant? Only a little smaller— I never exaggerate, even for effect. And he looks boneless, like a filet.

My wife, God bless her, I don't have to worry about; she's a gem in a crisis. One look at her son-in-law and she faints dead away. If I didn't know her better, if I wasn't absolutely certain that her simple mind contained no guile, I would have sworn she did it on purpose, to give everybody something to fuss about. Before we know what's happening, we're all in a tight, frantic conversation about what's the best way to bring her around. But while my daughter and her husband are in the bathroom looking for some deadly chemical, Sadie opens both eyes at once and stares up at me from the floor.

"What did I miss?"

"You didn't miss anything—you were only unconscious for fifteen seconds. It was a cat nap, not a coma."

"Say hello, Hector. Say hello to him or so help me I'll close my eyes for good."

"I'm very glad to meet you, Mr. Trumbnick," he says. I'm grateful that he's sparing me the humiliation of making the first gesture, but I pretend I don't see the stalk he's holding out.

"Smutual," I say.

"I beg your pardon?"

"Smutual. How are you? You look better than your pictures." He does, too. Even though his skin is green, it looks like the real thing up close. But his top lip sort of vibrates when he talks, and I can hardly bear to look at him except sideways.

"I hear you had some business this afternoon. My daughter never did tell me what your line is, uh, Morton."

"Daddy, his name is Mor. Why don't you call him Mor?"

"Because I prefer Morton. When we know each other better

63

I'll call him something less formal. Don't rush me, Lorinda; I'm still getting adjusted to the chopped liver."

My son-in-law chuckles and his top lip really goes crazy. "Oh, were you surprised? Imported meats aren't a rarity here, you know. Just the other day one of my clients was telling me about an all-Earth meal he had at home."

"Your client?" Sadie asks. "You wouldn't happen to be a lawyer?" (My wife amazes me with her instant familiarity. She could live with a tyrannosaurus in perfect harmony. First she faints, and while she's out cold everything in her head that was strange becomes ordinary and she wakes up a new woman.)

"No, Mrs. Trumbnick. I'm a—"

"—rabbi, of course," she finishes. "I knew it. The minute Hector found that skullcap I knew it. Him and his riddles. A skullcap is a skullcap and nobody not Jewish would dare wear one—not even a Martian." She bites her lip but recovers like a pro. "I'll bet you were out on a Bar Mitzvah—right?"

"No, as a matter of fact—"

"—a Bris. I knew it."

She's rubbing her hands together and beaming at him. "A Bris, how *nice*. But why didn't you tell us, Lorinda? Why would you keep such a thing a secret?"

Lorinda comes over to me and kisses me on the cheek, and I wish she wouldn't because I'm feeling myself go soft and I don't want to show it.

"Mor isn't *just* a rabbi, Daddy. He converted because of me and then found there was a demand among the colonists. But he's never given up his own beliefs, and part of his job is to minister to the Kopchopees who camp outside the village. That's where he was earlier, conducting a Kopchopee menopausal rite."

"A what!"

"Look, to each his own," says my wife with the open mind. But me, I want facts, and this is getting more bizarre by the minute.

"Kopchopee. He's a Kopchopee priest to his own race and a

64

rabbi to ours, and that's how he makes his living? You don't feel there's a contradiction between the two, Morton?"

"That's right. They both pray to a strong silent god, in different ways of course. The way my race worships, for instance—"

"Listen, it takes all kinds," says Sadie.

"And the baby, whatever it turns out to be—will it be a Choptapi or a Jew?"

"Jew, shmoo," Sadie says with a wave of dismissal. "All of a sudden it's Hector the Pious—such a megilla out of a molehill." She turns away from me and addresses herself to the others, like I've just become invisible. "He hasn't seen the inside of a synagogue since we got married—what a rain that night—and now he can't take his shoes off in a house until he knows its race, color and creed." With a face full of fury, she brings me back into her sight. "Nudnick, what's got into you?"

I stand up straight to preserve my dignity. "If you'll excuse me, my things are getting wrinkled in the suitcase."

Sitting on my bed (with my shoes on), I must admit I'm feeling a little different. Not that Sadie made me change my mind. Far from it; for many years now her voice is the white sound that lets me think my own thoughts. But what I'm realizing more and more is that in a situation like this a girl needs her father, and what kind of a man is it who can't sacrifice his personal feelings for his only daughter? When she was going out with Herbie the Hemopheliac and came home crying it had to end because she was afraid to touch him, he might bleed, didn't I say pack your things, we're going to Grossingers Venus for three weeks? When my twin brother Max went into kitchen sinks, who was it that helped him out at only four per cent? Always, I stood ready to help my family. And if Lorinda ever needed me, it's now when she's pregnant by some religious maniac. Okay—he makes me retch, so I'll talk to him with a tissue over my mouth. After all, in a world that's getting smaller all the time, it's people like me who have to be bigger to make up for it, no?

I go back to the living room and extend my hand to my son-in-law the cauliflower. (Feh.)

65

Winter's King

by Ursula K. LeGuin

When whirlpools appear in the onward run of time and history seems to swirl around a snag, as in the curious matter of the Succession of Karhide, then pictures come in handy: snapshots, which may be taken up and matched to compare the young king to the old king, the father to the son, and which may also be rearranged and shuffled till the years run straight. For despite the tricks played by instantaneous interstellar communication and just-sub-lightspeed interstellar travel, time (as the Plenipotentiary Axt remarked) does not reverse itself; nor is death mocked.

Thus, although the best-known picture is that dark image of a young man standing above an old one who lies dead in a corridor lit only by mirror-reflections in vague alcoves of a burning city, set it aside a while. Look first at the young king, the pride of his people, as bright and fortunate a man as ever lived to twenty-two; but when this picture was taken he had his back against a wall. He was filthy, he was trembling, and his face was blank and mad, for he had lost that minimal confidence in the world which is called sanity. Inside his head he repeated, as he had been repeating for hours or years, over and over, "I will abdicate. I will abdicate. I will abdicate." Inside his eyes he saw the red-walled rooms of the Palace, the towers and streets of Erhenrang in falling snow, the lovely plains of the West Fall, the white summits of the Kargav, and he renounced them all. "I will abdicate," he said not aloud and then, aloud, screamed as once again the man dressed in red and white approached him saying, "Sir! a plot against your

66

life has been discovered in the Artisan School," and the humming noise began again, softly. He hid his head in his arms and whispered, "Stop it, stop it," but the humming whine grew higher and louder and nearer, relentless, until it was so high and loud that it entered his flesh, tore the nerves from their channels and made his bones dance and jangle, hopping to its tune. He hopped and twitched, bare bones strung on thin white threads, and wept dry tears, and shouted, "Have them— Have them— They must— Executed— Stopped— Stop!"

It stopped.

He fell in a clattering chattering heap to the floor. What floor? Not red tiles, not parquetry, not urine-stained cement, but the wood floor of the room in the tower, the tower room where he was safe, safe from the old, mad, terrible man, the king, his father. In shadows there he hid away from the voice and from the great, gripping hand that wore the Sign-Ring. But there was no hiding, no safety, no shadow. The man dressed in black had come even here and had hold of his head, lifted it up, lifted on thin white strings the eyelids he tried to close.

"Who am I? Who am I?"

The blank black mask stared down, and the young king struggled, sobbing, because now the suffocation would begin: he would not be able to breathe until he gasped out the name, the right name—"Gerer!"— He could breathe. He was allowed to breathe, he had recognized the black one in time. "Who am I?" said a different voice, gently, and the young king groped for that strong presence that always brought him sleep, truce, solace. "Rebade," he whispered, "oh God! tell me what to do. . . ."

"Sleep."

He obeyed. A deep sleep and dreamless, for it was real: in reality he was dead. Dreams came at waking, now. Unreal, the horrible dry red light of sunset burned his eyes open and he stood, once more, on the Palace balcony looking down at fifty thousand black pits opening and shutting. From the pits came a paroxysmic gush of sound again and again, a shrill rhythmic eructation: his name. His name was screamed in his ears as a taunt, as a jeer. He beat his hands on the narrow brass railing and shouted to them, "I will silence you!" He could not hear his voice, only their voice, the pestilent mouths of the mob that feared and hated him, screaming his name. —"Come away, my lord," said the one gentle voice, and Rebade drew him away from the balcony into the vast, red-walled quiet of the Hall of Audience. The screaming ceased as if a machine had been switched off. Rebade's look was as always composed, compassionate. "What will you do now?" he asked.

"I will— I will ab- abdicate—"

"No," Rebade said calmly. "That is not right. What will you do now?"

The young king stood silent, shaking. Rebade helped him sit down on his iron cot, for the walls had darkened as they often did and drawn in all about him to a little cell. "Call—?"

"Call up the Palace Guards. Have them shoot into the crowd. Shoot to kill. They must be taught a lesson." The young king spoke rapidly and distinctly in a loud, high voice. Rebade said. "Good, my lord, a wise decision! Right. We shall come out all right: you'll see. Trust me, my lord."

"I do. I trust you. Get me out of here," the young king whispered, seizing Rebade's arm: but his friend frowned. That was not right. He had driven Rebade and hope away again. Rebade was leaving now, calm and regretful, although the young king begged him to stop, to come back, for the noise was softly beginning again, the whining hum that tore his mind to pieces, and already the man in red and white was approaching across a red, interminable floor. "Sir! a plot against your life has been discovered in the Artisan School—"

Down Old Harbor Street clear to the water's edge the street-lamps burned cavernously bright. Guardsman Pepenerer on his rounds glanced down that empty, slanting vault of light expecting nothing, and saw a creature staggering up it toward him. Pepenerer did not believe in porngropes, but he now saw a porngrope, sea-beslimed, staggering on thin webbed feet, gasping dry air—he could hear it gasping. . . . Old sailors' tales slid out of mind and he saw a man, sick or drunk or drugged, and he ran down Old Harbor Street between the blank grey warehouse walls, calling, "Now then! Hold on there!"

It was a tall young fellow, half naked and crazy-looking. Even as he gasped, "Help me," and the Guardsman reached a hand out to him, he lost his nerve, dodged away in rabid terror, and ran. He ran a few steps, stumbled, and pitched down slithering in the frost-slicked stones of the street. Pepenerer got out his gun and gave him .14 seconds of stun, just enough to keep him from thrashing about; then squatted down by him, palmed his radio and called the West Ward for a car. The fellow lay sprawled out meek as a corpse, eyes and mouth half open, arms flung wide as he had fallen. Both arms on the biceps and inner forearm were blotched with injection-marks. Pepenerer took a whiff of his breath, but got no resinous scent of orgrevy; likely he was not on a bender but had been drugged. Thieves, or a ritual clan-revenge. Thieves would not have left the gold ring on his forefinger: a massive thing, carved, as wide almost as the finger-joint. Pepenerer crouched forward to look at it, and then he turned his head and looked at the beaten, blank face in profile against the paving-stones, hard hit by the glare of the streetlamps. Pepenerer got a new quarter-crown piece out of his pouch and looked at the left profile stamped on the bright tin, and back at the right profile stamped in light and shadow and cold stone; then hearing the purr of the electric car turning down the Longway into Old Harbor Street he hastily put the coin away, muttering, "Damn fool."

King Argaven was off hunting in the mountains, anyhow, and had been for a couple of weeks; it had been in all the bulletins.

"You see," said Hoge the physician, "we can assume that he was mindformed; but that gives us almost nothing to go on. There are too many people in Karhide, and in Orgoreyn, for that matter, who are expert mindformers. Not criminals whom the police might have a lead on, but respectable teachers or physicians. And the drugs are available to any physician. As for getting anything from him, if they had any skill at all they will have blocked everything they did to rational access. All clues will be buried, the trigger-suggestions hidden, and we simply cannot guess what questions to ask. There is no way, short of brain-destruction, of going through everything in his mind; and even under hypnosis and deep drugging, which are dangerous, there would be no way now to distinguish implanted ideas or emotions from his own autonomous ones. Perhaps the Aliens could do something, though I doubt their mindscience is all they boast of; at any rate it's out of reach. We have only one real hope."

"Which is?" Lord Gerer asked, stolidly.

"The king is a quick and resolute man. At the beginning, before they broke him, he may have known what they were doing to him, and so put up some block or resistance, left himself some escape route. . . ."

Hoge's low voice lost confidence as he spoke, and trailed off in the silence of the high, red, dusky room. He drew no response from the old man who stood, black-clad, before the fire.

The temperature of that room in the King's Palace of Erhenrang was 54° F. where Lord Gerer stood, and 38° midway between the two big fireplaces; outside it was snowing lightly, a mild 22°. Spring had come to Winter. The fires at either end of the room roared red and gold, devouring thigh-thick logs. Magnificence, a harsh luxury, a wasteful splendor, fireplace, fireworks, lightning, meteor, volcano, such things satisfied the men of Karhide on the world Winter. But, except in Arctic colonies above the 35th parallel, they had never installed central heating in any building in the fifteen hundred years of their Age of Invention. Comfort came to them rare, welcome, and unsought: an accident, like joy.

Korgry, sitting beside the bed, turned glancing a moment at the physician and the Lord Councillor, though he did not speak. Both at once crossed the room to him. The broad, hard bed, high on gilt pillars, heavy with a finery of red cloaks and coverlets, bore up the king's body level with their eyes. To

Gerer it appeared a ship breasting, motionless, a swift vast flood of dark, carrying the young king into shadows, terrors, years. Then with terror of his own the old lord saw that Argaven's eyes were open, staring out a half-curtained, narrow window at the stars.

Gerer feared lunacy; idiocy; he did not know what he feared. Hoge had warned him: "He will not 'be himself,' Lord Gerer. He has suffered thirteen days of torment, intimidation, exhaustion, and mindhandling. There may be brain damage, there certainly will be side- and after-effects of several drugs." Neither fear nor warning parried the shock. Argaven's bright, weary eyes turned to Gerer and paused on him blankly a moment: then saw him. And Gerer, though he could not see the black mask reflected, saw the hate, the horror, saw his young king, infinitely beloved, gasping in imbecile terror and struggling with Korgry, with Hoge, with his own weakness in the effort to get away, to get away from Gerer.

Standing in the cold midst of the room where the tall prow-like head of the bedstead hid him from the king, the old lord heard them pacify Argaven and settle him down again. Argaven's voice sounded reedy, childishly plaintive. So the Old King, Emran, had spoken in his madness with a child's voice. Then silence, and the great fires burned.

Korgry the king's bodyservant yawned and rubbed his eyes. Hoge measured something from a vial into a hypodermic. Gerer stood in despair. My son, my son, my king, what have they done to you? So great a trust, so fair a promise, lost, lost . . . So the one who looked like a lump of half-carved black rock, a heavy, prudent, rude old man, grieved and was passion-racked, his love and service of the young king being the world's one worth to him.

Argaven spoke aloud: "My son—"

Gerer winced, feeling the words torn out of his own mind; but Hoge, untroubled by love, comprehended and said softly to Argaven, "The prince is well, sir. He and his mother are at Warlever Castle. We are in constant communication with the party by radio. The last time was a couple of hours ago. All well there."

71

Gerer heard the king's harsh breathing, and came somewhat closer to the bed, though out of sight still behind the red-draped headboard.

"Have I been sick?"

"You are not well yet, sir," the physician said, bland.

"Where—"

"Your own room, sir, in the Palace in Erhenrang."

But Gerer, coming forward though not to where Argaven could see his face, said, "You are home now. We do not know where you were."

Hoge's smooth face creased with a frown, though he dared not, physician as he was and so in his way master of them all, direct the frown at the Lord Councillor. Gerer's voice did not seem to trouble the king, who asked another question or two, sane and brief, and then lay still again. Presently Korgry, who had sat with him ever since he had been brought into the Palace (last night, in secret, by side doors, like a shameful suicide of the last reign, but all in reverse), Korgry committed lèse-majesté: huddled forward on his high chair he let his head droop on the side of the bed, and slept. The guard at the door yielded his post to a new guard, in whispers. Officials came and received a fresh bulletin for public release on the state of the King's health, in whispers. Stricken by severe symptoms of horm-fever while hunting in the High Kargav, the king had been rushed by private car to Erhenrang and was now responding satisfactorily to treatment, etc. Mr. Physician Hoge rem ir Hogeremme at the Palace has released the following statement, etc., etc. "God restore him," men said in small houses as they lit the fire on the altarhearth; old women said, "It comes of him roving around the city in the night and hunting up there in the snowy precipices, fool tricks like that," but they kept the radio turned on to catch the next bulletin. A very great number of people had come and gone and loitered and chatted this day in the great square before the Palace, watching those who went in and out, watching the vacant balcony; even now there were several hundred people down there, standing around patiently in the snow. Argaven XVII was loved in his domain. After the dull

72

brutality of his father Emran's reign that ended in the shadow of madness and the country's bankruptcy, he had come: sudden, gallant, young, changing everything; sane and shrewd, yet with a brilliance of magnanimity in all his acts. He had the fire, the splendor that suited his people. He was the force and center of a new age, a man born, for once, king of the right kingdom.

"Gerer."

It was the king's voice, and Gerer hastened, stiff and quick, through the hot and cold of the great room, the firelight and dark. "My lord?"

Argaven had got himself sitting up. His arms shook and the breath caught in his throat; his eyes burned across the dark air at Gerer. By his left hand, which bore the Sign-Ring of the Harge dynasty, lay the sleeping face of the servant, serene, derelict. "Gerer," the king said with effort and clarity, "summon the Council. Tell them, I will abdicate."

So crude, so simple? All the drugs, the terrorizing, the hypnosis, parahypnosis, neurone-stimulation, synapsepairing, spotshock that Hoge had described, for this blunt result? All the same, reasoning must wait. They must temporize. "As soon as your strength returns, sir—"

"Now. Call the Council, Gerer!"

Then he broke, like a bowstring breaking, and stammered in a fury of fear that found no sense or strength to flesh itself in; and still his faithful servant slept, deaf, beside his torment.

In the next picture things are going better, it appears: here is King Argaven XVII in good health and clothes, a handsome young man finishing a large breakfast. He talks with the nearer dozen of the forty or fifty people sharing or serving the meal (singularity is a king's prerogative, but seldom privacy), and includes all the rest in the largesse of his looks and courtesy. He looks, as everyone has said, quite himself again. Perhaps he is not quite himself again, however; something is missing, a certain boyish serenity, replaced by a similar but less reassuring quality, a kind of heedlessness. Out of it he rises in wit and warmth, but always subsides to it again, that darkness that absorbs him and makes him heedless: fear, pain, resolution?

Mr. Mobile Axt, Ambassador Plenipotentiary to Winter from the Ekumen of the Known Worlds, who had spent the last six days on the road trying to drive an electric car faster than 35 m.p.h. from Mishnory in Orgoreyn to Erhenrang in Karhide, overslept breakfast, and so arrived in the Audience Hall prompt, but hungry. The king had not yet come. The old Chief of the Council, the king's cousin Lord Gerer rem ir Verhen, met the alien at the door of the great hall and greeted him with the polysyllabic politenesses of Karhide. The Plenipotentiary responded as best he could; discerning beneath the eloquence Gerer's desire to tell him something.

"I am told the king is perfectly recovered from his illness," he said, "and I heartily hope this is true."

"It is not," the old man said, his voice becoming blunt and toneless. "My Lord Axt, I tell you this trusting your confidence; there are not ten other men in Karhide who know the truth. He is not recovered. He was not sick."

Axt nodded. There had of course been rumors.

"He will go alone in the city sometimes. He escapes his companions and guards. One night, six weeks ago, he did not come back. Threats and promises came, that same night, to me and the Second Lord of the Council. If we announced his disappearance, he would be murdered; if we waited in silence two weeks he would be returned. We kept silent, lied to the Spouse who was off at Warlever, sent out false news. Thirteen nights later he was found wandering on the waterfront. He had been drugged and mindformed. By what enemy or faction we do not yet know, we must work in utter secrecy, we cannot wreck the people's confidence in him—it is hard: we have no clue, and he remembers nothing whatever of his absence. But what they did is plain. They broke his will and bent his mind all to one thing. He believes he must abdicate the throne."

The tone remained low and plain; the eyes betrayed anguish. And the Plenipotentiary turning suddenly saw the echo, the match of that anguish in the eyes of the young king.

74

"Holding my audience, cousin?"

Argaven smiled but there was a knife in it. The old Councillor excused himself stolidly, bowed, left, an ungainly old man hurrying down a long red corridor.

Argaven stretched out both hands to the Plenipotentiary in the greeting of equals, for in Karhide the Ekumen was recognized as a brother kingdom, though no one had ever seen it. But his words were not the polite discourse that Axt expected. "Thank God you're here," he said.

"I left as soon as I received your message. The roads are still icy in East Orgoreyn and in the West Fall for miles after the border; I didn't make very good time. But I was very glad to come. Glad to leave, too." Axt smiled saying this, for he and the young king were on what might be called intimate diplomatic terms. What Argaven's abrupt personal welcome implied, he waited to see.

"Orgoreyn is a land that breeds bigots as a corpse breeds worms, as one of my ancestors remarked. I'm pleased that you find some relief here in Karhide. Though we have some bigots of our own. Gerer told you that I was kidnapped, and so forth? Yes. I've wondered if they were some of our own anti-Alien fanatics, who think your Ekumen is planning to enslave the earth. More likely one of the old clan-factions hoping to regain influence through me. Or the Nobles Faction. They came so near to outright control in my father's last years; I'm not very popular with the Nobles. . . . No telling, yet. It's strange, to know that one has seen these men face to face, and yet can't recognize them. Who knows but I see those faces daily? Well, no profit in such thoughts. They wiped out all their tracks. I am sure of only one thing. *They* did not tell me that I must abdicate."

He was striding beside the Plenipotentiary up the long, immensely high room toward the dais and chairs at the far end. The windows were little more than slits, as usual on this cold world; fulvous strips of sunlight fell from them diagonally to the red-paved floor, dusk and dazzle in Axt's eyes. He looked up at the young king's face in that somber, shifting radiance. "Who then?"

"I did."

"When, my lord, and why?"

"When they had me, when they were remaking me to fit their mold and play their game. Why? So that I can't fit their mold and play their game! Listen, Lord Axt, if they wanted me dead they'd have killed me: they want me to live, to rule, to govern, to be king. As such I am to follow the orders imprinted in my brain, gain their ends for them. I am their tool: ignorant, but ready to use. Why else should they have let me live?"

All this came hard and fast on Axt's understanding, but he was quick of understanding, that being a minimal qualification of a Mobile of the Ekumen; besides, the affairs of Karhide, the stresses and seditions of that lively kingdom, were well known to him. Remote and provincial though Winter was, its dominant nation, Karhide, was as large as any Ally nation of the Ekumen in these disjointed times, and more vigorous than many. Axt's reports were discussed in the central Councils of the Ekumen eighty light-years away; the equilibrium of the Whole rests in all its parts. Thus Axt understood and thought quickly, and he said, as they sat down in the great stiff chairs on the dais, "In order—perhaps—for you to abdicate?"

"Leaving my son as heir, and a Regent of my own choice? They would not gain much from that."

"Your son is an infant, and you are a very strong king. . . . Whom would you name as Regent?"

The king frowned. In a rather hoarse voice he said, "Gerer."

Axt nodded. "He is no faction's tool, certainly."

"No. He is not," Argaven replied, though with no warmth. A pause. "Is it true that the . . . science of your worlds might undo what was done to me, Lord Axt?"

"Possibly. In the Institute on Olull. But if I sent for a specialist tonight, he'd get here twenty-four years from now. . . . You're not aware of a change in any specific attitude—"
But a lad, coming in a side door behind them, set a small table by the Plenipotentiary's chair and loaded it with dishes of fruit, sliced bread-apple, a silver tankard of ale. Argaven

had noticed that his guest had missed his breakfast. Though the fare on Winter, mostly vegetable and that mostly uncooked, was dull stuff to Axt's taste, he set to gratefully; and as serious talk was unseemly over food, Argaven shifted to generalities. "Once you said something, Lord Axt, which seemed to imply that all men on all worlds are blood kin. Did I mistake your meaning?"

"Well, so far as we know, which is a tiny bit of dusty space under the rafters of the Universe, all the men we've run into are in fact men. But the kinship goes back some five hundred and fifty thousand years, to the Fore-Eras of Hain. The ancient Hainish settled a hundred worlds."

Argaven laughed, delighted. "My Harge dynasty has ruled Karhide for seven hundred years now. We call the times before that 'ancient.'"

"So we call the Age of the Enemy 'ancient,' and that was less than six hundred years ago. Time stretches and shrinks; changes with the eye, with the age, with the star; does all except reverse itself—or repeat."

"The Powers of the Ekumen dream, then, of restoring that truly ancient empire of Hain; of regathering all the worlds of men, the lost worlds?"

Axt nodded, chewing bread-apple. "Of weaving some harmony among them, at least. Life loves to know itself, out to its farthest limits. To embrace complexity is its delight. All these worlds and the various forms and ways of the minds and lives on them: together they would make a really splendid harmony."

"No harmony endures," said the young king.

"None has ever been achieved," said the Plenipotentiary. "The pleasure is in trying." He drained his tankard, wiped his fingers on the woven-grass napkin.

"That was my pleasure as king," said Argaven. "It is over."

"Sir—"

"It is finished. Believe me. I will keep you here, Lord Axt, until you believe me. I need your help. I must not rule this country. I cannot abdicate against the will of the Council. They will vote against me. If you cannot help me, then I

77

will have to kill myself." He said it reasonably, but Axt well knew that in Karhide suicide was held to be the ultimately contemptible act, inexcusable, beneath pity.

"One way or another," said the young king.

The Plenipotentiary pulled his heavy cloak closer round him; he was cold; he had been cold for seven years, since he came to Winter. "My lord," he said, "I am an alien on your world, with a handful of aides, and a little device with which I can hold conversations with other aliens on remote worlds. I represent power, but have none, despite my title. How can I help you?"

"You have a ship on Horden Island."

"Ah, I was afraid of that," said the Plenipotentiary, imperturbable. "My lord, that ship is set for Ollul, twenty-four light-years away. Do you know what that means?"

"My escape from my time, in which I have become an instrument of evil."

"Escape—there's no escape," said Axt, his imperturbability giving way a bit. "No, my lord. Forgive me. Absolutely not— I could not consent to this—"

Icy rain of spring rattled on the stones of the tower, wind whined at the angles and finials of the roof. Inside it was quiet, shadowy. One small shielded light burned outside the door. The nurse lay snoring mildly in her bed, the baby head down and rump up in his crib. The father stood beside the crib. He looked around the room, or rather saw it without looking, knowing it utterly even in the dark; he too had slept here as a little child, it had been his first domain. Then cautiously, slipping his broad hand under, he lifted up the small downy head and put over it a chain on which hung a massive ring carved with the tokens and signs of the Lords of Harge. The chain was far too long, and Argaven knotted it shorter, thinking that it might twist and choke the baby. So obeying that small anxiety he tried to allay the great fear and wretchedness that filled him. He put his face against the baby's cheek, whispering, "O my son, live long, rule well. . . ." Then he turned and quietly left the tower room, the heart of a lost kingdom.

He knew several ways of getting out of the Palace unperceived. He took the surest, and then made for the New Harbor through the bright-lit, sleet-lashed streets of Erhenrang, alone.

Now there is no seeing him. With what eye will you watch a process that is one hundred millionth percent slower than the speed of light? He is not now a king, nor a man; he is translated; you can scarcely call fellow-mortal one whose time passes seventy thousand times slower than yours. He is incalculably isolate. It seems that he is not, any more than an uncommunicated thought is; that he goes nowhere, any more than a thought goes. And yet, at very nearly but never quite the speed of light, he voyages. He is the voyage. Quick as thought. He has doubled his age when he arrives, less than a day older, in the portion of space curved about a dust-mote, Ollul by name, the fourth planet of a yellowish sun. And all this has passed in utter silence.

With noise now, and fire and meteoric fury enough to satisfy a Karhider's lust for splendor, the clever ship makes earthfall, setting down in flame in the precise spot it left some fifty-five years ago; and presently, visible, unmassive, uncertain, he emerges from it, and stands a moment in the exitway shielding his eyes from the light of a hot, strange sun.

Axt had sent notice of his coming, of course, by instantaneous transmitter twenty-four years ago, or seventeen hours ago depending on how you look at it; and Powers and Aides of the Ekumen were on hand to meet him. Pawns did not go unnoticed by those players of the great game, and this man who had come into their hands was not a pawn. One of them had spent some months of the twenty-four years in learning Karhidish, so that Argaven could speak to someone. His first speech was a question: "What news from Karhide?"

"Mr. Mobile Axt and his successor have sent regular summaries of events, and certain private messages for you; you'll find all the material in your quarters, Mr. Harge. Very briefly, the Regency was uneventful, after a depression in the early years. Your Arctic settlements were abandoned then, but Orgoreyn has recently begun such an experiment on the south polar continent. Your son was enthroned at eighteen, so he has ruled now for seven years."

"Yes, I see," said the man who had kissed that year-old son last night.

"I am to tell you, Mr. Harge, that whenever you see fit, the specialists at our Institute over in Belxit—"

"As you wish," said Mr. Harge.

They went into his mind very gently, very subtly, opening doors. For locked doors they had delicate machines, that always found the combination. They found the man in black, who was not Gerer, and compassionate Rebade, who was not compassionate; they stood on the Palace balcony with him, and climbed the crevasses of nightmare with him up to the room in the tower; and at last he who was to have been first, the man in red and white, approached him saying, "Sir! a plot against your life—" And Mr. Harge screamed in abject terror, and woke up.

"Well! That was the trigger, I think. The signal to begin tripping off the other instructions and determine the course of your phobia. An induced paranoia. Really beautifully induced, I must say. Here, drink this, Mr. Harge. No, it's just water. You might well have become a remarkably vicious ruler, more and more obsessed by fear of plots and subversions, more and more disaffected from your people. Not overnight, of course. It would have taken several years for you to become really intolerably tyrannic; though they no doubt planned some boosts along the way. Well, well, I see why Karhide is well spoken of, over at the Clearinghouse. If you'll pardon my objectivity, this kind of skill and patience is quite rare. . . ." So the doctor, the mindmender, the hairy greenish-black man from some Cetian world, went rambling on while the patient recovered himself.

"Then I did right," said Mr. Harge at last.

"You did. Suicide, abdication, or escape were the only acts of major consequence which you could have committed of your own volition. They counted on your moral veto forbidding you suicide, and the Council's veto forbidding you abdication. But being possessed with ambition themselves they discounted the possibility of abnegation; and left one door open for you. Only a strong-minded man (if you'll pardon my literalness) could have availed himself of that one alternative, as you did. . . . Well, I expect they'll be wanting you to look in at the Clearinghouse soon, to discuss your future, now that we've put your past back where it belongs—eh?"

"As you wish," said Mr. Harge.

He talked with certain personages there in the Clearinghouse of the Ekumen for the West Worlds; and when they suggested that he go to school, he assented readily. For among those mild persons whose chief quality seemed a cool, profound sadness indistinguishable from a warm, profound hilarity—among them, the ex-king of Karhide knew himself a barbarian, unlearned and unwise.

He attended Ekumenical School. He lived with other onworlders and aliens in barracks near the Clearinghouse in Vaxtsit City. Never having owned much that was his only, and never having had any privacy at all, he did not mind barracks life. He did not mind anything much, getting through the works and days with vigor and competence but always a certain heedlessness. The only discomfort he noticed as such was the heat, the awful heat of Ollul that rose to 85° F. sometimes in those blazing interminable seasons when no snow fell for two hundred days on end. Even when winter came he still sweated, for it never got below 20° or so outside, and the barracks were kept sweltering at forty degrees above that. He slept on top of his bed, naked and thrashing, and dreamed of the snows of the Kargav, the ice in Old Harbor, the ice scumming one's ale on cool mornings in the Palace, the cold, the dear and bitter cold of Winter.

He learned a great deal. He had already learned in his first few days on Ollul that the Earth was, here, called Winter, and Ollul was the Earth: one of those facts which turn the universe inside out like a sock. He had learned that fish were not necessarily warm-blooded, that it is better not to accept the loan of a Perifthenian's spouse, that a meat diet causes diarrhea in the unaccustomed gut, and that when he pronounced Ollul as Orrur some people laughed. He tried also to unlearn that he was a king. Once the Powers of the Ekumen took him in hand, he learned and unlearned much more. He was led, by all the machines and devices and experiences and (simplest and most demanding) words that the Ekumen had to use, into an intimation of what it might be to understand the nature and the history of a kingdom that was a million years old and thousands of millions of miles across. When he had begun to guess the immensity of this kingdom of men and the durable pain and monotonous waste of its history, he began also to see what lay beyond its borders in space and time, and among naked rocks and furnace-suns and the shining desolation that goes on and on, he glimpsed the sources of hilarity and serenity, the inexhaustible springs. He learned a great many facts, numbers, myths, epics, proportions, relationships, and so forth, and saw beyond the borders of what he had learned the unknown again, a splendid immensity. In this augmentation of his mind and being there was great satisfaction; yet he was unsatisfied. Nor did they always let him go on as far as he would have liked into certain fields, mathematics and the physical sciences for instance. "You started late, Mr. Harge," they said, "we must build on the foundations laid earlier. You weren't formed to be a student, but a doer, and we want to keep you in subjects which you can put to use."

"What use?"

They—the ethnographer Mr. Mobile Gist represented Them at the moment, across a library table—looked at him sardonically. "Do you consider yourself to be of no further use, Mr. Harge?"

Mr. Harge, who was generally reserved, spoke with sudden fury: "I do, Mr. Gist."

"A king without a country," said Gist in his heavy Terran accent, "self-exiled, believed dead by spouse and son and all his people, I suppose might feel himself a trifle superfluous.

. . . But then why do you think we're bothering with you?"

"Out of kindness," said the young man.

"Oh, kindness . . . However kind we are, we can give you nothing that would make you happy, Mr. Harge, except . . . Well. Waste is a pity. You were indubitably the right king for Winter, for Karhide, for the purposes of the Ekumen. You have a sense of equilibrium. You would probably have unified the planet, and you certainly wouldn't have regimented your local state, as your son seems to be doing. However, no unweaving that web. Only consider our hopes and needs, Mr. Harge, and your qualifications, before you despair of your life. Fifty, sixty more years of it you have to get through. . . ."

A last snapshot taken by alien sunlight: erect, in a Hainish-style cloak of grey, a handsome man of thirty-odd stands, sweating profusely, on a green lawn beside the chief Power of the Ekumen in the West Worlds, the Stabile, Mr. Hoalans of Alb, who can change and to some extent control the destinies of forty-two worlds.

"I can't order you to go there, Argaven," says the Stabile. "Your own conscience—"

"I gave up my kingdom to my conscience, twelve years ago. It's had its due. Enough's enough," says the younger man. Then he laughs suddenly, so that the Stabile also laughs; and they part in such harmony as the Powers of the Ekumen desire among men.

Horden Island, off the south coast of Karhide, was given as a freehold to the Ekumen by the Kingdom of Karhide during the reign of Argaven XV. No man lived there. Yearly generations of seawalkies crawled up on the isle's barren rocks, and laid and hatched their eggs, and nursed their young, and finally led them back in long single file to the sea. But once every ten or twenty years fire ran over the island and the sea boiled on the shores, and if any seawalkies were on the beaches then, they died.

When the sea had ceased to boil, the Plenipotentiary's little electric launch approached. The starboat ran out her gossamer-steel gangplank to the deck of the launch, and a man started to walk up it as a man started to walk down it, so that they met in the middle, in midair, between sea and land, an ambiguous meeting.

"Mr. Ambassador Horrsed? I'm Harge," said the one from the starboat, but as he spoke the one from the seaboat knelt down and said aloud, in Karhidish, "Welcome, Argaven of Karhide!"

As he straightened up he added in a quick whisper, "You come as yourself— Explain when I can—" Behind and below him on the deck of the launch stood a sizeable group of men, gazing up at the newcomer with grim faces. All were Karhiders by their looks; several were old.

Mr. Harge stood for a minute, two minutes, three minutes, erect and perfectly motionless though his grey cloak tugged and riffled in the cold wind that was blowing. He looked once at the dull orange sun to the west, once at the grey land northward across the water, back again at the silent men who watched him. Then he strode forward so suddenly that the Plenipotentiary Horrsed had to get aside in a hurry. He stepped onto the deck amidst the silent men, and spoke to one of the old ones. "Are you Ker rem ir Kerheder?"

"I am."

"I knew you by that, Ker—the lame arm." He spoke clearly; there was no guessing what emotions he felt. "Guessed you, rather. Are there others of you I knew? I cannot recognize you. Sixty years—"

They were all silent. He said nothing more.

All at once one of them, a man scored and scarred with age like wood that has been through fire, got down laboriously on his knees. "My Lord King, I am Bannith of the Guard of the King's Household, you served with me when I was Drillmaster, and you a boy, a young boy," and he bowed down his bald head in homage or to hide quick senile tears. Certain others knelt then, stiff and frail, bending down bald and grey and white heads; the voices that hailed him as king quavered with emotion and with age. One, Ker of the crippled arm, lifted his fierce, furrowed face (Argaven had known him as

84

a timid boy of thirteen) and spoke to those who still stood unmoving, watching Argaven: "This is he. I have eyes that have seen him, and that see him now. This is the King."

One or two of the younger men also knelt. Most did not. Argaven looked at them, from face to face, one after another.

"I am Argaven," he said. "I was king. Who reigns now in Karhide?"

"Emran," one answered.

"My son?"

"Your son Emran," said old Bannith, but Ker cried fiercely, "Argaven, Argaven reigns in Karhide: I have lived to see the bright days return. Long live the King!"

One of the younger men looked at the others. "So be it," he said. "Long live the King!" He knelt, and they all knelt.

Argaven took their homage unperturbed, but when later a moment came he turned on Horrsed the Plenipotentiary, demanding, "What is this? What has happened to my country? Did the Stabile expect this to happen, and not warn me? I was sent here to assist you, as an Aide from the Ekumen—"

"That was twenty-four years ago," said the Plenipotentiary. "Things go ill with your country, and King Emran has broken relations with the Ekumen. I'm not really sure what the Stabile's purpose in sending you here was, at the time he sent you; but at present, we're losing our game here; and so the Powers on Hain suggested to me that we might move out our king."

"But I am *dead*," Argaven said. "I have been dead for sixty years, man!"

"The King is dead," said Horrsed, "long live the King."

Then, as some of the Karhiders approached, Argaven turned from the Plenipotentiary and went over to the rail. Grey water bubbled and slid busily by the ship's side. The shore of the continent lay now to their left, grey patched with white. It was cold: a day of early winter in the Ice Age of a bleak world where men lived only in the tropics, and the seasons varied from cold to colder. The ship's engine purred softly. Argaven had not heard that purr of an electric engine for a dozen years now, the only kind of engine Karhide's slow and stable Age of Invention had chosen to employ. The sound of it was very pleasant to him.

He spoke abruptly without turning, as one who has known since infancy that there is always someone there to answer: "Why are we going east?"

"We're making for Kerm Land, sir."

"Why Kerm Land?"

It was one of the younger men, a bright-eyed, stout fellow, who replied. "Because that part of the country is in open rebellion against the—against King Emran, sir. I am a Kermlander: Perreth ner Sode, at your service."

"Is the king in Erhenrang?"

"Erhenrang was taken by Orgoreyn six years ago. The king is in the new capital, east of the mountains—the Old Capital, actually, Rer."

"He lost the West Fall?" Argaven said, and then turning full on the stout nobleman, "He lost the West Fall? He surrendered Erhenrang?"

Perreth quailed, but answered promptly, and with a sudden gleam as of conviction in his eyes, "We've been hiding behind the mountains for six years, sir."

"Is the uprising still on?"

"King Emran signed a treaty with the Confederation of Orgoreyn five years ago, ceding them the western provinces."

"A shameful treaty, sir!" old Ker broke in, fierce and quavering. "A fool's treaty! Emran dances to the drums of Orgoreyn. We, here, are all rebels and exiles—the Ambassador there is an exile with a price on his head!"

"He lost the West Fall," said Argaven. "We took the West Fall for Karhide seven hundred years ago—" He looked round on the others again with his strange, keen, unheeding gaze. "What kind of king is he?" he demanded; but when none dared answer he dismissed the question and asked, "How strong are you in Kerm Land? What provinces are with you? What forces have you? Where do the Nobles stand?"

"Against us, sir; the country with us, mostly."

Argaven was silent awhile.

"Has he a son yet?"

"He had. The Prince was killed in the western battles, six years ago."

"He served with the Guard, as you did, sir," old Bannith put in. "Killed in the retreat from Erhenrang, at seventeen years old—"

"The heir is Girvry Harge rem ir Orek, sir," said Perreth.

"Who the devil is he? —What was the Prince's name? The king had no son, when I began my journey here."

"His name was Argaven."

Now at last comes the dark picture, the snapshot by fire-light—firelight, because the power plants of Rer are wrecked, the trunk lines cut, and half the city is burning. Snow flurries heavily down above the flames and gleams red for an instant before it melts in midair, hissing faintly.

Snow and ice and partisans keep Orgoreyn at bay on the west side of the Kargav Mountains. No help came to the Old King, Emran, when his country rose against him. His army fled and his city burns, and now at the end he is face to face with the usurper. But he has, at the end, something of his father's arrogance: he pays no heed to the rebels. He stares at them and does not see them, lying on his back in the dark hallway, lit only by mirrors that reflect distant fires, where he killed himself.

Stooping over him Argaven lifts up his hand, an old man's hand, broad and hard, and starts to take from the forefinger the massive, carved gold ring. But he does not do it. "Let him keep it," he says, "let him wear it." For a moment he bends yet lower, as if he whispered in the dead man's ear or laid his cheek against that rough, cold face. Then he straightens up, and stands awhile, and presently goes out through dark corridors, by windows bright with distant ruin, to set his house in order and begin his reign: Argaven, Winter's king.

The Time Machine

by Langdon Jones

The cell is not large. There is just room for a small bunk along one wall, and a small table on the other side, a stool in front of it. The table and the stool have once been painted a glossy red, but their finish has long been spoiled by time, and now light wood shows through the streaks of paint. The floor is flagged, and the walls are made of large blocks of stone. The stone has streaks of dampness across its surface, and in the air is a sweet smell of decay. There is a window high in the far wall, set with bars of rusted iron, and through it can be seen a patch of blue sky, and a wisp of yellow cloud. Sometimes, not very often, a bird flashes across the space like a brief hallucination. In the opposite wall there is a large metal door, with a grille set into its surface. Behind the grille is a shutter, so that those outside may, when they wish, observe the prisoner from a safe distance.

The bunk is made of metal, and is fixed permanently to one wall. It is painted green, and this color is interrupted only where the rusty nuts and bolts extrude. On one side the bunk is bolted to the wall, and on the other it is supported by two metal legs, which have worn little depressions in the stone floor. Above the bunk, crudely scratched into the wall, are various drawings and messages. There are initials, dates, obscenities and phallic drawings. Set a little apart from the others is the only one which does not make immediate sense. It is engraved deeply into the wall, and consists of two words, set one above the other. The engraving obviously took a great deal of time to complete. The upper of these words is "TIME," the lower, "SOLID."

The bunk is covered by rumpled grey blankets, which smell of the sweat of generations of prisoners. Sitting at the foot of the bunk is the prisoner. He is leaning over, his elbows on his knees, his back hunched, looking at a photograph in his hands.

The photograph is of a girl. It is just a little larger than two inches square, and is in black and white. It is a close-up, and the lower part of her arms, and her body below the waist are not revealed. Her head is not directly facing the camera, and she appears to be looking at something to one side, revealing a three-quarter view of her face. Behind her is a brick wall—a decorative wall in Holland Park on that day after the hotel and after the morning in the coffee shop; soon they were to part again at the railway station.

Her dark hair was drawn back, and she had a calm but emotional expression on her face. Her face was fairly round, but her high cheekbones caused a slight concavity of her cheeks, giving her always a slightly drawn look which he had always found immensely attractive, ever since he had first known her. Her features were somewhat negroid—"a touch of the tar brush, as my mother used to put it," she had said in one of her letters—large dark eyes, and large lips which, when she smiled, gave her a look of ironic sadness. Occasionally she also had the practical look of a Northern housewife, and her energy was expressed in her face and her body. Her body was very slim, and her flesh felt like the flesh of no other woman on earth. When he had first seen her she had been wearing a black dress at a party, a dress which did nothing to conceal the smallness of her breasts, and which proudly proclaimed her slightness. This had captivated him immediately. It was something which accented her femininity, although doubtless she had not considered it in this way, and he saw her that first time as the most beautiful thing on earth.

He would meet her in Leicester. He would set off early on Sunday and take a train to Victoria, and walk among the few people about at this time on a Sunday morning to the coach

89

station. He could never understand why it was—as he sat in the cafeteria with a cup of coffee—that the people all about appeared so ugly. The only people that morning who were at all pleasing to the eye were a family of Indians who had sat near him—the women in saris, and the men bewhiskered and proud in turbans. Perhaps it was all subjective, and everyone appeared ugly because he knew that this morning, in little more than three hours, he would be meeting her again. The weather was not impossibly cold—they wanted to make love, and many things were against it that week. At nine-fifteen he would walk over, past the coaches for Lympne airport and France, to the far corner of the yard, where the Leicester coach would be waiting.

He got in the coach. There were never more than eight or nine people who wanted to go to Leicester early on a Sunday morning, and he would walk down to the back of the coach and sit on the left-hand side. Why always the left, he didn't know. At nine thirty-five the vehicle would set off, pouring out clouds of diesel smoke, emerging from its home like a mechanical dragon. As they passed Marble Arch, Swiss Cottage, and headed for the M1, he was conscious of a mounting tension. Partly sexual—partly the knowledge that soon he would see her again, and partly because he knew that *he* knew. What was going to happen this time? He could visualize that one morning she wouldn't come, but he would, and instead of loving there would be hatred and fighting. She had told him during the week, and he had been very upset. But he wanted her to continue, for he knew what it would do to her to have to stop now. What had been set into action was a series of circumstances that had to run a certain course until it was possible to break it. And the breaking would be hard—was hard.

The sun was shining, and the fields that they passed became transformed, as they always did, by her proximity in time. Everything around him was beautiful. It was as if he could see the scene through the coach window with an intensity that would not be possible normally. It was as if together they were one being, and that apart from her he was less than half a person. But there were four other people who depended on her as well. Two little boys, one little girl and one adult man. A family is a complete entity as well. Later he would go to her home in West Cutford, and see her with her children, and feel himself to be a malevolent force, a wildly destructive element that didn't belong here, and yet, seeing at the same time an image of what might have been; how close was this reality to the one he wanted.

When the coach left the motorway, it was only half an hour before he would be in Leicester, and three quarters before they would be together, their proximity having an as-tronomical rightness, as implacably correct as the orbit of the earth. The watery January sun shone onto the brown brick buildings that told him that soon he would be at their meeting-place—the coach station in Southgate Street. This place had a special significance for him; it was like the scene of some great historical event. But most of the places were; not the hotel, where the coming and going of other people obscured the sig-nificance of their own, but their little shed at Groby Pond, their room at the top of a house in West London. All these places deserved some kind of immortality.

Now the tension was very strong; his muscles were clenched all over his body and his hands were shaking. The coach approached some traffic lights, turned left, bumping over a rough road surface, and went down a grim street, full of half-demolished buildings. Further down were some other build-ings composed of reddish-brown brick, except for a modern pub which was opposite a large flat area surrounded by metal railings. The coach turned into this concrete area, for this was Southgate Street. As the coach slowed up the few people inside began to rise, putting on overcoats and collecting their luggage. He looked intently through the windows to see if she had arrived. She wasn't here yet. The coach was early; it was only quarter-past twelve. There was six and a half hours of the day left. This was always the most difficult part. Before he had felt that he was going toward her; that he could feel the distance between them lessening. But now all the movement was up to her and he could no longer be directly aware of it.

He climbed down from the coach and went to the other side of the road, waiting for her car to arrive. Looking across at the coach station, he knew that he would remember this place for the rest of his life whatever happened. In one month, seventeen days and six hours they would say goodbye for the last time.

Cars were passing in groups; there would be a time when nothing was on the road at all, then later twenty cars would come along together, and his eyes would move as he looked at first one, then the next. A cold wind was blowing, and he was shivering uncontrollably. A couple of girls walked past on the other side of the street, talking and laughing together. A car came along that looked like hers, but inside it was a large, white-haired man. This was impossible. He turned and walked round to the entrance of the pub. This was The Shakespeare, the same name as another pub that had featured in their lives; it was as if their whole existence was marked out by commonplace things that were all cryptograms, that all had hidden significance. Their love made everything more real, and at the same time turned the world into a devious collection of symbols.

He pushed through the doors of the pub and went into the lounge bar. He ordered a drink, and then went to sit by one of the windows. If he stood up and looked through the net curtains he could just see part of the coach station. Parked outside was a car, but from here it did not look like hers. He sat down, and regarded the shiny surface of the table in front of him.

Things were obviously bad for her at home. Her letters had told him what had been going on. She could not get away from this situation; she would part from him and then go back to a person who was being hurt, a person whose life was being threatened by their love—a love that seemed innocent and inevitable. That first night, when they suddenly found themselves in bed together, when a few hours before they had been little more than friendly strangers, it had all seemed so right.

They both knew that life was now going to become difficult, but still wanted it to happen. He stood up, and peered through the window. The parked car was still there, and she was not in sight. He sat down again. But how much stress could one stand? How much could this man stand? He understood the situation, but how long would it be before his control broke down, and he came with nothing in his brain but an urge to destroy? How would he react to this? How could he possibly try to physically hurt a man he had hurt so much already? He stood up and looked through the window again. Suddenly finding it impossible to wait in the pub any longer, he abruptly walked toward the door and went outside in the cold again. The parked car was not hers. It was nearly half-past twelve. He crossed the road and went back inside the coach station. He sat down on a bench with his back to the road. In his bag was a book, and he took it out. It was very cold. He began to read.

The sun had passed the point at which it shines directly into the cell. Now dark shadows are creeping across the floor, and it is becoming colder. The prisoner lifts his feet from the floor and lies back on his bunk, holding the photograph above him. At the time the photograph had been taken they had spent two days in a room in a hotel in London, doing little but making love, going out occasionally for food. It had been a fairly cheap hotel, and the room had looked, at first, rather bare. But in two hours it had become transformed into a jeweled palace. The red bed-cover had glowed with the mystical luminosity of a robe in a Flemish painting. When they had left the hotel, they had gone to Holland Park, aching to make love again, full of an insatiable desire to repeat an experience so good it should have been unrepeatable. He felt vaguely surprised that the exposed flesh of her face and neck did not show any signs of his love. He felt that his hands and lips and tongue should have left visible tracks on her skin that would show that this woman was loved. Perhaps there was a gentleness in her eyes, a quirk of her lips; but perhaps he was imagining these signs.

He held the photograph close to his eyes so that he could

see the grain, and the slight fuzziness of her individual hairs. Now he was conscious of the photograph as a record only. A piece of paper that was not even there at the time. Recorded tracks of light that had reflected from her at that time into the lens of a camera. This contact with her was so nebulous, and yet the photograph somehow solidified the events, gave them a concrete reality, as if at some time or some place they were together in Holland Park, she in front of him, apologizing for her tiredness and the untidiness of her hair, saying "Just after making love is not the best time for taking a picture of me," and then being quiet and looking to one side, and the shutter opening, slowly, slower, and then freezing, wide open, this "time" a tangible material like film going through a camera, that can be wound on, stopped and taken out.

Their love affair was now like a piece of sculpture, an object that plainly begins at one point and ends at another, but which may be seen as a single object in space, which may be looked at closely, details expanding, may be examined from different angles, touched, embraced, wept upon.

The last time in the hotel had been good, so good that he could now remember nothing but an ecstatic feeling of life and death and her cries regularly punctuating the quiet of the room, and his own gasped sounds joining hers in a complex of rhythm, and then nothing but his own engulfment in a torrent of whiteness.

Caroline Howard. First just a name, and then a name that was a woman, and then a name that was so intertwined with his own existence it became a million things, was a part of him. Just the sound of her name, reflected softly from the stone walls, was enough to bring back a whole series of memories and associations; it must be like the lifetime's memories of a drowning man. In a fraction of a second it was all there to be seen, touched, tasted, smelled. Caroline Howard Caroline Howard Caroline Howard—a bright orgasm in morning sunlight.

The time machine operates on an organic, electrochemical basis, with mineral connections. It is operated by means of a circulating substance that is sometimes fluid and sometimes gaseous, passing through an infinite number of stages of creation. This substance becomes finer and finer in form, eventually phasing from the limits of existence to great solidity and density, beginning the cycle again. The implications of this cycle, with the relative nature of its stages, provide the basic crystallizing power of the machine. The apparatus is also provided with gross mechanical parts, cogs, motors and chains, which are essential to the smooth transport of its medium through all the stages of metamorphosis. The machine deals with relationships, patterns and similarities. Some of the implications of the time machine are almost metaphysical in nature.

It may easily be seen that the machine is not like any other of the mechanical constructions that have been made up to now. While the operation of the machine may be analyzed in detail, the reader of such a description will not be able to understand at all the functions of its cycles. Also the mechanically-minded reader will notice immediately that there are components which he would deem unnecessary and uneconomic, and he will undoubtedly comment too that more components seem to be essential for the machine to work at all, and that in its present state it would be capable of doing absolutely nothing. The time machine is capable, in fact, of operation in a number of different ways. On the other hand it may work in a more general sense for one, or any number of separate observers. Also, the machine may, and does, operate entirely on its own, unobserved; it does this constantly, the separate parts of the construction existing at different and all points of time.

It is to be understood that time is not a moving stream. Time is a minor quality of the continuum, common only to living creatures, and consists of an involuntary change of attention. The consciousness of a creature is an infinitely restricted series of sense-impressions, operating in three dimensions only. The universe consists of a four dimensional geometric form, which, in cross-section, contains all the physical facts of matter, and is curved so that it eventually rejoins

95

itself, forming a four-dimensional ring shape. Thus, a cross-section of any part of this ring will produce the universe at any particular point in "time." This "time" is merely the attention of the creature observing the shape about him, and is due to his being able to be aware of only one infinitely small part of the shape. His attention is constantly and involuntarily operating on a different part of the ring, giving the impression of movement and animation to what is in fact a static object, and also giving him the false impression of temporal extension. If one draws a wavy line, and follows this line with one's eyes, it will appear to move up and down, whereas with a widening of attention the line can immediately be appreciated as an unmoving and complete object. The time that each of us experiences is common only to us, and is an internal psychic operation rather than a measurable physical fact.

If we stand at one end of a room and walk across to the other, this restricted attention is all that gives the impression of movement. In fact movement is an aspect of time, and to someone lacking this restriction of attention, it would be obvious that the movement was only an impression in the mind of the person concerned and that his body, as it crossed the room, was merely a solid and static object.

We can see now that time is not the barrier it was once thought to be, and that as a psychic mechanism it may be radically altered, or completely destroyed. It is surprising that this was not realized before; the time-dilation or time-destruction observed by takers of the "mind-expanding" hallucinogenic drugs has been often noted, as well as the more usual distortions of time during various common mental states.

The time machine, by operating in terms of relationships of pattern, is able to crystallize the attention of the observer, producing a concrete *déjà vu,* and in the solidity of its wheels and pistons we find reflected the tangibility of the universe, in all its states of being.

He looked up from the book. And saw her. She was talking to two bus men, asking them if they knew whether the London bus had arrived yet. He hurriedly put the book away, and as he stood she saw him. She was wearing her black fur coat, and her face, as she came toward him, was his own face, as familiar as the face he shaved each morning, a face that was more than the sum of all the faces he knew; his own, his parents', his friends', more than anything else he would ever find. Her face was troubled. They approached each other slowly, not running with joyful exuberance as they had the last time they had met here, or moving quickly with desperation to clasp each other, to shut off the world in the closeness of each other's arms as they would later. He took her gently in his arms, and they kissed softly, and then embraced, holding each other tightly. She exhaled his name in a sigh, a drooping inflection that suggested pressure that had been building up suddenly released. Now was right; everything was infinitely right. His face was pressed against her neck, the scent of her hair was filling his nostrils, her body was warm in his arms. Now he was alive, and he did not want to move from this position ever again. His hands ran over her back, and he felt her lips at his neck; he was melting into a state of complete being, a state that had intolerable tensions and unformulated desires, that caused his breath to be exhaled explosively, hearing the sounds he made, they both made, to be like miniature versions of the sounds crushed from their bodies by the dazzling pressure of orgasm. Waves of pressure ran round his body; his head moved, lips brushing her cheek, her ear, her neck. Their heads drew apart, and he looked into her eyes. He felt his head moving with the impossible surging of communication of emotions impossible to communicate. His eyes moved as he tried to take in all the details of her face at once. He smiled, and saw an answering smile on her face, a reflection of his own feelings. They kissed for a long time, and then slowly drew apart.

"How have things been at home?"

"Not too good. Difficult."

They began to walk out of the coach station, their arms round each other.

"Do you mind if we go for a drink first? I do feel that I need it."

"Of course not."

They walk across the road, and into The Shakespeare. They sit at the table with drinks, and she opens her coat to reveal her grey dress. He tells her that he is very fond of the dress, and they tell each other "I love you," a universal reassurance, always needed. Soft lips against his. Unhappiness in her eyes. In memory, not much is said. A letter is discussed, and one or two sentences are actually verbalized, although in a constantly varying way. "He can accept the whole thing intellectually, and he doesn't want to stop it, for my sake. He knows I'm seeing you."

"I know."

"No, I mean today. He saw me off, and watched me drive away in the car." A feeling of mute horror that stays the same, despite the changing pattern of the words. "What with my period and everything, all my energies are at a low ebb. I'm in the most schizophrenic state. There's part of me that can't bear the thought of having an affair, and the rest of me wants nothing but you." He says nothing. There is nothing but the sound of her voice, and he watches her lips moving, sees the flecks of mascara on her cheeks, feels terror at his innocent power of inflicting pain.

Later they leave the pub, at one o'clock, and drive off to Groby Pond, the place at which they arrived the last time, his first trip to Leicester, after driving off twelve miles in the wrong direction, laughing at the confusion into which they were both plunged by their mutual proximity. They take a wrong turning this time, and the next time. At Groby Pond was a disused quarry where they had come before, to be alone under an enormous sky, a sky that made no judgments, condemned no one, and was content to be.

The city is devoted to the appreciation of beauty—Rolling architecture is spread out in autumn sunlight—The city has patterned trees set out among the plazas—High towers pillars for the sky—Spotlights are situated along the kerbs to show the human bodies on the pavements to their best advantage—Last year a man was found wearing clothes and was executed

—Soft winds blow scents of musk into the market—In the main square is a gigantic golden representation of a single testicle— the sounds of the people are the muted voice of summer holidaymakers—laughter on a tennis court—Parks are rolling grassland with bowers supplied for making love, which must be made aesthetically—the main crime is committing offenses against the soul, for which the penalty is instant, and beautiful, decapitation—Birds shriek into the sun, protesting at the loss of their virgin cruelty—Sleek, fat cats assume poses in the gutters—Men urinate only from the tops of high buildings— The government headquarters consists of five red towers, standing up in the city like the fingers of a bloody hand—All the pubs have yards where one may sit with one's love and drink together for the last time—the courtyards are like seas— there are no lavatories—illness is forbidden by state decree— Sculptures are designed to be orgasms in steel—In a park in the center of the city is a large brick shed with a light on its side—Serious musicians play only some Mozart and some Berg —Beaches and pavilions glisten like mirrors in the sun—The city beats like a bird's wing—People float in aerial choreography, like the sinking drowned—Metal is woven in great garlands and shines throughout the city—Capsules of mescalin are set in trays at every point—The city is the city of time— the city knows no time—the city is the city of soft people— the city of flags and paintings that move—the city is the city of the afternoon—mown grass falls from the sky like rain—the City is the city of beautiful decay, where all is young—the city is the city of the sky—the city of eternal surprise—the city of long dark hair—the city of eggs with marble shells—the city is a diffraction grating, and from a height of three hundred feet can be seen only as a blaze of color—it is the city of high parabolas—the city of impossible waterfalls—the city of melting silver blades—the city is the city of brooks—they weave their way everywhere—all the time is the sound of bubbling water . . .

The time machine utilizes certain objects for its various operations: a skull cap with electrodes, attached to a machine designed for the artificial production of sexual orgasm; the miniature score of Messiaen's *Chronochromie;* a magnetic tape, two thousand, four hundred feet long, containing nothing but the voice of a man repeating the word "time"; a reproduction of Dali's landscape, *Persistence of Memory;* a bracket clock by Joseph Knibb.

He enters the time machine, giving himself up to its embrace, feeling his normal consciousness changing, the widening of his perceptions. Colors flow over his body like a smooth sheet of water—blue sparks ignite in his brain—he is conscious of the pattern his body makes in space-time—He moves his finger and sees the resultant wiggling shape, his finger like an electroencephalograph pen—Words float in his mind, picked out in violet fire—Long steel fingers fiddle about in his brain like the legs of robot spiders—he falls asleep and wakes up three hundred times a second—His feet are removed by steel hands and placed neatly under his bed—His arms are broken off with mechanical deftness—his body is taken completely apart by the mechanical fingers, and he slides in pieces through the conveyor belts of the machine.

They pulled up at the pond, with the front of the car only a few yards from the water's edge. There were several other cars parked here too; this was a fairly popular beauty spot. A few people were outside their cars, braving the January weather, throwing pieces of bread to the ducks on the water. They sat for a while, he with his arm around her, his face pressed to her hair, stroking her with slow fingers, their voices low as they spoke to each other, both of them weighed down by circumstances so vast that they could not be seen all at one time. She had brought along a bottle of wine, cheap red wine with brandy added, a box of sandwiches, and also a thermos flask of coffee. They filled the cup of the flask with wine, and took it in turns to sip from it. "You realize that these are only delaying tactics on my part? I feel so low. If I really wanted to make love, I wouldn't want food or anything." He nodded, for he knew. It was up to her to make the move today. She offered him a small sandwich, but at the moment he was unable to eat; his stomach was locked with tension. But he watched her eating, looking at her as if looking could lock her forever within him, knowing that in time the outlines of her features would fade, until one day, alone, he would re-member only a composite picture of her face, not looking as she looked on this day at any time. But still he looked at her intensely, watching the movements of her hands, her glances and her dark eyes.

They packed away the food, and she came into his arms again. "In a minute we can go and make love."

"Do you want a cigarette first?" She took a cigarette, and they stayed smoking for a moment, now and then drinking from the cup.

Now was the time to leave the car, and they went round to the boot, where she had stored an enormous bundle of blankets out of the house so that they should at least be com-fortable. As he helped her with the bundle, he was very con-scious of the people about, as if they knew that it was full of blankets. Last time they had climbed over a wide green gate that led to the quarry, but now they could see a car parked by the gate, full of people looking out at the sheet of silver that was Groby Pond. This time, they decided, they should go over a stile a little further down, set into a low stone wall. They walked along, he with one arm clasping the bundle, the other round her, his fingers buried in the fur of her collar. The last time they had been here they had gone over the green gate, ignored a small path leading to the left towards a brick shed and some other buildings in a little dip, and had taken the right-hand path up to the top of the quarry, and had lain in the brambles in this incredibly open place, in which it seemed there was nothing but a huge sky and great vistas of grey stone cliffs. Later they would go through the gate and would turn left, down the small path, and they would never go over this stile again. He pushed the blankets under the bottom rung and climbed over, helping her as she followed. There was a tortuous path leading downwards through the trees and un-dergrowth, in the direction of a brook. They began to go down the path, he leading the way and holding onto her hand, sliding, being whipped by branches and circumnavigating patches of mud. Laughing they came to a little river of mud, and clambered across it. Now the way ahead looked even more impenetrable, and even less likely to lead up to the top of the quarry. He suggested that she wait here, while he would go to see what was ahead.

His perspective changes—He rushes along corridors of people, the same people, in quanta of time, each one slightly different from the last, like a cine film—A mad express, lights reflecting from the walls of life.

The time machine poses problems.

Why? Why did they take this path, that second time, when later they would find a much easier way to get to their little shed? Why did they not brave the stares of the people in the car, and avoid this tortuous journey? Why, the first time, did they go over the green gate but completely ignore the path that led to their refuge? The shed at Groby Pond was so important to them. They even called it their "den." It was a little enclosed world of three sides, in which they could shut out the knowledge of pain and the niceties of balance that were necessary for them to stay whole. They could observe this world outside through an open fourth side, only partly masked by stringy bushes, and could hear its water bubbling nearby. Why did they, then, choose not to go down the small path on these two occasions? It is not only in love, but in all life that people often act with the blind illogicality of the insane. What is this quality called "time" that makes them act so? How can one assess an adulterous love affair seen now in terms of shape?

He emerged into a clearing. There were some brick buildings to the right, a couple of sheds and a cottage with boarded-up windows. He went over to try the doors but found them locked. He found that he was concentrating on this moment of being alone, living it with a perverse kind of enjoyment, like the enjoyment of being cold just before stepping into a warm bath.

He turned. Behind him was a shed with three sides. It was about five feet high and very roomy. The front was half-concealed by straggly bushes and the darkness inside should hide the glimmer of two bodies, unless someone got too close. He walked across to the shed, and went inside. He was rather disappointed by the interior, which was gloomy and damp. He came out of the shed again, wondering whether or not it would be suitable. He decided to use the opportunity of this solitude to urinate, smiling, as he unzipped his fly, at this un-expected modesty of his, and feeling rather ashamed of it at the same time. Hearing her coming, he forced the process even faster and barely finished before she appeared from behind the buildings. Feeling a little like a guilty schoolboy, he zipped up his trousers and went towards her. "I've found a place," he said, "but you may find it a bit sordid." She walked across to the shed and looked inside. "Why, it's perfect. But will we be seen from the road?" He stepped back until he was a long way away. He could see her now only as a vague patch of lightness in the shed. "No," he called, "it's fine!" He came back, and picking up the bundle of blankets he carried it inside the shed. He put the bundle down, and then took her in his arms. They kissed, their bodies pressed together, and his general tension was suddenly transformed into sexual desire, his body responding to hers with a swiftness that spoke of their long absence. They drew apart, and she squatted on the floor and began to unroll the bundle. Inside were two large blankets, and he was amused to see that she had even had the fore-thought to bring a red towel with her. They spread out the ground-sheet, and arranged the blankets into an improvised double bed. He took off his sweater and arranged it to serve as a pillow. Now when they spoke their voices were hushed, and quietly they both took off their shoes, lifted the blankets, and slid side by side into their bed in the shed at Groby Pond, while outside the brook bubbled past.

The time machine caresses with soft winds—it deafens the mind with brave light—slow blind worms stretch their bodies through time—straight files of fingers tap on miles of desks—grey vines are shrined in fog and kick and scream like young horses—wings are torn from my *back!*

Gas springs from eight star-formed arms
Which revolve like pink wheels
"Ghost" gas is leaked off into the spandrels
Pressuring a container which explodes
Pulling a chain which pulls a claw
Which plucks the tine of a tuning fork
Sounding a clear A
Which reorganizes the constituents of the gas
Stars wheels and spandrels
Form a double hexagon of mystical significance
And the gas throbs with the deep blue glow
Of an unnatural agency
The shapes of the spandrels—
Cherubs' faces with foliage—
Reform the organization of the gas
Which rings and metamorphoses
Into lead

The time machine taps his body with a thousand fingers which play over his skin like a row of pianists. The fingers have little needles in the tips, which are feeding a special electrically conductive ink. This ink is tattooed into his body in a complex pattern, and soon the whirls and curlicues will flow with an electrical force. Time drips from a faucet like dark green treacle.

Later they were going to lie together naked in this shed, but this time the coldness and the likelihood of detection made them agree beforehand to keep on as many clothes as possible. Their bodies twisted together, her hands running over him, he kissing her ear, her neck, her throat. They whimper together with the delight of this long-delayed contact. He slides his leg between hers, pressing it high, and feels the muscles of her thighs clenching in response. He unzips her dress behind, and lowers his face to the flesh of her shoulders and back, this feeling of her flesh against his coming as an actual physical relief, as if, for the rest of his life, when not with her, he would always miss the feel of her body. He slid the dress down, exposing the soft dark skin of her chest and arms, and the little brassiere. His mouth found the sweetness of her shoulders, and his lips lingered there. Her hands were on his thighs, and then his shirt was unbuttoned, and her lips were against his stomach. He helped her hands with his belt and trousers, sliding his clothes from his legs completely, and shuddering under the ecstatic pressure of her hands. He felt that their lovemaking could never become banal; each time they came together it was a mutual exploration of pleasure. Each possible contact of their bodies could be repeated a million times. Her dress was now round her neck, and his hands ran over the smooth warm flesh. This time of lovemaking was all times of lovemaking, the little soft mounds of her breasts, her arching stomach, always receiving the caresses of his hands and mouth, never any other. The afternoon was the afternoon of her body; there was nothing else in time or space, nothing but her limbs and her flesh, nothing but the pressure of her hands on his skin. They kissed as if their mouths were drawn together magnetically, until their faces were covered with saliva, and there was nothing but a wide wet world of voluptuous love. Their arms around each other, their bodies surged together at the hips. He slid her pants down over her legs, caressing the smooth skin of her limbs, until the scrap of silk disappeared into the blankets. And now their bodies pressed together with nothing between them, the feel of their naked flesh making their kisses even more urgent. His hand circled, running over her skin, her belly, her thighs, running through a nest of hair between her legs, circling smaller until it found puckered flesh, moving up and down slowly, pressing deeper, until his finger finally entered a soft dark electrical place, and she gasped, and arched her body still more. He was vaguely expecting to find a string in the way, but he could feel none, and then forgot about it. This was Caroline; now she could understand, and so could he. Time passed, and none was comprehended. Nothing mattered but the feel of her body. He slid two fingers inside her, and she caught her breath. His tongue ran over her stomach, and he rotated his wrist, his fingers moving in a soft wet place, curves of muscle pressing them. Her hands were on him, driving everything from his mind but the consciousness of her and of this exquisite pressure. He felt a different quality in the wetness of her vagina, and a long time later realized that there was a profuse flow of blood. When he finally withdrew his hand, he slowly moved it up, arching his wrist so that his fingers did not touch the bedclothes and brought his hand to the light. His first two fingers were covered from top to bottom in thick, bright red blood. She was watching his hand too; it had suddenly assumed a position of paramount importance, like an object framed by perspective lines in a photograph. What had been an unobtrusive movement had become a dramatic gesture. He felt as though he had just been probing a terrible wound in her body, and he had a brief moment of horror. "Have you got a piece of rag?" She indicated a packet of sanitary pads that he hadn't noticed before, and he took one, and quickly wiped the blood from his fingers. She felt his erection beginning to subside, and asked, "Are you sure you want to make love?" He nodded, not thinking of asking her the same question, thinking of nothing but loving her. His hands ran over her again, and soon his body found itself moving over her, now above her, now sliding into the dampness of her.

Now there was a pause.

Now they were together.

He looked down at her face, and kissed her slowly on the lips, running his hands in little repetitive caresses over her bare shoulders. Slow movements began, like the movements of glaciers, years of time translated into flashes of fire. Then faster, now a rhythm. A single strand of bright steel, a long rod that flashed brightly, twirling in the bright electrical air, wider and wider, filling the world with silver. And then he paused, looking down at her face, raising his eyebrows slightly. She smiled. "We haven't seen each other often enough, have we?" He began to move again, feeling the focus of their bodies damply sliding together, the warmth of her flesh next to his.

The world revolved about him. He lifted his head, feeling the movement like a ritual of intense importance. And thin strands of wire string out, joining together, forming thicker strands, ropes of wire, less and less, until there is only one rod, gleaming brightly, shining and glittering, twisting and coruscating, growing wider and wider . . . He stopped his movements again, and then started, slowly. Moving in her he could feel his skin all over his body, his limbs warm, and a nostalgic, dropping emptiness in his stomach. He concentrated on these feelings, trying to blot out the other feeling from his mind—the feeling of sharpness, a diffused sweet whiteness that was even now making itself more manifest, becoming more and more powerful, almost overwhelming. He stopped again, suddenly. He kissed her gently on the lips and spoke. "It's obviously going to be like this all the time. Will you mind us pausing like this?" "No, no, that's all right." They kissed again, their tongues trembling together, damp surfaces all over their bodies in contact. And he felt his body moving again.

The city is the city of broken festivals—city of changing carpets and the August moon—spires dance in the squares—in the city the night is velvet—instead of drains, set along the gutters are bowls of wild flowers—cats sing among headstones—drunken women in bright flared skirts dance among piles of petals—the city is full of soft waters that fall slowly from the moon—in the center of the city is a tall steel rod that grows wider and wider, opening out at the top into an enormous white umbrella—colored banners are set from building to building, covering the city in bursts of flame—skeletons dance in the city's lights—the festival is a jubilee of eternity—vendors of violet shadows move in a concourse through the streets—crowds of people move like slow pink phantoms—long white worms coil about the lamp standards—the city revolves in the fire of night—stainless steel fingers spread to receive the dawn—festivities ring out among the spider struts—all the people are spread with daffodils . . .

Their bodies lay together. They were now one being, neither male nor female, but just a complete body of a strange, lethargic creature that twitched, regularly contracting itself under some blankets. He moved in her, feeling her soft moisture, feeling the folds of voluptuous muscle holding him. When they stopped again, they lay over to one side. Now he could caress her, and his hand moved over her back, along her thighs, feeling acres of flesh, fields that he could explore at leisure, feeling too the damp blows at his hips, the feeling of the underside of her body against his abdomen, his testicles rolling back and forth and bumping her. His hand probed beneath her, feeling the wetness that had run from her and the pucker of her anus, trying to ingest the whole of her body, his stomach sinking and his body melting into hers, pausing, moving again. Once he had to stop suddenly, and all his muscles became rigid with the effort of shutting off, his arms shaking, feeling a spurt of semen, and then the feelings receding, and now moving vigorously, knowing that they would not return for a long time, looking down at her face, her swollen lips, her mouth half-open, her breath exhaled in little sighs, each movement of his body echoed by hers, a shuddering over the whole of her.

The city shimmers like glass—waltzes fade in dark alcoves—the sun shatters and falls to the sea like tumbling drops of blood—wire springs nod in the morning air—grass dies in profuse movements—fountains are spurting, their water viscous in death—skulls rattle on pavements—the city is brown, and the stones crack—flowers are growing from genitals—the pavements are littered with dying blooms—the air is sweet with the death of flowers—dye drips from the banners, bleaching them to pure white . . .

A sound of water, dim light, and leaves and stones on the ground. It was as if he was seeing everything with a preternatural clarity, watching the stones to keep his mind away from the mass of physical sensations in which he was floating. Their bodies writhed together on the ground, and he felt that this

108

movement, this strange dance, had been going on for eternity, that there had never been any other life, that he had been born in this woman and would die in her embrace. His body was floating, he was conscious of vast chemical reactions going on in the universe. Her breath was coming in loud gasps now, and he knew that it wouldn't be long. But he might have to stop, and it might escape again. A white wedge inserted itself, growing more and more prominent, and his body began to erupt in a silver anguish. He stopped. He was breathless and covered with sweat. Lying still in her he looked at her face. She was breathing heavily, and as he watched her face changed, moving from side to side, all the marks of normal human life dropping away, her head going back, her mouth open. Her cries began, slow regular cries, and he began to move again, letting the feelings blossom, opening the floodgates, dropping, dropping, a silver line blooming inside him, higher, higher, but not quite high enough, and then breaking, their movements frenzied, resignation, dimly hearing his own voice, feeling his head dropping, and then only a world of whiteness.

The city implodes, the towers, spires and struts of metal raining to the center like a waterfall—liquid pours in on the dead city—whirlpools of vegetation—dead people dance in the water—all that is left is a floating mass of flowers and machines.

They lay together quietly, and he kissed her, feeling his body warm and relaxed, with no tension in him anywhere. She opened her eyes, looking worried. "I wanted to give you something you could remember, like that time in the hotel . . ." "It's all right; nothing went wrong. It was good for me." She smiled at him. "That sometimes happens. It just starts when I am relaxed." They lay together some more, and smoked a cigarette. He slowly withdrew from her, and she handed him the towel as he kneeled upright. He rubbed the towel over the front of his body, suddenly realizing that it was pitch dark. He could feel clots of blood on his flesh, and rubbed energetically. He lit a match to see how much blood there was on him. There were a few stains left, and he wiped at them. In the dim light of the match he could see the pallid skin of his body, and looking at his half-erect penis he suddenly felt a revulsion for his own flesh, and shook out the match. There was congealed blood all over his hairs, feeling uncomfortable, but he realized that it would have to stay there until he had time to wash. They began to search for their clothes by match-light. "We said we were going to keep on our clothes, but I managed to lose all mine except my dress, and that was round my neck!" They laughed together as they searched. While they were dressing they were quiet, and he wondered if she too felt this strange melancholy that had settled on him. He lit another match, and looked at his watch. "It's half-past five; we were quite a long time. It gives us just long enough to sit in the car for a while and then get back to Leicester." They gathered together their possessions, rebundled the blankets, and emerged from the little shed, walking slowly past the line of buildings, holding hands, up toward the road.

They moved carefully through the blackness, seeing nothing but the dark shapes of trees against the dim sky. A car briefly flooded the road above with light. As they got to the higher ground there was a large black shed, with a single light on the side. The ground was yellow in this light, which shone onto the surrounding trees, making them look like pale ghosts. They stood together watching this light, conscious of the smallness of their bodies and feeling a strong and inexplicable sadness. The light made everything cold and unreal, an analytical light that transformed familiar trees into symbols of unconsummated love and inevitable death. Her hand tightened round his, and they stood watching the light for a long time. He knew that one day he would find the events of this day quite amusing, but at the moment he felt only a sadness fed by the yellow light. They turned, and walked quickly to the green gate, climbing over hurriedly. The lake was dark as they walked past, and all was quiet but for the sound of water lapping at the shore. There was a car parked near hers, and as they passed they saw a couple kissing. "Let's tell them that we know a much better place!" she said, and he laughed as he helped her squeeze the bundle into the boot.

They could both keenly feel the cold, and he shivered as she got in the car and unlocked his door. Inside the car she switched on the light, and then got out the box of sandwiches. Now he felt hungry, and he ate quickly. There was congealed blood round his fingernails, but he didn't want to clean it off, wanting to carry her substances as long as he could. They sat and talked lethargically, kissing each other gently. In each other's eyes they could read the urgent question: "What are we to *do?*" Now there was very little of the day left. At quarter to six, one hour before they were due to part again, the car backed out and turned onto the road, leaving Groby Pond behind it.

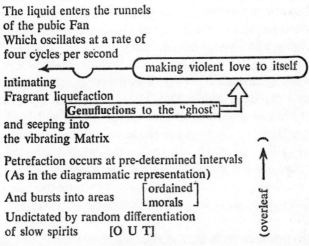

The car drew up outside the coach station. The London coach, a bright looming monster, was ready to leave, and would shortly be drawing out of the station on its way to the M1. As the car pulled up outside The Shakespeare, they turned and fell into each other's arms. Her lips were frantic on his, and they pressed tightly to each other, wanting to make love again, wanting to hold each other and never to let go. Soon, very soon, they would leave, and the distance be-

111

tween them would expand rapidly, at a combined rate of one hundred and twenty miles an hour. His right hand was under her coat, running over her shoulder and back, trying to impress the feel of her on his mind forever. She pulls the front of her sweater out of her skirt and thrusts his cold hand up against the warmth of her body. They meet for polite conversation in a pub. She sits over an armchair, her legs dangling over one arm, listening to Messiaen's *Trois Petites Liturgies*. They talk together in the yard of Henekey's in Portobello Road on a bright sunny day, thinking that time was more crucial to them then than ever before, their words measured now only in hundreds. Cogs turn, and the time machine performs a ritual osculation at the foot of a metal apparition. The city swirls in autumn tides, its drowned coiling like ropes, the bodies illuminated by the sunny greenness of the water, hair forming moving curves, skin shredding off in twisting rinds, fixed by the sun above in a moment of coiling, gentle—beauty. They meet again, hurriedly taking off their clothes and making love on a living room carpet. They die. They are born. The birds of night flap through years, their large black wings dripping yellow drops of poison. The universe rolls through the aether like a dead whale. They kiss, trying to merge into each other, tongues searching for this union which will bind them forever. The car door opens. He leaps out and walks quickly across to the coach. He sits by a window, and a girl sits beside him. As the coach moves off he watches her car, and sees her sitting inside in the darkness, watching the coach.

They do not wave to each other.

The prisoner feels in the right-hand pocket of his denim suit. He pulls out a small leather wallet, and puts the photograph into one of the compartments, transferring it back to the pocket. Now it is evening; the stone walls are touched with gold. He lies on his back on the bunk, watching the ceiling, and the rippling spider webs. A little while later there is a rattling sound at the door. Soon it opens, and his warder walks in. He turns his head on the bunk and looks at the warder.

The man clears his throat and then begins to speak, as if speaking is an effort.

"There has been a general decree. All the prisoners are to be released. You are free to go."

Configuration of the North Shore

by R. A. Lafferty

The patient was named John Miller.
The analyst was named Robert Rousse.
Two men.
The room was cluttered with lighting, testing, and recording equipment. It held several sets of furniture that conferred together in small groups, sofas, easy chairs, business chairs, desks, couches, coffee tables, and two small bars. There were books, and there was a shadow booth. The pictures on the walls were of widely different sorts.
One setting. Keep it simple, and be not distracted by indifferent details.

"I have let my business go down," Miller said. "My wife says that I have let her down. My sons say that I have turned into a sleepy stranger. Everybody agrees that I've lost all ambition and judgment. And yet I *do* have a stirring ambition. I am not able, however, to put it into words."

"We'll put it into words, Miller, either yours or mine," Rousse said. "Slip up on it right now! Quickly, what is the stirring ambition?"

"To visit the Northern Shore, and to make the visit stick."

"How does one get to this Northern Shore, Miller?"

"That's the problem. I can locate it only very broadly on the globe. Sometimes it seems that it should be off the eastern tip of New Guinea, going north from the D'Entrecasteaux Islands and bypassing Trobriand; again I feel that it is off in the Molucca Passage toward Talaud; and again it should be

114

a little further south, coming north out of the Banda Sea by one of the straats. But I have been in all those waters without finding any clue to it. And the maps show unacceptable land or open sea wherever I try to set it."

"How long?"

"About twenty-five years."

"All in what we might call the Outer East Indies and dating from your own time in that part of the world, in World War II. When did it become critical?"

"It was always critical, but I worked around it. I built up my business and my family and led a pleasant and interesting life. I was able to relegate the Thing to my normal sleeping hours. Now I slow down a little and have less energy. I have trouble keeping both sets of things going."

"Can you trace the impression of the North Shore to anything? Transfigured early memory of some striking sea view? Artform-triggered intuition? Can you trace any roots to the evocative dream?"

"I had an inland childhood, not even a striking lakeview in it. And yet the approach to the North Shore is always by a way recognized from early childhood. I don't believe that I have any intuition at all, nor any sense of art forms. It is simply a continuing dream that brings me almost to it. I am rounding a point, and the North Shore will be just beyond that point. Or I have left ship and wade through the shallows; and then I have only a narrow (but eerie) neck of land to traverse to reach the North Shore. Or I am, perhaps, on the North Shore itself and going through fog to the place of importance, and I will have the whole adventure as soon as the fog clears a little; but it doesn't. I've been on the verge of discovering it all a thousand times."

"All right. Lie down and go to dreaming, Miller. We will try to get you past that verge. Dream, and we record it."

"It isn't that easy, Rousse. There's always preliminaries to be gone through. First there is a setting and sound and smell of a place near the surf and a tide booming. This watery background then grows fainter; but it remains behind it all. And then there is a little anteroom dream, a watery dream

115

that is not the main one. The precursor dream comes and goes, sharp and clear, and it has its own slanted pleasure. And only then am I able to take up the journey to the North Shore."

"All right, Miller, we will observe the amenities. Dream your dreams in their proper order. Lie easy there. Now the shot. The recorders and the shadow booth are waiting."

Shadow booths reproduced dreams in all dimensions and senses, so much so that often a patient on seeing a playback of his own dream was startled to find that an impression, which he would have said could be in no way expressed, was quite well expressed in shadow or color or movement or sound or odor. The shadow booth of the analyst Rousse was more than a basic booth, as he had incorporated many of his own notions into it. It reproduced the dreams of his patients very well, though to some extent through his own eyes and presuppositions.

First was given the basic, and Rousse realized that for his patient Miller this was New Guinea, and more particularly Black Papua, the stark mountain land full of somber spooky people. It was night; the area seemed to be about fifty yards from the surf, but every boom and sigh was audible. And there was something else: the tide was booming underground; the ocean permeated the land. Guinea, the mountain that is an island, was a mountain full of water. The roots of the mountain move and sigh; the great boulders squeak when the hammer of the tide hits them; and on the inside of the cliffs the water level rises. There is the feeling of being on a very large ship, a ship a thousand miles long.

"He has captured the Earth-Basic well," the analyst Rousse said. Then the basic faded back a bit, and the precursor dream began.

It was in a flat-bottomed rowboat from some old camping trip. He was lying on his back in the bottom of the boat, and it was roped to a stump or tree and was rocking just a little in the current. And here was another mountain full of water, but an inland one of much less bulk, and the ice-cold springs ran out of its sides and down its piney shoulders to the shingle

116

of the creek bank. Fish jumped in the dark, and blacksnakes slid down the hill to drink. Bullfrogs echoed, and hoot owls made themselves known; and far away dogs and men were out possuming, with the baying carrying over the miles. Then the boy remembered what he must do, and in his dream he unroped the boat and shoved into the stream and ran his trot line. From every hook he took a fish as long as his arm till the boat was full and nearly swamped.

And from the last hook of all, he took a turtle as big as a wagon wheel. He would not have been able to get it into the boat had not the turtle helped by throwing a booted leg over the side and heaving himself in. For by this time it was not so much a turtle but more like someone the boy knew. Then he talked for a while with the turtle that was not exactly a turtle any more. The turtle had a sack of Bull Durham and the boy had papers, so they rolled and smoked and watched the night clouds slide overhead. One of them was named Thinesta and one was named Shonge, which chased the first and would soon have him treed or caught, if they did not run into the mountain or the moon first.

"Boy, this is the life!" said the turtle. "Boy, this is the life!" said the boy.

"He's a poet," said Rousse, and this puzzled him. He knew himself to be a cultured man, and he knew that Miller wasn't.

Then the little precursor dream slid away, and there began the tortuous and exhilarating journey to the North Shore. It was coming around a point in an old windjammer on which all the men were dead except the dreamer. The dead men were grinning and were happy enough in their own way. They had lashed themselves to rails and davits and such before they had died. "They didn't want it bad enough," the dreamer said, "but they won't mind me going ahead with it." But the point was devilish hard to turn. There came on wind and driving spray so that the ship shuddered. There was only ashen light as of false dawn. There was great strain. The dreamer struggled, and Rousse (caught up in the emotion of it) became quite involved and would have been in despair if it were not for the ultimate hope that took hold of him.

A porpoise whistled loudly, and at that moment they rounded the point. But it was a false point, and the true point was still up ahead. Yet the goal was now more exciting than ever. Yet both the current and the wind were against them. Rousse was a practical man. "We will not make it tonight," he said. "We had better heave to in this little cove and hold onto what advantage we have gained. We can make it the next time from here." "Aye, we'll tie up in the little cove," one of the dead men said, "we'll make it on the next sortie." "We will make it *now*," the dreamer swore. He jammed the windjammer and refused to give up.

It was very long and painful, and they did not make it that night, or that afternoon in the analyst's office. When the dream finally broke, both Miller and Rousse were trembling with the effort—and the high hope was set again into the future.

"That's it," Miller said. "Sometimes I come closer. There is something in it that makes it worthwhile. I have to get there."

"We should have tied up in the cove," Rousse said. "We'll have blown backwards some ways, but it can't be helped. I seem to be a little too much in empathy with this thing, Miller. I can see how it is quite real to you. Analysis, as you may not know, has analogs in many of the sciences. In Moral Theology, which I count a science, the analog is Ultimate Compensation. I am sure that I can help you. I have already helped you, Miller. Tomorrow we will go much further with it."

The tomorrow session began very much the same. It was Guinea again, the Earth Basic, the Mountain Spook Land, the Fundament permeated with Chaos which is the Sea. It boomed and sighed and trembled to indicate that there are black and sea-green spirits in the basic itself. Then the basic adjusted itself into the background, and the precursor dream slid in.

The boy, the dreamer was in a canoe. It was night, but the park lights were on, and the lights of the restaurants and little beer gardens along the way. The girl was with him in the canoe; she had green eyes and a pleasantly crooked mouth. Well, it was San Antonio on the little river that runs through the parkways and under the bridges. Then they were beyond the parkway and out of town. There were live-oak trees overhanging the water, and beards of spanish moss dragged the surface as though they were drifting through a cloud made up of gossamer and strands of old burlap.

"We've come a thousand miles," the girl said, "and it costs a dollar a mile for the canoe. If you don't have that much money we'll have to keep the canoe; the man won't take it back unless we pay him." "I have the money, but we might want to save it to buy breakfast when we cross the Mississippi," the boy said. The girl's name was Ginger, and she strummed on a stringed instrument that was spheroid; it revolved as she played and changed colors like a juke box. The end of the canoe paddle shone like a star and left streaks of cosmic dust on the night water as the boy dipped it.

They crossed the Mississippi, and were in a world that smelled of wet sweet clover and very young catfish. The boy threw away the paddle and kissed Ginger. It felt as though she were turning him inside out, drawing him into her completely. And suddenly she bit him hard and deep with terrible teeth, and he could smell the blood running down his face when he pushed her away. He pushed her out of the canoe and she sank down and down. The underwater was filled with green light and he watched her as she sank. She waved to him and called up in a burst of bubbles. "That's all right. I was tired of the canoe anyhow. I'll walk back." "Damn you, Ginger, why didn't you tell me you weren't people?" the dreamer asked.

"It is ritual, it is offering, the little precursor dreams that he makes," Rousse said.

Then the precursor dream glided away like the canoe itself, and the main thing gathered once more to mount the big effort. It was toward the North Shore once more, but not in a windjammer. It was in a high hooting steamship that

119

rode with nine other ships in splendid array through one of the straats out of what, in concession to the world, they had let be called the Banda Sea.

"We come to the edge of the world now," the dreamer said, "and only I will know the way here." "It is *not* the edge of the world," one of the seamen said. "See, here is the map, and here we are on it. As you can see, it is a long way to the edge of the world." "The map is wrong," the dreamer said, "let me fix it." He tore the map in two. "Look now," the dreamer pointed, "are we not now at the edge of the world?" All saw that they were; whereupon all the seamen began to jump off the ship, and tried to swim back to safety. And the other ships of the array, one by one, upended themselves and plunged into the abyss at the edge of the water. This really was the edge of the world, and the waters rushed over it.

But the dreamer knew the secret of this place, and he had faith. Just in time he saw it, right where he knew it must be, a narrow wedge of high water extending beyond the edge of the world. The ship sailed out on this narrow wedge, very precariously. "For the love of God be careful!" Rousse gasped. "Oh hell, I'm becoming too involved in a patient's dream." Well, it *was* a pretty nervous go there. So narrow was the wedge that the ship seemed to be riding on nothing; and on both sides was bottomless space and the sound of water rushing into it and falling forever. The sky also had ended—it does not extend beyond the world. There was no light, but only ashen darkness. And the heavy wind came up from below on both sides.

Nevertheless, the dreamer continued on and on until the wedge became too narrow to balance the ship. "I will get out and walk," the dreamer said, and he did. The ship upended itself and plunged down into bottomless space; and the dreamer was walking, as it were, on a rope of water, narrower than his boots, narrow as a rope indeed. It was, moreover, very slippery, and the sense of depth below was sickening. Even Rousse trembled and broke into cold sweat from the surrogate danger of it.

But the dreamer still knew the secret. He saw, far ahead,

120

where the sky began again, and there is no sky over a void. And after continuing some further distance on the dangerous way, he saw where the land began again, a true land mass looming up ahead.

What was dimly seen, of course, was the back side of the land mass, and a stranger coming onto it would not guess its importance. But the dreamer knew that one had only to reach it and turn the point to be on the North Shore itself.

The excitement of the thing to come communicated itself, and at that very moment the watery rope widened to a path. It was still slippery and dangerous, it still had on each side of it depths so deep that a thousand miles would be only an inch. And then for the first time the dreamer realized the fearsomeness of the thing he was doing. "But I always knew I could walk on water if things got bad enough," he said. It was a tricky path, but it was a path that a man could walk on.

"Keep on! Keep on!" Rousse shouted. "We're almost there!" "There's a break in the path," said Miller the dreamer, and there was. It wasn't a hundred feet from the land mass, it wasn't a thousand feet to the turning of the point and the arrival at the North Shore itself. But there was a total break. Opposite them, on the dim land mass, was an emperor penguin.

"You have to wait till we get it fixed," the penguin said. "My brothers have gone to get more water to fix it with. It will be tomorrow before we get it fixed." "I'll wait," the dreamer shouted.

But Rousse saw something that the dreamer did not see, that nobody else had ever seen before. He looked at the shape of the new sky that is always above the world and is not above the abyss. From the configuration of the sky he read the Configuration of the Northern Shore. He gasped with unbelief. Then the dream broke.

"It may be only the quest-in-itself motif," Rousse lied, trying to control himself and to bring his breathing back to normal. "And then, there might, indeed, be something at the end of it. I told you, Miller, that analysis has its parallels in

121

other sciences. Well, it can borrow devices from them also. We will borrow the second-stage-platform from the science of rocketry."

"You've turned into a sly man, Rousse," Miller said. "What's taken hold of you suddenly? What is it that you're not saying?"

"What I am saying, Miller, is that we will use it tomorrow. When the dream has reached its crest and just before it breaks up, we'll cut in a second-stage booster. I've done it before with lesser dreams. We are going to see this thing to the end tomorrow."

"All right."

"It will take some special rigging," Rousse told himself when Miller was gone. "And I'll have to gather a fair amount of information and shape it up. But it will be worth it. I am thinking of the second stage shot in another sense, and I might just be able to pull it off. This isn't the quest-in-itself at all. I've seen plenty of them. I've seen the false a thousand times. Let me not now fumble the real! This is the Ultimate Arrival Nexus that takes a man clean out of himself. It is the Compensation. If it were not achieved in one life in a million, then none of the other lives would have been worthwhile. Somebody has to win to keep the gamble going. There has to be a grand prize behind it all. I've seen the shape of it in that second sky. I'm the one to win it."

Then Rousse busied himself against the following day. He managed some special rigging. He gathered a mass of information and shaped it up. He incorporated these things into the shadow booth. He canceled a number of appointments. He was arranging that he could take some time off, a day, a month, a year, a lifetime if necessary.

The tomorrow session began very much the same, except for some doubts on the part of the patient Miller. "I said it yesterday, and I say it again," Miller grumbled. "You've turned sly on me, man. What is it?" "All analysts are sly, Miller, it's the name of our trade. Get with it now. I promise that we will get you past the verge today. We are going to see this dream through to its end."

There was the Earth Basic again. There was the Mountain booming full of water, the groaning of the rocks, and the constant adjusting and readjusting of the world on its uneasy foundation. There was the salt spray, the salt of the Earth that leavens the lump. There were the crabs hanging onto the wet edge of the world.

Then the Basic muted itself, and the precursor dream slid in, the ritual fish.

It was a rendezvous of ships and boats in an immensity of green islands scattered in a purple-blue sea. It was a staging area for both ships and islands; thence they would travel in convoys to their proper positions, but here they were all in a jumble. There were LST's and Jay Boats, cargo ships and little packets. There were old sailing clippers with topgallants and moonscrapers full of wind, though they were at anchor. There was much moving around, and it was easy to step from the ships to the little green islands (if they were islands, some of them were no more than rugs of floating moss, but they did not sink) and back again onto the ships. There were sailors and seamen and pirates shooting craps together on the little islands. Bluejackets and bandits would keep jumping from the ships down to join the games, and then others would leave them and hop to other islands.

Piles of money of rainbow colors and of all sizes were everywhere. There were pesos and pesetas and pesarones. There were crowns and coronets and rix-dollars. There were gold certificates that read "Redeemable only at Joe's Marine Bar Panama City." There were guilders with the Queen's picture on them, and half-guilders with the Jack's picture on them. There were round coins with square holes in them, and square coins with round holes. There was stage money and invasion money, and comic money from the Empires of Texas and Louisiana. And there were bales of real frogskins, green and sticky, which were also current.

"Commodore," one of the pirates said, "get that boat out of the way or I'll ram it down your throat." "I don't have any boat," said the dreamer. "I'm not a commodore; I'm an army sergeant; I'm supposed to guard this box for the lieutenant." Oh hell, he didn't even have a box. What had happened to the box? "Commodore," said the pirate, "get that boat out of the way or I'll cut off your feet."

He did cut off his feet. And this worried the boy, the dreamer, since he did not know whether it was in the line of duty or if he would be paid for his feet. "I don't know which boat you mean," he told the pirate. "Tell me which boat you mean and I'll try to move it." "Commodore," the pirate said, "move this boat or I'll cut your hands off." He did cut his hands off. "This isn't getting us anywhere," the dreamer said, "tell me which boat you want moved." "If you don't know your own boat by now, I ought to slit your gullet," the pirate said. He did slit his gullet. It was harder to breathe after that, and the boy worried more. "Sir, you're not even a pirate in my own outfit. You ought to get one of the sailors to move the boat for you. I'm an army sergeant and I don't even know how to move a boat."

The pirate pushed him down in a grave on one of the green islands and covered him up. He was dead now and it scared him. This was not at all like he thought it would be. But the green dirt was transparent and he could still see the salty dogs playing cards and shooting craps all around him. "If that boat isn't moved," the pirate said, "you're going to be in real trouble." "Oh, let him alone," one of the dice players said. So he let him alone.

"It's ritual sacrifice he offers," Rousse said. "He brings the finest gift he can make every time. I will have to select a top one from the files for my own Precursor."

Then it was toward the North Shore again as the Precursor Dream faded.

It was with a big motor launch now, as big as a yacht, half as big as a ship. The craft was very fast when called on to be. It would have to be, for it was going through passes that weren't there all the time. Here was a seacliff, solid and without a break. But to one who knows the secret there *is* a way

124

through. Taken at morning half-light and from a certain angle there was a passage through. The launch made it, but barely. It was a very close thing, and the cliffs ground together again behind it. And there behind was the other face of the sea-cliff, solid and sheer. But the ocean ahead was different, for they had broken with the map and with convention in finding a passage where there was none. There were now great groupings of islands and almost-islands. But some of them were merely sargasso-type weed islands, floating clumps; and some of them were only floating heaps of pumice and ash from a volcano that was now erupting.

How to tell the true land from the false? The dreamer threw rocks at all the islands. If the islands were of weed or pumice or ash they would give but a dull sound. But if they were real land they would give a solid ringing sound to the thrown rock. Most of them were false islands, but now one rang like iron.

"It is a true island," said the dreamer, "it is named Pulo Bakal." And after the launch had gone a great way through the conglomerate, one of the islands rang like solid wood to the thrown rock. "It is a true island," said the dreamer, "it is named Pulo Kaparangan."

And finally there was a land that rang like gold, or almost like it (like cracked gold really) to the thrown rock. "It is true land, I think it is," said the dreamer. "It is named Pulo Ginto, I think it is. It should be the land itself, and its North Shore should be the Shore Itself. But it is spoiled this day. The sound was cracked. I don't want it as much as I thought I did. It's been tampered with."

"This is it," Rousse urged the dreamer. "Quickly now, right around the point and you are there. We can make it this time."

"No, there's something wrong with it. I don't want it the way it is. I'll just wake up and try it some other time."

"Second stage called for," Rousse cried. He did certain things with electrodes and with a needle into Miller's left rump, and sent him reeling back into the dream. "We'll make it," Rousse encouraged. "We're there. It's everything you've sought."

"No, no, the light's all wrong. The sound was cracked.

What we are coming to—oh no no, it's ruined, it's ruined forever. You robbed me of it."

What they came to was that little canal off the River and into the Sixth Street Slip to the little wharf where barges used to tie up by the Consolidated Warehouse. And it was there that Miller stormed angrily onto the rotten wooden wharf, past the old warehouse, up the hill three blocks and past his own apartment house, to the left three blocks and up and into the analyst's office, and there the dream and the reality came together.

"You've robbed me, you filthy fool," Miller sputtered, waking up in blithering anger. "You've spoiled it forever. I'll not go back to it. It isn't there any more. What a crass thing to do."

"Easy, easy, Miller. You're cured now, you know. You can enter onto your own full life again. Have you never heard the most beautiful parable ever, about the boy who went around the world in search of the strangest thing of all, and came to his own home at the end, and it so transfigured that he hardly knew it?"

"It's a lie, is what it is. Oh, you've cured me, and you get your fee. And slyness is the name of your game. May somebody some day rob you of the ultimate thing!"

"I hope not, Miller."

Rousse had been making his preparations for a full twenty-four hours. He had canceled appointments and phased out and transferred patients. He would not be available to anyone for some time, he did not know for how long a time.

He had his hideout, an isolated point on a wind-ruffled lake. He needed no instrumentation. He believed he knew the direct way into it.

"It's the real thing," he told himself. "I've seen the shape of it, accidentally in the dream sky that hung over it. Billions of people have been on the earth, and not a dozen have been to it; and not one would bother to put it into words. 'I have seen such things—' said Aquinas. 'I have seen such things—' said John of the Cross. 'I have seen such things—' said Plato.

And they all lived out the rest of their lives in a glorious daze.

"It is too good for a peasant like Miller. I'll grab it myself."

It came easy. An old leather couch is as good a craft as any to go there. First the Earth Basic and the Permeating Ocean, that came natural on the wind-ruffled point of the lake. Then the ritual offering, the Precursor Dream. Rousse had thrown a number of things into this: a tonal piece by Gideon Styles, an old seascape by Grobin that had a comic and dreamlike quality, Lyall's curious sculpture "Moon Crabs," a funny sea tale by McVey and a poignant one by Gironella. It was pretty good. Rousse understood this dream business.

Then the Precursor Dream was allowed to fade back. And it was off toward the North Shore by a man in the finest craft ever dreamed up, by a man who knew just what he wanted, "The Thing Itself," by a man who would give all the days of his life to arrive at it.

Rousse understood the approaches and the shoals now; he had studied them thoroughly. He knew that, however different they had seemed each time in the dreams of Miller, they were always essentially the same. He took the land right at the first rounding of the point, leaping clear and letting his launch smash on the rocks.

"There will be no going back now," he said, "it was the going back that always worried Miller, that caused him to fail." The cliffs here appeared forbidding, but Rousse had seen again and again the little notch in the high purple of them, the path over. He followed the path with high excitement and cleared the crest.

"Here Basho walked, here Aquin, here John de Yepes," he proclaimed, and he came down toward the North Shore itself, with the fog over it beginning to lift.

"You be false captain with a stolen launch," said a small leviathan off shore.

"No, no, I dreamed the launch myself," Rousse maintained. "I'll not be stopped."

"I will not stop you," said the small leviathan. "The launch is smashed, and none but I know that you are false captain."

Why, it was clearing now! The land began to leap out in its richness, and somewhere ahead was a glorious throng. In the throat of a pass was a monokeros, sleek and brindled.

"None passes here and lives," said the monokeros.

"I pass," said Rousse.

He passed through, and there was a small moan behind him. "What was that?" he asked.

"You died," said the monokeros.

"Oh, so I'm dead on my couch, am I? It won't matter. I hadn't wanted to go back."

He went forward over the ensorceled and pinnacled land, hearing the rakish and happy throng somewhere ahead.

"I must not lose my way now," said Rousse. And there was a stele, standing up and telling him the way with happy carved words.

Rousse read it, and he entered the shore itself.

And all may read and enter.

The stele, the final marker, was headed:

Which None May Read and Return

And the words on it—
And the words—
And the words—

Let go! You're holding on! You're afraid! Read it and take it. It is *not* blank!

It's carved clear and bright.

Read it and enter.

You're afraid.

Paul's Treehouse

by Gene Wolfe

It was the day after the governor called out the National
Guard, but Morris did not think of it that way; it was the
morning after the second night Paul had spent in the tree,
and Morris brushed his teeth with Scotch after he looked into
Paul's bedroom and saw the unrumpled bed. And it was hot;
though not in the house, which was airconditioned.

Sheila was still asleep, lying straight out like a man on the
single bed across from his own. He left her undisturbed, filling his glass with Scotch again and carrying it out to the patio
at the side of the house. The sun was barely up, yet the metal
furniture there was already slightly warm. It would be a hot
day, a scorcher. He heard the snip-snack of Russell's shears
on the other side of the hedge and braced himself for the
inevitable remark.

"It's going to be a hot one, isn't it?" Sticking his head over
the top of the hedge. Morris nodded, hoping that if he did not
speak Russell would stay where he was. The hope was fruit-
less. He could hear Russell unlatching the gate, although he
purposely did not look.

"Hotter than the hinges of hell," Russell said, sitting down.
"Do the gardening early, that's what I told myself, do it early
while it's cool, and look at me. I'm sweating already. Did you
hear what they did last night? Beat a cop to death with golf
clubs and polo mallets out of a store window."

Morris said nothing, looking up at Paul's treehouse. It was
on the other side of the yard, but so high up it could be seen
above the roofline of the house.

"Beat him to death right out on the street."

"I suppose some of them deserve it," Morris said moodily.

"Sure they do, but it's *them* doing it. That's what gets to me.
. . . Drinking pretty early, aren't you?" Russell was tall and
gangling, with a long neck and a prominent Adam's apple;
Morris, short and fat-bellied, envied him his straight lines.

"I guess I am," he said. "Like one?"

"Since it's Saturday . . ."

It was cool in the house, much cooler than the patio, but
the air was stale. He splashed the cheaper "guest" whisky into
a glass and added a squirt of charged water.

"Is that your boy Paul's?" When he came out again Russell
was staring up at the treehouse just as he himself had been
doing a moment before. Morris nodded.

"He built it on his own, didn't he? I remember watching
him climb up there with boards or something, with his little
radio playing to keep him company." He took the drink. "You
don't mind if I walk around and have a look at it, do you?"

Reluctantly Morris followed him, stepping over the beds of
flame-toned, scentless florabundas Sheila loved.

The tree at the other side of the house gave too much shade
for roses. There was nothing under it except a little sparse
grass and a few stones Paul had dropped.

Russell whistled. "That's way up there, isn't it? Fifty feet
if it's an inch. Why'd you let him build it so high?"

"Sheila doesn't believe in thwarting the boy's natural in-
clinations." It sounded silly when Morris said it, and he
covered by taking another sip of the whisky.

Russell shook his head. "If he ever falls out of there he'll
kill himself."

"Paul's a good climber," Morris said.

"He'd have to be to build that thing." Russell continued to
stare, craning his body backward. Morris wished that he
would return to the patio.

"It took him almost two weeks," Morris said.

"He swiped the lumber off the housing project, didn't he?"

"I bought him some of it." For an instant Morris had seen

Paul's small, brown head in one of the windows. He wondered if Russell had noticed it.

"But he swiped most of it. Two-by-fours and four-by-fours; it looks solid."

"I suppose it is." Before he could catch himself he added, "He's got buckets of rocks up there."

"Rocks?" Russell looked down, startled.

"Rocks about the size of tennis balls. Paul built a sort of elevator and hauled them up. He must have eight or ten buckets full."

"What's he want those for?"

"I don't know."

"Well, ask him." Russell looked angry at having his curiosity balked. "He's your kid." Morris swallowed the last of his second drink, saying nothing.

"How does he get up there?" Russell was looking at the tree again. "It doesn't look as if you *could* climb it."

"He cut off some of the branches after he got the place built. He has a rope with knots in it he lets down."

"Where is it?" Russell looked around, expecting to see the rope tangled in the tree's branches somewhere.

It was bound to come out now. "He pulls it up after him when he goes in there," Morris said. The Scotch was lying like a pool of mercury in his empty stomach.

"You mean he's up there now?"

Neither of them had heard Sheila come out. "He's been up there since Thursday." She sounded unconcerned.

Morris turned to face her and saw that she was wearing a quilted pink housecoat. Her hair was still in curlers. He said, "You didn't have to get up so early."

"I wanted to." She yawned. "I set the clock-radio for six. It's going to be hot in town and I want to be right there when the stores open."

"I wouldn't go today," Russell said.

"I'm not going down *there*—I'm going to the good stores." Sheila yawned again. Without makeup, Morris thought, she looked too old to have a son as young as Paul. He did himself, he knew, but Sheila usually looked younger to him; especially

131

when he had had something to drink. "Did you hear about the National Guard, though," she added when she had finished the yawn.

Russell shook his head.

"You know how somebody said they were shooting at everything and doing more damage than the rioters? Well, they're going to protest that. I heard it on the radio. They're going to hold a march of their own today."

Russell was no longer listening. He leaned back to look at Paul's treehouse again.

"Ever since Thursday," Sheila said. "Isn't that a scream?"

Morris surprised himself by saying, "I don't think so, and I'm going to make him come down today." Sheila looked at him coolly.

"How does he live up there?" Russell asked.

"Oh, he's got a blanket and things," Sheila said.

Morris said slowly, "While I was at the office Thursday he took blankets out of the linen closet and a lot of canned food and fruit juice out of the pantry and carried it all up there."

"It's good for him," Sheila said. "He's got his radio and scout knife and what not too. He wants to get away and be on his own. So let him. He'll come down when he's hungry, that's what I tell Morris, and meanwhile we know where he is."

"I'm going to make him come down today," Morris repeated, but neither of them heard him.

When they went away—Sheila to start breakfast, Russell, presumably, to finish clipping his side of the hedge—Morris remained where he was, staring up at the treehouse. After two or three minutes he walked over to the trunk and laid a hand on the rough bark. He had been studying the tree for three days now and knew that even before Paul had looped some of its limbs it had not been an easy tree to climb. Walking only a trifle unsteadily, he went to the garage and got the stepladder.

From the top of the ladder he could reach the lowest limb by stretching himself uncomfortably and balancing on the balls of his feet with his body leaning against the trunk. Suddenly conscious of how soft his palms had become in the last fifteen years, how heavy his body was, he closed his hands around the limb and tried to pull himself up. Struggling to grip the tree with his legs, he kicked the ladder, which fell over.

From somewhere below Russell said, "Don't break your neck, Morris," and he heard the sound of faint music. He twisted his head until he could see Russell, with a transistor radio clipped to his belt, righting the ladder.

Morris said, "Thanks," gratefully and stood panting at the top for a moment before coming down.

"I wouldn't do that if I were you," Russell said.

"Listen," Morris was still gulping for breath, "would you go up there and get him?" It was a humiliating admission but he made it: "You ought to be able to climb better than I can."

"Sorry," Russell touched his chest, "doctor's orders."

"Oh. I didn't know."

"Nothing serious, I'm just supposed to stay away from places where I might take a bad fall. I get dizzy sometimes."

"I see."

"Sure. Did you hear about the fake police? It came over our radio a minute ago."

Morris shook his head, still panting and steadying himself against the ladder.

"They're stripping the uniforms off dead cops and putting them on themselves. They've caused a lot of trouble that way."

Morris nodded. "I'll bet."

Russell kicked the tree. "He's your kid. Why don't you just tell him to come down?"

"I tried that yesterday. He won't."

"Well, try again today. Make it strong."

"Paul!" Morris made his voice as authoritative as he could. "Paul, look down here!" There was no movement in the treehouse.

"Make it strong. Tell him he's got to come down."

"Paul, come out of there this minute!"

The two men waited. There was no sound except for the

tuneless music of the radio and the whisper of a breeze among the saw-edged leaves.

"I guess he's not going to come," Morris said.

"Are you sure he's up there?"

Morris thought of the glimpse of Paul's head he had seen earlier. "He's up there. He just won't answer." He thought of the times he had taken the pictures his mother had given him, pictures showing his own childhood, from their drawer and studied them to try and discover some similarity between himself and Paul. "He doesn't want to argue," he finished weakly.

"Say." Russell was looking at the tree again. "Why don't we chop it?" He dropped his voice to a whisper.

Morris was horrified. "He'd be killed."

The radio's metallic jingling stopped. *"We interrupt this program for a bulletin."* Both men froze.

"Word has reached our newsroom that the demonstration organized by Citizens For Peace has been disrupted by about five hundred storm troopers of the American Nazi Party. It appears that members of a motorcycle club have also entered the disturbance; it is not known on which side."

Russell switched the radio off. Morris sighed, "Every time they have one of those bulletins I think it's going to be the big one."

His neighbor nodded sympathetically. "But listen, we don't have to cut the tree clear down. Anyway, it must be nearly three feet thick and it would take us a couple of days, probably. All we have to do is chop at it a little. He'll think we're going to cut it with him in it, and climb down. You have an ax?"

Morris shook his head.

"I do. I'll go over and get it."

Morris waited under the tree until he had left, then called Paul's name softly several times. There was no reply. Raising his voice, he said, "We don't want to hurt you, Paul." He tried to think of a bribe. Paul already had a bicycle. "I'll build you a swimming pool, Paul. In the back yard where your mother has her flowers. I'll have men come in with a bulldozer and dig them out and make us a swimming pool there." There was no

134

answer. He wanted to tell Paul that they weren't really going to chop down the tree, but something prevented him. Then he could hear Russell opening the gate on the other side of the house.

The ax was old, dull and rusted, and the head was loose on the handle so that after every few strokes it was necessary to drive it back on by butting it against the trunk of the tree; each blow hurt Morris's already scraped hands. By the time he had made a small notch—most of his swings missed the point of aim and fell uselessly on either side of it—his arms and wrists were aching. Paul had not come down or even looked out one of the windows.

"I'm going to try climbing again." He laid down the ax, looking at Russell. "Do you have a longer ladder than this one?"

Russell nodded. "You'll have to come over and help me carry it."

Russell's wife stopped them as they crossed Russell's patio and made them come inside for lemonade. "My goodness, Morris, you look as if you're about to have heat prostration. Is it that warm out?" Russell's house was airconditioned too.

They sat in the family room, with lemonade in copper mugs meant for Moscow Mules. The television flickered with scenes, but Russell's wife had twisted the sound down until Morris could hear only a faint hum. The screen showed a sprawling building billowing smoke. Firemen and soldiers milled about it. Then the camera raced down suburban streets and he saw two houses very like his own and Russell's; he almost felt he could see through the walls, see the two of them sitting and watching their own houses—which were gone now as police fired up at the windows of a tall tenement. Russell, winking and gesturing for silence, was pouring gin into his mug to mix with the lemonade now that his wife had gone back to the kitchen.

He felt sick when he stood up, and wondered dully if Sheila were not looking for him, angry because his breakfast was getting cold. He steadied himself on the doorway as he

135

followed Russell out, conscious that his face was flushed. The heat outside was savage now.

They moved cans of paint and broken storm windows aside to uncover Russell's extension ladder. It was as old as the ax, dirtied with white and yellow splashes, and heavy as metal when they got it on their shoulders to carry outside.

"This'll get you up the first twenty feet," Russell said. "Think you can climb from there?"

Morris nodded, knowing he could not.

They hooked the two sections together and leaned them against the tree, Russell talking learnedly of the proper distance between the bottom of the ladder and the base of the object to be climbed. Russell had been an engineer at one time; Morris had never been quite sure of the reason he no longer was.

The ladder shook. It seemed strange to find himself surrounded by leaves instead of looking up at them, having to look down to see Russell on the ground. At the very top of the ladder a large limb had been broken off some years before and he could look straight out over the roof of his own home and all the neighboring houses. "I see smoke," he called down. "Over that way. Something big's burning."

"Can you get up to the boy?" Russell called back.

Morris tried to leave the ladder, lifting one leg gingerly over the stub of the broken limb. Giddiness seized him. He climbed down again.

"What's the matter?"

"If I had a rope," Morris gestured with his hands, "I could put it around my waist and around the trunk of the tree. You know, like the men who climb telephone poles." Sirens sounded in the distance.

"I've got some." Russell snapped his fingers. "Wait a minute."

Morris waited. The noise of the sirens died away, leaving only the talk of the leaves, but Russell did not return. Morris was about to go into the house when the truck pulled up at the curb. It was a stake-bed truck, and the men were riding on it, almost covering it. They were white and brown and black;

136

most of them wore khaki shirts and khaki trousers with broad black leather belts, but they had no insignia and their weapons were clubs and bottles and iron bars. The first of them were crossing his lawn almost before the truck had come to a full stop, and a tall man with a baseball bat began smashing his picture window.

"What do you want?" Morris said. "What is it?"

The leader took him by the front of his shirt and shook him as the others circled around. A stone, and then another, struck the ground and he realized that Paul was throwing them from his treehouse trying to defend him, but the range was too great. Someone hit him from behind with a chain.

The Price

by C. Davis Belcher

The green Chevrolet was stalled at the corner of Washington and Pine Streets. Behind it, the truck driver felt his patience drain away until, with a curse, he shifted gears and rolled his huge truck backward. The protruding sheets of steel sliced through the Volkswagen behind him and through the head of the driver, John Phillpott Tanker.

The ambulance drivers who brought him in had little hope. The nurses in the Emergency Room had less. The residents struggled on, patching torn blood vessels, giving transfusions, wrapping his head in a new plastic bag, and trying every other trick any one of them could think of before they too admitted it was hopeless.

Walter Sturbridge heard about it Sunday evening when an old friend, an elevator operator at University Hospital, called him on the phone. Sturbridge set a record for the trip in. Trotting down the basement corridors toward the north side of the hospital, he saw old Loomis waiting for him.

"How is he?" Sturbridge said.

"He's messed up pretty bad." Loomis steered him toward his elevator. "Let's take this thing up to three where we can sit and talk a bit." They settled, lit cigarettes. Sturbridge waited.

"What they want, Mr. Sturbridge, is to transplant Mr. Tanker's heart."

Sturbridge slouched down in the oversized red plastic chair that he had pulled into the patch of light from the elevator door. He stared back at Loomis. The deserted hospital office, empty since Friday, still held the lingering smells of the girls who worked here.

"They got this fellow, Rowalski, they're just achin' to put a new heart in. Been in and out of here since high school. Four, five years ago they did a valve job. Worked for a little while," Loomis said, "then went to pieces. These doctors do them transplants have to wait and wait. Sometimes work for days on someone and see them die before they can find what they need. They got maybe a dozen waiting, so they're always looking."

Was he a feature writer, Sturbridge thought, or a stupid cub reporter feeling sorry for himself? So it was a hot night and he had missed the Ed Sullivan Show. This was University Hospital and not the Tankerville *Herald*. When they said, "What can we do for Tanker?" and got back a big fat "Nothing," someone had surely asked, "What can we do with Tanker?" A healthy thirty-two-year-old with his head smashed by a truck. And all Sturbridge could think about was that ten million dollars rated a mighty big funeral. But not the characters in here that looked for wrecks like Tanker.

Old Loomis wandered around the dark office looking for a wastebasket he could spit in. "Shakes you up when it's someone you know," he said. "They ain't heartless, these fellers. Otherwise. Anything they could do for Mr. Tanker they would gladly do. But when it's like this, they get to thinking about the ones needing transplants, and start nagging the office to get permission."

Years of war and newspaper reporting had toughened Sturbridge outwardly, but he remained tenderhearted. Thinking of John Phillpott Tanker being cannibalized for spare parts like a wrecked car made him ill. When they had first seen him, they had known this was it. Right away someone had said, "Who owns Tanker? When he's dead, that is." Someone had said, "Get the papers signed so we'll be all set to go." As if Tanker were some casual bit of wreckage.

The elevator buzzed and the big "7" lit up. "They're getting ready up there," Loomis said. "I'll drop you off on six."

The corridors, crowded and endless, overwhelmed him with

139

a dozen different hospital smells as he moved from ward to ward. What rankled in Sturbridge was that Hartman, that old poop of a family lawyer, had glimpsed this and brought along his partners to help with the family, while Sturbridge, the fair-haired boy of the Tankerville *Herald,* the lad from the big city, sat on his fat ass sketching out a flowery obituary.

Everybody else around here from old Loomis on up knew what was going on. Sturbridge ground his teeth so hard he bit his tongue. What a jerk he appeared! Kidding himself it counted to let the family see Walter Sturbridge on the job, while all the time these country cousins were getting ready to give Tanker the lead in a damn big show to which Sturbridge didn't even have a ticket.

He had found a corner in the Visitors' Room and taken off his coat, loosened his shoes and tie, stretched out in a chair and lit a cigarette when Hartman came hopping over. Lawrence Jennings followed, puffing his usual cigar. He was Sturbridge's boss on the Tankerville *Herald.* The son of Tanker's dead sister, he was ten years older than Tanker but was his nephew. He would be worth millions, Sturbridge thought, struggling to see Jennings from this fresh viewpoint.

"It's this way," Hartman said. "They hold out no hope for John. He may die any time. They want to use his heart and maybe other things for transplants. You get around. What do you think?"

Praise God, Sturbridge thought, Loomis had already told him. He didn't have to sit there with his mouth open, like some country bumpkin being taken in by a shell game. "They can't change their minds afterwards," he said.

"I'm surprised at you, Walter," said Jennings. "I thought you were more modern. This second-thought business cuts both ways. If we don't say yes now, we can't say it later. We think John would want us to say yes."

Jennings chewed fiercely on his cigar and looked around the room. Sturbridge's eyes followed, taking in the clusters of family. Ordinary people, he thought. They hadn't expected to get anything except Christmas dinner out of John Phillpott Tanker until it was far too late to do them any good. He figured the hospital would have a downhill fight convincing this collection of heirs that they would be talked about as progressive citizens, freed of ancient superstitions, if they signed away all of Tanker that anyone seemed to want.

"Write something on this transplant business if you can, Walter," Jennings said. "Everyone will be curious, and the family would like to see the right story in our own paper."

Sturbridge nodded. "Anybody know Rowalski?"

Jennings did not reply. Hartman, whose eyes were shifting about the room, following his partners as they distributed releases for the heirs to sign, finally said, "Rowalski is about John's age. His father was an engineer, worked for Crewes and Lloyd—you'll remember them, down at the end of Water Street. The father died quite young. Accident, if I remember right. Anyhow, he left his wife with four small children and not much else. This one, Sidney his name is, has been sickly since high school."

"Let's hope this will be a break for him," Jennings said as he moved away. "Call me tonight if anything bothers either of you."

When the lawyers left, Sturbridge glanced at his watch—quarter of eleven—he had been in the hospital an hour and a half. Dimly he recalled there were two real good movies on the late shows. By twos and threes, the heirs slipped away. Soon Sturbridge was alone in the Visitors' Room. They would write themselves a little note to remember the funeral and flowers, he thought, and so much for John Phillpott Tanker.

He stubbed out his cigarette, tied his shoelaces, and went to the men's room to wash his face. Glasses off, he stared at himself in the mirror, cheered because he was still very much among the living. He tried to remember whether he had left a razor in his car.

He got into Tanker's room by following two aides wheeling a big machine. Concealed by a swarm of doctors who were tapping needles, muttering at the blinking lights, and peering into the green faces of cathode-ray tubes, the man on the bed had become plain Tanker. Though barely alive, he was a patient, and a rich one. The blood would continue to drip, the

141

needles to flicker, and the oxygen to hiss through the hoses until the very end. There would be no fooling about that. Sturbridge saw a nurse staring at him and left.

To kill time, he went down to the bottom floor and bought a sandwich at a vending machine. It was cool down there; he slipped off his coat and tie and walked around to the small waiting room by the emergency office. Old Loomis was inside, eating sandwiches, with a young fellow wearing a white uniform. Loomis called out, "Come over with us, Mr. Sturbridge. Want you to meet Danny Gruber, he's one of our technicians up on seven. Told him about you. Can I get you some coffee?" The old man scuttled away.

"Pretty busy up there, ain't you?" Sturbridge asked.

"We're about ready now. We'll really clean house tonight, if they don't fool around too long in Recovery."

"You just have to wait until he dies, don't you?"

"Until he's pronounced dead. Can't say just when the end is."

"How come?"

"Well, when is a man dead—when he stops breathing, or his heart stops beating, or when there's irreversible brain damage, or what? In the old days, no problem. You could just let the body lie around until the neighbors came in with the police. That was when you could let a person get really dead dead, Mr. Sturbridge. But the liver, kidneys, heart, and all that don't wait around. They get dead dead pretty fast, too. You've got to be pretty spry. Not so spry there's any loose talk about murder or manslaughter, but still spry enough so that you have some chance your transplant might take. They have a committee," Gruber added.

Great suffering God, Sturbridge thought, another committee. A committee to decide if you were dead. Not dead dead. Just dead enough.

Loomis came in with coffee. He poised there for a moment like a startled old seagull. "Gotta get back," he said.

"Can you take a minute," Sturbridge asked, "and tell me about Rowalski?"

"Gruber here knows him better. I just see him in the

142

elevator, but Gruber here, his wife and Rowalski's wife, both nurses here one time. About four years ago when he had the valve job done, looked like he was going to be fine, and he and this nurse fall for each other. Nice girl, she was. Got two kids, ain't they?" He looked at Gruber, who nodded. "Sure hope he does well tonight." He tottered off toward his elevator.

Sturbridge lit another cigarette. Gruber didn't smoke. "When does the committee get in on a business like this?"

"Been in close to an hour," Gruber said. "Five of them. They cover everything. All kinds of electrocardiograms and electroencephalograms, and down on the second floor there's a special little lab for tests."

Sturbridge looked at his feet. That was how it was done, he thought. Sitting in the middle of all this data, they were pretty certain just how alive a fellow like Tanker was. The tough part was to decide how little alive Tanker needed to be in order to be dead enough to be legal. Committee members allied with the surgical transplant teams, with millions of dollars in malpractice insurance standing between them and any finger-pointers, might see death come earlier than others.

He looked at Gruber. "You wait until they make up their minds?"

"For the final green light," Gruber said, "but our spies tell us when it's getting close."

"So it's not close now?"

"No. If it was, that little light would be blinking sevens instead of fours. If it started on seven I'd be out of here like a bullet. I'm going back up anyhow, Mr. Sturbridge. Would you like to come up and see a little bit of what getting ready is like?"

Leaving the service elevator, they stepped over a recent litter of empty cartons and bottles. Gruber opened a small door and eased Sturbridge in. The place was like a gigantic airplane cockpit with the odor of intricately processed wire and metal, smelling like nothing else whatever, and he breathed this in like fresh air on a mountaintop. His gaze swept across the precise confusion of this array of dials, lights, meters and gauges, blended into that incredible symmetry possessed only by things that somehow worked. Gruber moved along the panel with a technician's certainty. He pushed a button. "Is everything all right, Miss Lord?" he said.

"Fine, Mr. Gruber, but Dr. Lutz wants the temperature of the liver tank raised one degree."

"O.K., Miss Lord, I'll take care of it."

He was busy for a minute adjusting dials. Then he beckoned. Standing beside him, looking through the plate-glass viewing port, Sturbridge could see the entire operating room. Doctors and nurses, masked, gowned and gloved, stood ready.

The waiting men and women reminded Sturbridge of a painting of communicants at some ancient rite. Here they stood, patiently, many barely out of childhood, with years spent in training, eager to wield the instruments and say the words which are the incantations of their modern magic. Their faith had saved and would save again. In his mind Sturbridge saw other men and women gathered in remote rooms the world over, communing with those powers whose force they respected, waiting, waiting for someone like Tanker. The idea was so overwhelming that his mouth would only say something silly. "What if someone has to take a leak?"

"No problem. Someone is always scrubbing. They go to the john, drink coffee, yak a little, the young ones may get in a little necking, and then they scrub and gown up again. It may go on for hours." He smiled. "You know, my wife was a nurse here, and my brother is one of the doctors out there somewheres. I get it from all sides."

Christ, Sturbridge thought, this transplantation business was how Gruber made a living. He liked it. *I bet the first thing he'll tell his wife will be how he raised the temperature one degree on the liver tank.*

A door slammed on the other side of the partition behind them. "What do you mean visible, you goddamned fool?" a gruff voice said. "That polymyograph they hooked onto him is so damned sensitive, it would give a higher reading hooked onto an old horse turd than it's giving hooked onto Tanker. You scientific hotshots give me a pain in the ass."

There was a pause before a softer, smoother voice replied,

144

"If that boss of yours wasn't so damned anxious to get a new kidney into that worthless son of old man Krillus so he can nick him about twenty thousand, you wouldn't be breathing down all our necks to pronounce this poor devil dead."

"You miserable hypocrite. Would you play God and pass judgment on Krillus' boy just because he has a little tough luck, and deny him a chance to live? We've had both his kidneys out for a week now."

"I'm not hypocrite enough to say this man's dead when a student nurse can look at the dials and see he's alive."

"Dials, my butt. Pull that damn plug out of the wall, and that whole show will stop in two seconds. We've got seven operating rooms ready to go up here, with nurses and doctors killing time playing with each other until you make up your feeble mind this man is dead."

Gruber smiled. He walked along checking the panel, humming happily. "Things always get a little tight in the committee at the end," he said.

Committees were committees, Sturbridge thought. When the high priests of Egypt got together in a back room of the temple, they probably had things to say to each other. He said, "Tell me about Rowalski."

"Good man, always trying. We both studied electronics, and took some courses together. He's a solid technician. After he had the valve job and got married, things looked good for a while and he thought some of getting a job with us here."

"So what does he do?"

"He has a little radio and TV repair shop at home. Picks up a few dollars but not a living. The agencies help him out."

"Not much of a life," Sturbridge said.

"He lost his gumption after the valve job went bad, and hasn't been the same Rowalski. His wife has the jitters and takes four kind of tranquilizers and smokes three packs of cigarettes a day. She can't sleep, so things have been going to hell. There's a lot of us wishing him luck tonight."

Sturbridge nodded. "I never thought of it from Rowalski's point of view. Just Tanker's." He rose. "You've been kind," he said, shaking hands, "and thanks, but I better get out of your way now."

Back on Recovery, Sturbridge tried to mix in and get inside Tanker's room for a quick look, but a nurse spotted him and shooed him away. He sat in a phone booth trying to reach his paper and heard outside, "John, for Christ's sake, old man, we've been set up there for over three hours. Good God Almighty, how long is it going to take you to convince these stupid bastards—" The doctors moved away.

They were working men with a job to do, Sturbridge thought. They knew Tanker's goose was cooked. They had all these cases in here needing transplants, and ever since Tanker was tagged It, they'd been going. Taking blood out of Tanker for matching as fast as they ran it in. How did they know they were matching against Tanker and not some skid-row bum who had swapped his blood for a few dollars? Probably did the best they could. In ancient days they robbed graves so they could study bodies. Now, upstairs, they waited, poised like a suspended shot on television, aiming to cheat death when they started. He was an alien standing there: still he could sense the pressure as it seeped down the stairways and down the elevator shafts and flowed into Recovery.

He yawned. Despite the air conditioning, his clothes were sticky. He needed a shave. Most of all he was tired, tired really of being an onlooker, sneaking peeks through keyholes and unshaded windows.

Perhaps he could see Rowalski, he thought. He dialed the hospital. The central desk said no. Maybe he'd gone up.

Back in the Visitors' Room, he found the little light but now it was flashing three. They weren't on top yet, he thought. He went through his coat, tie, shoes and cigarette routine like an enfeebled actor, condemned forever to rehearse an unsatisfactory and misunderstood role. He pulled out a notebook and did the one thing he knew how to do.

He took off his glasses to rub his eyes, lit a fresh cigarette, and felt sorry for himself. The little light was flashing sevens. So now it was close. Upstairs the last cups of coffee were being

146

drunk, last visits to the john were being made, sleepers were being awakened. Around the high sinks it was scrub, scrub, scrub, as each crew's reinforcements moved up, kidding and joking to ease the tension of the hours ahead, like troops, in the last hour before dawn, moving up to the line of battle.

He didn't try to get close to Recovery. Outside Tanker's room three doctors stood in a small, tired, and solemn cluster. Soon there was a fourth. It was 4:15. Sturbridge wondered if all the patients waiting for Tanker were already on seven, or if they were now saying goodbye to their tearful families. Near him an elevator came up and was locked with open door. Aides appeared with long low carts and reels of electric cable.

Then Sturbridge felt a surge of pity and understanding for the fifth man on that committee, who now must be excruciatingly aware that his own squeamishness, conscience, or sense of fitness had condemned him to be the one who finally said Tanker was dead enough. Sturbridge could picture him dragging himself from one dial to another, staring at one group of flashing lights and then another, hoping to find there some mechanistic magic that would relieve him of his burden. For he must know full well that by now University Hospital waited on him.

Sturbridge saw him come out. Hours earlier, he must have been called from a dinner party. Now in his disheveled suit he resembled a sad and bedraggled penguin. He stepped toward the other four and with an oddly appealing gesture threw up his hands.

The long low carts, the reels of cable, more doctors, more nurses, moved into Tanker's room and soon, as if moved by a will of his own, Tanker's bed appeared, still covered and surrounded by tubes and needles, tanks and flashing lights. It moved, in what seemed to Sturbridge a poignantly solemn procession, past the tormented five and into the waiting elevator. The door closed.

Sturbridge heard the nurse. "Desk," she said, "this is Recovery. Patient John Phillpott Tanker expired four thirty-seven A.M."

147

Sturbridge called his paper and gave them the time of death. Driving through the early dawn, he thought it would be nice to get home where he could take off his clothes and be comfortable.

When he had typed about half a page, the smell of frying bacon overwhelmed him. God, he hadn't realized he was that hungry. As he ate, he told Maisie all about it. Then he fell asleep over the typewriter. Maisie let him doze a little while, then woke him and he finished the piece. He called it "The Night John Phillpott Tanker Died," and Maisie took it down to the paper while he went to bed.

Even Lawrence Jennings went out of his way to flatter him. "They keep telephoning, Walter. They like it. We need some more. Can you keep them coming?"

Gruber's brother, other doctors, and a lawyer friend coached him. He explained the problems so the ordinary man could see them. He called his second article "Legal Death." Letters poured in screaming, "A man is dead when he's dead and any fool knows that." Others showed more understanding.

He visited families made wretched by their burdens: invalids who neither died nor recovered nor adjusted. Instead they lived with the hopes and monstrous despairs of the near-dead, bound to life by an umbilical cord woven by modern science. He knew these families well. He wrote and wrote, and called it "The Hopeful Supplicants."

All supplicants might not be equally deserving. In Gruber's control room, the night Tanker died, he had heard the name Krillus. Faintly he recalled a scandal, but could not pin it down. One of the regular reporters, Hank Coggins, filled him in.

"That boy Krillus is a completely no-good son of a bitch. Not just raping three teenage girls and killing two people with his car. Let's face it, some kids are pretty wild. A young boy, full of piss and vinegar, he can do a lot of rough things, but eventually, if he grows up a decent sort of man, people forgive him. But this Krillus boy, Tony they call him, he's just a mean bastard. Always has been. Gutted cats. Beat up small kids. His daddy's money bought him out of everything. But he got sick and ended up with lousy kidneys. They got infected, and a week or so before Tanker died they either had to take his kidneys out or he was going to die. And they took them out."

Sturbridge nodded. "I've seen the artificial kidney machine they used to keep him alive until Tanker showed up."

"That right? Well, Krillus only had this one boy. His wife's dead years now. He's just a contemptible old fart himself, no self-respecting doctor would put his kidney in anything but a dirty pickle jar, and anyhow he's too old and they had to wait." Hank paused to light a cigarette. "Early that morning when Tanker died, they put one of his kidneys in Tony Krillus and it just worked fine. He takes medicine and some kind of treatment, but three weeks after they put it in, he was running around like you and me and has been ever since."

Sturbridge tried to interview Rowalski, who was doing well, but the hospital would permit no visitors. He drove out one day to see Rowalski's wife. The heat wave had broken; there had been rain and the trees and fields were green. Rowalski's lawn was a litter of bottles, papers, old tires, discarded plastic toys, and a broken cart struggling valiantly to hide the rampant weeds. The iron gate hung awry from a broken hinge. Beyond the cracked and pitted concrete, the porch door stood ajar.

To the left a bench, some tools, and a few disemboweled and dust-covered television sets marked the limits of what had once been Rowalski's shop. A battered baby carriage, a cot, a small basket filled with apples, another filled with tomatoes now intruded on these. On the cot a huge yellow tiger cat flashed green eyes filled with suspicion at Sturbridge, but collapsed into purrs when petted.

He heard the house door open, and turned. The cat repaid this neglect by sinking two large claws into his hand. He made his peace and introduced himself. There were no chairs, so he sat with the cat. Mrs. Rowalski brought out the baby which she put in the carriage, a small child which she sat on the porch, a coffee percolator and the necessary things, a bottle for the baby, cigarettes, and finally a camp stool for herself. She was only about twenty-five, he thought, but he could see how the grinding years had etched her face. They sat there enjoying their smoke, the nice afternoon, the quiet children, and waited for the coffee.

Her hair was brushed back and tied with a piece of candy-box ribbon. She was clean but unadorned. He asked her about her childhood.

Her pregnant mother had fled Germany while the rest of the family were on the way to the gas chambers, and died in Brooklyn of tuberculosis when the little girl was four. From orphanage to foster home to foster home had been the child's dreary round until she became a student nurse at University Hospital.

Her cheerless childhood had left her dull in social situations. She could not joke or flirt easily. Unlike the other student nurses, she had not flexed her emotions by falling in love with at least two medical students, interns, residents, laboratory technicians, elevator operators, or personable male patients.

When Sidney Rowalski was admitted for repair of a defective heart valve, her needs and his met. Their marriage was a monument testifying that he and she had made it. If the valve job had held up, they would have done as well as most.

She checked the baby, then brought out a glass of milk and a cookie for the little girl.

"How do you feel about things now?" he asked her.

She looked at him seriously. He could see the fatigue lines around her eyes and lips. "I can't be sure," she said. "If I could just believe we could be happy."

"And can't you believe this?" he asked.

"I don't know," she said.

On the way home he stopped at the chain drug store. Bill would be coming home from military school this weekend; he bought a box of peanut brittle. Then he went to the corner where the old man sold flowers, and bought a big bunch of yellow roses. Maisie would feel faintly jealous and suspect him of patting some secretary at the Tankerville *Herald*. He couldn't help that.

Publication of "The Hopeful Supplicants" changed Sturbridge's life. Lawrence Jennings stopped him in the hall to pound him on the back and say, "Man, you can really write." The lawyer, Hartman, stopped him on the street, took him to lunch, and talked and talked about how much he and his wife had enjoyed the articles. Things were looking up, Sturbridge thought; at least it didn't look as if he had to worry about his job. Then UPI asked to syndicate his articles. At last, Sturbridge admitted, he could taste money, he could smell money, and, God willing, he would damn soon have some.

He was working hard on his fourth article, which he called "By These Hands." He hoped to convey something of what he had glimpsed through the window in Gruber's control room the night Tanker died. And the things Gruber and his brother had told him since. At the Hartmans' for dinner, the Sturbridges met a nurse from University Hospital, Gladys Peterson, an old friend of Mrs. Hartman's. "Mr. Sturbridge needs your help, Gladys," Mrs. Hartman said. "He needs to know just what went on."

Gladys took a big swallow of her bourbon and started in. She was a big blond blustery sort of girl, good-natured and willing. She had an eye for what counted. She took Sturbridge through the developing drama of the operating floor as the patients came up. She followed them as they were moved to different rooms and told him what the rooms contained. With the arrival of the body of John Phillpott Tanker, the overall show faded out, because she was in the room where the heart transplant from Tanker to Rowalski was being done.

"A thing like that is real exciting, Mr. Sturbridge. I mean even when you've worked around hospitals for years like I have, still there's something about putting another heart in a person that makes the shivers run up my spine. I'm just not tough enough, I guess." She paused for a swallow of her bourbon, a quick fluff fluff to her hair, a glance around to see that she was holding her audience.

"They had Rowalski up in the operating room for, oh, a good hour or more before Mr. Tanker finally died. They were checking up all the time back and forth with Recovery, because they had to get Rowalski connected to the heart-lung machine in plenty of time, but yet not too early because it don't do them any good to be on one of those heart-lung machines a minute longer than they need to." She finished her bourbon and Mrs. Hartman brought her another. Gladys took a good swallow. "I tell you, Mrs. Hartman, I just couldn't be a scrub nurse today. I just couldn't stay with it. When I was a scrub nurse, just one doctor did the operating and the other doctors helped him by keeping things back out of the way so he could see what he was doing. And if they started in trying to do any of the operating, they got a good sharp rap on the fingers from the doctor that was doing it. But it's not like that now. What with hooking up the heart-lung machine and maybe doing a tracheotomy, that's putting a tube in their neck to hook up to the anesthesia machine, and then opening them up so you can get at the liver or kidney or heart or whatever you are going to transplant, why you may have three or four people cutting and sewing at the same time. There is so much to do and it goes fast, fast, fast, and the girls that are scrubbed just have to be quick and pay real strict attention, because when those young squirts stick out their hand for something they want it right now. A nurse may have been out necking with that same doctor the night before, but she better be right on her toes in that operating room. She won't be out necking with that doctor and she won't be in there giving him the wrong instruments, either, if she can't stay with it.

"You know, Mr. Sturbridge, the really spooky part for me was when they had taken Rowalski's heart out but they hadn't put Mr. Tanker's heart in yet. That's when you really looked at that heart-lung machine over there with the blood running down through the big cellophane bag and the oxygen bubbling up through it. You can hear the pumps going chunk-chunk-chunk-chunk, and see the blood flow into those plastic hoses that run from the machine down across the floor to Mr. Rowalski. Then they take Mr. Tanker's heart out of the perfuser and they have it up there trimming it so it will fit exactly and you know I wanted to holler at those pumps—don't stop —don't stop—don't stop—because you could just see that that pump was all there was."

"By These Hands" was reprinted across the country, and Sturbridge had the rare and delightful pleasure of seeing and hearing himself quoted. When *Readers' Digest* wrote requesting reprint rights, he found that even the fullest cup could hold a little more. Sturbridge's style had appeal. UPI asked him to write a column, once a week to start, on transplant problems. UPI felt it might go if he wanted to give it a try.

His concern for Rowalski's family was genuine. Lawrence Jennings agreed to give plenty of publicity to any local groups that would help out, and between the veterans' organizations, the lodges, the churches, and Rotary, they made a howling success of cleaning up and painting the place. The Legion rearranged its car lottery so that Mrs. Rowalski, with everyone forewarned, got one of the cars. Rowalski, doing well, was being considered for a trial visit home.

Later that week the reporter, Hank Coggins, came up. "That Krillus boy ain't changed none. Killed another kid this morning with his damned car."

"What happened?"

"He hit a kid named Andrews. Family lives down by the brick kilns. Killed him instantly."

The next day Hank was back. "There's more to that story if you want it."

"Dump your bag," Sturbridge said.

"It's a mixed-up deal. Tony Krillus had a row with his old man and moved in with a friend in the old Packer Apartments down by the railroad station. Usually if a family has money, there isn't too much trouble about killing a kid down in that neighborhood. But this time old man Krillus wasn't having any. Seems Tony had his own car and he's over twenty-one and the old man either canceled the insurance or it run out, so there isn't anything to pay the Andrews family with. So the family got a lawyer, that new fellow, Yates, and he's had Tony Krillus arrested until he posts bond. Yates swears somebody is going to pay."

Sturbridge wrote a column on the hazards of keeping criminals or insane people alive by transplants. The liver transplant died, and he did a little more work on his fifth big

153

article, which he called "On Borrowed Time." Then one day he saw Hartman boil up the stairs as if outrunning a subpoena server and duck into Lawrence Jennings' office. A few minutes later Sturbridge's phone rang and Jennings asked him to come over.

Jennings' face was flushed, his lips tightly pursed. "Walter," he said, "you're the nearest thing to an expert we've got around here on this transplant business. Have you ever heard anyone argue against declaring a man dead because his kidney or heart was still alive in someone else?"

Sturbridge stared at him. "Well, no. The early transplants were kidneys taken from identical twins, and the question didn't come up. When they started doing hearts and lungs and more and more kidneys, they had to use organs from people who were legally dead, but they had to work fast. Of course all kinds of releases are signed, and I've never heard of any legal tangle about it."

"I told you so," Hartman cried, jumping up and waving his hands at Jennings. "John Phillpott Tanker was legally dead. Five doctors at University Hospital said so. No whiz-kid lawyer can change that."

"Is that so?" said Jennings. "Well, how about the fellows who were hung by the neck until some doctor said they were dead, but the relatives took them down and revived them; how about the ones that came to in an undertaker's shop after some trusty sawbones said all was over; do they have to stay legally dead? Hell, no. You know that and I know that."

"The whole body was revived," Hartman cried. "The same person was still there. The doctor's mistake was obvious."

"Does it have to be the whole body?" Jennings demanded.

"How about filling me in?" Sturbridge said. "I can hear the shooting but what are you shooting at?"

"It's the damnedest thing," Jennings said. "You know about Tony Krillus. Well, Yates is determined to get money. Old man Krillus won't part with any. Holly here"—he pointed at Hartman—"is in Probate Court starting on John's estate. Yates has brought in this New York fellow, and Holly can't even get the death certificate admitted. They argue that it is an inaccurate and unsatisfactory statement inasmuch as Tanker just isn't totally dead."

Hartman snorted. "I never expected in all my days to sit in a courtroom and hear it argued that a man wasn't totally dead when he's been out in Spring Valley for months with a big marble stone on top of him. I feel like I'm watching one of those way-out television shows."

"Damn it all, Holly," Jennings said, "transplanting hearts and kidneys was way-out television just a damned short while ago. I don't want any calm superior legal air about this. This is my ass. I expect to inherit a damn big chunk of John's estate as you both well know. Anything, and I mean anything, God damn it, that threatens to get in my way is a matter of deep personal concern."

There was a pause.

"What does Yates hope to gain with all this hoopla about the death certificate?" Sturbridge asked.

"Now you're getting to the nub of it," Jennings said. "My spies tell me that Yates has dreamed up the idea of filing suit against the Tanker estate. He is going to claim that without Tanker's kidney Tony Krillus would be dead. So what Yates is going to say is that if Tony Krillus killed the Andrews boy, he did it only because Tanker's kidney kept him alive to do it. So he is going to sue the hell out of Tanker. So what I am asking Holly is, does the whole body have to be revived? I'm worried as hell about this. A man can lose an arm or a leg or even both arms and both legs and his eyes and the Lord knows what else and still be John B. Citizen. But can a kidney or a heart lose everything else and keep on living and be John B. Anybody? Or just what the hell is the situation?"

Sturbridge couldn't take his eyes off Hartman. *God*, he thought, *he's really got the wind up*. He watched a muscle jump in Hartman's cheek beneath the handkerchief he was rubbing over his face.

Hartman cleared his throat and got a grip on himself. "I think you are getting excited without good reason, Lawrence. Judge Cotton has to let them present whatever arguments they

155

want, but you'll see he'll throw the whole business out fast enough. The estate will be settled just about as you expect."

"I'm not sure Judge Cotton gives a damn," Jennings said. "He's due to retire soon. What do you think, Walter?"

"He's going to be sitting on a case that's hotter than the Scopes monkey trial," Sturbridge said. "If the old boy has to write new law or change old law, he's going to do his damnedest to make sure the Supreme Court finally says he's right."

"Damn it all," Jennings said, "my wife will skin me alive. And you too, Holly. We figured we were all set. Now everything makes me feel worse and worse. Holly, how little of a person is still that person? Hell, with accidents and operations nowadays you lawyers must have some irreducible bit in mind."

"No," Hartman said. "As long as there's anything there it's a person. They can be deaf, dumb, blind, and completely paralyzed and still be a legal person. But with this transplant business, I just don't know. I want to call up a few people and do a little reading. I'll find something." He stood up, watching Jennings.

"O.K., Holly, do the best you can." Jennings waved him away and watched him out of the office. "He's damn near as scared as I am, and I'm not kidding you one single bit, Walter, when I tell you I'm scared as hell. Last few months you've had a little taste of money, the way those articles of yours have been selling. I see your new car and things like that and I'm glad for you. But just ask yourself, Walter, how you'd feel if you had been looking at five million dollars as being so nearly your own that you could feel it in the way people spoke to you, the way your wife treated you, the way you treated yourself, and then you just begin to smell faintly, like a far-off forest fire, the chance that you may lose it."

He lifted his big body out of the chair and went into his office and returned with two cold bottles of beer. He looked at Sturbridge. "Got any ideas, Walter?"

"None that are much help," Sturbridge said. "I'm no lawyer but my first guess would be that transplants will be thrown out and the estate will be whacked up in the usual fashion."

"I'd like that," Jennings said. "But how're they going to throw it out? You might like to disown your father or your brother but you can't do it. The relationship is a fact. Tony Krillus is part John Tanker. Tanker was worth ten million bucks. It's new. It's different. But I don't see how you can say they'll throw it out."

Sturbridge held up his hand. "What I really meant to say is that it's just going to be too confusing. Next thing you'll be saying this Tony Krillus is somehow related to the fellow that got Tanker's other kidney or even his heart or liver."

"That's just the point," Jennings said. "Isn't he? What do we mean by related? Events don't care how confused we are. The lawyers might figure a Martian space ship should be covered by the laws of trespass, but will that make any damn difference to the Martians? You have a new kind of person here and the lawyers are just blowing smoke out their ears when they talk as if present law will cover everything."

Jennings looked tired, but he was able to pound the table with his half-empty beer bottle. "I have to face it, Walter," he said. "That bunch of quacks at University Hospital is so damned anxious to get a Nobel Prize, they'd put the balls from a bull on a refugee eunuch and lease him out for stud if they thought that would do it. Why, Christ, from what I read in our paper, they can't even say for sure Tanker was dead and make it stick. When I think of that smoothie from the hospital office giving us that 'everything for science' bit and rolling his eyes toward the ceiling like some damned undertaker's assistant, while all the time John was in Recovery fighting for his life, I tell you, Walter, it makes my blood boil. The fact is I've been screwed—and my wife and all my relatives will soon be shouting it at me—I've been screwed. Should have listened to you at the hospital that night. You smelled a rat—probably just instinct. But Holly, he was so damned happy with all those papers and being the big father advisor, he never even stopped to wonder what he might be getting my ass into."

Jennings finished his beer and struggled to his feet. "Might as well go home and face the music."

Sturbridge told Maisie later, "Believe me, Jennings has really got it in for the hospital. Figures it's all their fault. If Tanker had been allowed to die complete and natural as God intended, there wouldn't be any trouble, as he sees it. He's lining up all the heirs and if this deal costs them money, they'll get it out of the hospital if they can. Legal costs, mental anguish, loss of time—they'll hit them for all of that and any money they may lose from the estate."

Sturbridge leaned on his elbows. "The hell of it is, three weeks ago that bunch of heirs were thick as thieves going over plans for new houses and picking out interior decorators, and now they hate each other. Everyone thinks someone should have stopped the transplants. And they all agree it's Jennings' and Hartman's fault. But I was feeling a little teed off that night because they were going to get all that money, so I didn't sound very enthusiastic. Now they all think if they had listened to me they'd be home free. And they would. So we're ahead. Maisie, let's go to bed."

Sturbridge basically did not care whether the Tanker heirs or the Tanker transplants got the estate, or how they shared it. With Tony Krillus, however, he had to recognize that a transplant wasn't just a surgical stunt ending in success or failure. After stewing it over for several days, he wrote a fifth article. "They Live Again" was syndicated nationwide and brought in sacks of mail. He had touched a nerve.

The Tanker case became *the* subject in Tankerville. To get an expert opinion, place a bet, or get your face kicked in for expressing your own view too freely was easy. Believing that in union there was strength, Yates had everyone who had received a transplant from Tanker convinced he was entitled to part of the estate. Those patients who had died were represented by their families. Anyone who had kept part of Tanker alive or was still keeping part of him alive was a relative; this was the line on which the battle would be fought.

The hospital called and asked for a conference. Sturbridge was relieved, because Jennings had been getting more and more fidgety. They met in Lawrence Jennings' office: five of

158

them. Dr. Wingate, Chief of Surgery; Cutler, Chief Attorney; Hartman, Jennings, and Sturbridge.

Jennings said, "None of us have any idea where we really stand, so no sense sitting here trying to bluff each other. Do you agree with me that what we want is some way to kill this whole silly lawsuit? If we can do that, we have no problem. If we can't, we won't know for several months or years, and then we can settle down to our mutual bloodletting."

There was a certain amount of huffing and puffing by the lawyers, during which Jennings distributed drinks and beer and put out potato chips and peanuts; then he called the meeting to order by saying, "Bullshit, Holly. Let's get down to real cases. Can the hospital make the diagnosis of legally dead stand, and if they can will you lawyers be able to get the court to accept it so we can go ahead and probate Tanker's will?" He looked around. "What do you think, Doc?"

Dr. Wingate was a spare alert man in his early forties. His eyes twinkled. "I think we're being led up a damned daisy trail by this lawyer, Yates," he said. "To the legal mind a man is either dead or alive. Not so. We've got instruments sensitive enough to detect electrical and chemical changes in a dead man in the ice box in the morgue. The law says when a licensed physician pronounces a man legally dead, he is dead. Doctors have made mistakes and can still make mistakes. Everyone in the transplant business is afraid of arguments about this. So we set up a committee. Just remember that, Mr. Jennings, five of our best doctors said Mr. Tanker was dead. If the court says that won't do, that we have to wait until every possible evidence of activity is gone, then that is the end of the transplant business."

"I don't want to be unpleasant," Jennings said, "but suppose they come right out and say you were a little bit quick about taking parts out of John. What then?"

"They've been through this in other places," said Cutler, the hospital attorney. "The releases they sign are pretty comprehensive."

Jennings looked at the two lawyers. "Do you fellows feel

that with the permits and the evidence of the five doctors, you can knock this out of court?"

The two lawyers buzzed together, then Hartman said, "As the law stands now we're in. If the judge decides to dream up a new law, then God alone knows."

Jennings took a swallow of beer, wiped his mouth, and looked around the table. His gaze settled on Sturbridge. "Walter," he said, "you got anything to offer?"

"Yes," Sturbridge said, "but it doesn't help any and you won't like it."

"I can't see how we can be any worse off," Jennings said. "Shoot."

Sturbridge said, "I'm not a doctor, lawyer, or Indian chief but I am a reporter, and I would like to ask Dr. Wingate a few questions to clear up what I want to say."

"Go to it," Dr. Wingate said.

"Everyone, subconsciously, thinks of a person as actually living in his head somewhere. Certainly not in his liver or heart. We were talking about it and realized that a person can lose arms, legs, gall bladder, spleen, appendix, and can be deaf, dumb and blind but we regard them as still being the same person. But suppose you take their head off and keep all the rest of the body living—would it still be the same person, Dr. Wingate?"

"We've never done that," Dr. Wingate said.

"Just suppose, Doctor," Sturbridge said.

Wingate looked at him and smiled. "I'll be damned if I know."

Sturbridge turned to the lawyers. "How about you?" he asked.

They buzzed some more. "Maybe," they said.

"Then let's take it a step further," Sturbridge said, "and imagine that Dr. Wingate and his team over at University Hospital take the head off John Brown and put it on the body of Bill Smith and the operation is a perfect success. What's the name of the survivor? What are his legal rights to the two estates, to the estate of John Brown, whose head he has, and to the estate of Bill Smith, whose body he has?" He looked at Hartman.

"He's still John Brown and he owns whatever John Brown owned and that's it," Hartman said.

"Now let's imagine that John Brown, who contributed the head, isn't worth a nickel, but that Bill Smith, who put in the body, is worth ten million dollars. How would you feel about that?" Sturbridge looked at Cutler, the hospital attorney.

Cutler stuck his lower lip out. "There would be one hell of a lawsuit."

"That's what you're going to have," Sturbridge said, looking around. "While I'm being my poisonous self, I've got one more. Tell me, Dr. Wingate, doesn't any bunch of cells whether they're in a plant, or a heart, or a kidney have a natural right to live by whatever means they can?"

"It's the struggle for existence," Dr. Wingate said. "All evolution depends on it."

"Right," Sturbridge said. "So tell me, who has the authority to sign away this natural right of Tanker's heart or kidneys to try and keep on living? Even if the only way they can find to do it is to get Dr. Wingate to put them in somebody else? Does anybody? And if nobody can, then why can't Tanker's heart or kidney look to Tanker's estate for food, shelter, amusement and medical care, even though the host Dr. Wingate selected—even if it's Tony Krillus—has to receive all these things at the same time?"

"Your question makes me realize I'm just a surgeon and damn glad of it," Dr. Wingate said.

A few nights later, Maisie invited the Hartmans and Gladys Peterson to dinner. "That Sidney Rowalski was back for a checkup," Gladys said. "When I think of the times I've seen him lying in an oxygen tent ready to breathe his last, and now, my, he looks good."

Mrs. Hartman sniffed. "Poor thanks the Tanker family are getting, after all they did for him."

"The lawyers will have to find a way to take care of that," Gladys said. "People aren't going to keep on burying perfectly good hearts and lungs and kidneys, if they got sick kids or relatives that can be kept alive by using them. Stands to reason. People will settle this and settle it right."

Her certainty impressed Sturbridge. He wanted to finish his sixth article, which he called "On Borrowed Time." He knew he would have to say a great deal about the medical and legal difficulties associated with transplants, but he did not want to say anything that would keep the work from going ahead. The idea that the people would decide what was right became the keystone. It was wonderfully well received.

Some weeks later the word seeped around that old Judge Cotton was finally going to come up with a decision. Sturbridge met Jennings outside the old courthouse. Together they climbed the dirty wet granite steps, bending their heads to the gusts of wind and rain, until they reached the huge doors, which opened reluctantly into the wind to let them slide through into the lobby.

Sturbridge was struck once again by the contrast between the dream of justice and its working reality. Lawyers and clients were scattered about, dripping from their sodden coats. The marble walls were discolored with smoke and grime. The light from the dirty bulbs in the huge candelabras disappeared into dingy darkness.

The bailiff, red-cheeked and puffy with his moment of importance, was shouting, "Hear ye—Hear ye—" and they scrambled to their feet. The coughing ceased. Judge Cotton was a small man nearly lost behind the huge oaken bench, until he clambered into view on a high stool. He turned and nodded at the bailiff, and Sturbridge noticed the dandruff scattered over the back of his faded robe. "Even though he's retiring pretty soon, he could loosen up enough to buy a new robe," Jennings said, as they sat down again.

The judge was perched up there between the flags, which hung listlessly from their poles. Behind and above him a huge gilded eagle had moulted in great white patches. The judge looked up. A sigh and then silence as everyone waited. Then a glut of lawyers and clerks surrounded the bench: the dank audience, condemned to limbo, picked their noses, loosened their ties, and squirmed in the eternal human effort to fit a hard bottom to a hard oak seat.

Then another sigh. The lawyers and clerks had been driven back. The judge was alone. Silence fell.

"I find in the case before us," he said, in a voice as dry and serene as the whispering of leaves in the early morning, "that the recipients of tissue transplants from John Phillpott Tanker should share with the legitimate heirs in the distribution of his estate. They cannot replace these heirs but they cannot be excluded. The degree of sharing will be determined by future argument before this court."

Jennings looked at Sturbridge and sighed with relief. "I was scared, Walter, that he might leave the family out entirely. This I can live with. We'll have to work out a settlement because none of us will want to wait forever. I have to call my wife."

That night Sturbridge watched Sidney Rowalski on television. Rowalski was asked about the lawsuit. "After all," he said, "God knows, I'm grateful I got Mr. Tanker's heart. I'd be dead probably if I hadn't, because I couldn't have hung on much longer. I had rheumatic fever when I was a boy and what heart I had left was going to pieces. But still I feel queer. Part of me is really Mr. Tanker and most of the rest of Mr. Tanker is gone. It's different somehow from having a plastic or a metal heart, I think. I never had one, but you could imagine it being part of yourself, like glasses, or false teeth. But my heart belongs to Tanker and I'm not trying to be funny."

Later he was asked about the money. "Well, I'm glad," Rowalski said. "At first, I admit I had a funny feeling I was being ungrateful somehow and that just getting Mr. Tanker's heart should be enough. My wife argued with me, pointing out that although I felt pretty good right now I had no way of telling what lay ahead. And then there was the children. If I was going to keep myself going I had to take care of Mr. Tanker's heart, and if Mr. Tanker's heart was going to keep going it had to take care of me. We were both in me together.

I never knew Mr. Tanker, but I finally decided he would want his heart and me mighty well taken care of."

Right on the heels of his column on the court decision, Sturbridge was notified he had won the Pulitzer Prize. Lawrence Jennings told him at work, sent out for sandwiches and coffee for everyone, and gave Sturbridge a cold glass of beer. Sturbridge called Maisie and she cried. There at the paper everyone came up to his office and it was a nice party.

He went home and petted Maisie until she stopped crying. Bill had gone AWOL from military school and thumbed his way home. The afternoon paper carried Sturbridge's picture and then people started coming. Everybody. Bringing food, bringing liquor, bringing good wishes. They came from the hospital led by the Grubers, from the paper led by Lawrence Jennings, and from the town led by the Hartmans. Sturbridge was completely and utterly satisfied. It was three in the morning before they were gone. He was in a tremendous glow. He could hear Maisie reclaiming her kitchen, which the other women had taken over for the evening. Bill was trying to finish one last piece of chocolate cake. Sturbridge looked at him with great affection.

"You know, Bill," he said, "if you put a heart and a lung, and a kidney and a liver there on the table I doubt if I could tell them apart. But I'm mighty grateful to them, yes sir, mighty grateful. They sure did all right by me." He pulled himself up and started for the stairs.

Maisie called from the kitchen, "I'll be right up, dear."

"You better be," Sturbridge said.

And Bill laughed as only a sixteen-year-old can laugh.

The Rose Bowl-Pluto Hypothesis

by Philip Latham

Crack!

Six men came charging down the track, elbows churning, legs driving. Two of the blue-clad Tech men took an early lead, but at the halfway mark one of their rivals was gaining fast. The three flashed across the tape in a photo finish that had the little crowd in the Pasadena Rose Bowl yelling its head off.

"I think one might be safe in describing that as an uncommonly rapid hundred," Alyson said, speaking with that same air of guarded reserve that he ordinarily used for superior themes in his English Lit course. Zinner, his companion, was anything but reserved. At the moment, however, he appeared to be trapped in a stationary state of exceptionally long lifetime.

"Know what the time was for that hundred?" Zinner asked, staring glassy-eyed at his stop watch.

Alyson shook his head. "My waterclock sprung a leak."

"Eight point nine-two seconds is what I read it."

"So one of 'em broke the nine-second barrier?"

"*One* of 'em? *Three* of 'em!" Zinner retorted. "No wind either."

The hundred was only the first of a series of incredible performances on the cinder path that April afternoon. By the time the two professors left the Rose Bowl they had witnessed a 20.5-second furlong, a 45.8 quarter mile, and an 8:35.3 two mile. The mile was run in only 4:09.7, but then the winner hadn't been pushed.

165

Back at Tech they strolled across the campus in animated argument that had nothing to do with their scholastic activities.

"And remember this wasn't the Olympic Games," Zinner was protesting. "It was only a lousy little dual meet."

"There is only one explanation," Alyson said.

"I'd like to hear it."

"The track men today are better than we were forty years ago."

"That I will not admit," said Zinner. "There's something funny going on."

"But how can you deny it?" Alyson demanded. "Back in the twenties anybody who could break ten seconds in the hundred was a whiz. The world's record for the mile was four-ten-four. Now every high school's got some kid who can break ten seconds. They run the mile under four minutes every month. Might as well swallow your pride, old man. We just naturally weren't so good."

"Why should track athletes be any better today?" Zinner asked.

Alyson considered.

"Well, I don't know exactly," he said. "The human race is improving—"

"Like hell it is!"

"Vitamins."

"You get all the vitamins you need at the dinner table."

"Superior training methods . . . weight lifting . . ."

"You know perfectly well hoisting a barbell wouldn't help a bit running the mile. And look at the fight game. Boxers aren't any better."

Alyson reviewed the dismal situation in the heavyweight division. "All right then, how do *you* explain that hundred today?"

"It wasn't a hundred."

They had halted by the lily pond where sophomores used to throw recalcitrant freshmen before the student council adopted more enlightened methods of indoctrination.

"You mean it was rigged? It wasn't a full hundred yards?"

"Oh, it was a full hundred yards all right. Only the hundred yards of today are not the hundred yards of yesterday."

"I don't follow."

"Because space is not the same. It's shrunk."

Zinner paused to allow time for this statement to exert its full effect.

"The solar system is passing through a region in which space has undergone a shrinkage of approximately ten per cent. The assumption of such a coefficient of contractility satisfactorily accounts for all the observed phenomena."

"Next time why don't you get a tape and measure the hundred?"

"Waste of time. Tape measure's shrunk too."

A chill wind from Los Angeles was blowing over the campus, rattling the eucalyptus leaves and bending the yellow calendulas.

"You really believe that?" Alyson asked.

Zinner did not flinch. "Such is my considered opinion."

"This is much too big a subject for discussion here by the lily pond," Alyson said. "Only in front of my fireplace over a long drink can we do it proper justice."

"A *very* long drink," Zinner added. "To make up for the shrinkage over the last forty years."

The close friendship between the two was remarkable, for aside from their mutual interest in track, they had little in common. (Although there were some on the faculty who maintained that the less you had to do with the members of your own department, the better you got along with them.) Zinner had once held the school record in the hundred of 9.8 seconds, an achievement which he cherished in the same way that a child clings to an old doll. Some years ago with the approach of his fiftieth birthday, he had seriously considered having himself timed in a hundred. He even went so far as to come home one evening with a new pair of sprint shoes under his arm, raising strong doubts in his wife's mind concerning his sanity. Only when the family physician, after listening to his heart and taking his blood pressure, had shaken his head and reached for his prescription pad, did he reluctantly give it up. And so the sprint shoes had gone to join Those Things That Are Definitely In the Past, another melancholy reminder of man's transitory existence on this planet.

Why Zinner looked back with such nostalgia on his track career was puzzling, when he had so many other things going for him. He was the world's undisputed authority on the planet Pluto. His value for the size of that distant object,

$$\text{Diameter Pluto} = 0.518 \times \text{Earth}$$
$$= 6610 \text{ km}$$
$$= 4110 \text{ mi}$$

had been officially accepted by the International Astronomical Union as the best available. There was no second choice.

This figure was the result of pouncing upon Pluto whenever its path chanced to fall across some star. Considering the millions of faint stars revealed by a large telescope, it might seem that the planet would have difficulty missing them. On the contrary, observable occultations of a star behind the disk of Pluto were exceedingly rare events. Most years there were none at all. One occultation was really good. And if there were two, it was like hitting the jackpot. Much of Zinner's success could be attributed to the photometric technique he had developed for measuring the light intensity of star and planet during such close encounters.

Alyson had come to Tech from Michigan where he had run a respectable mile. Unlike Zinner, however, his chief concern had been to get under the wire on the thesis for his Ph.D. degree—*John Donne: His Middle Period*. Once through with John Donne he could take this job at Tech and get married. He accomplished both. It was an arrangement that had proven perhaps more satisfactory than stimulating.

The following week the track team went to San Diego, so there was nothing doing in the Rose Bowl that Saturday. It had been agreed that Alyson was to pick Zinner up at five sharp, drive home for cocktails and dinner with their wives, leaving them ample time to make the curtain at the Music Center by 8:30. But on this occasion Alyson, a stickler for punctuality, was late by half an hour. He arrived at Zinner's office badly out of breath from hurrying up the stairs, only to find the astronomer in his shirtsleeves, completely oblivious of the clock.

"Got pinched on the way over," Alyson explained. "Cops followed me. Had to take it easy."

Zinner was all sympathy. "Too bad."

"Wasn't my fault. Claimed I was doing fifty in a thirty-mile zone."

"Why don't you come clean and admit you're guilty as hell?"

"I'll swear I wasn't doing over forty."

"That's what they all say."

"Said they checked my speed by radar."

"That's the trouble with science today. Always finding some damn practical use for it."

Having disposed of that subject, Zinner returned to the books and papers scattered over his desk.

"Spent the afternoon collecting data on the velocity of light. Turned out to be quite a job."

"Look, Zin, this is no time to be fooling with the velocity of light," Alyson said. "The girls'll be worried—"

"Let 'em worry. Probably haven't got their faces on yet."

He picked up one of the sheets, holding it so Alyson could see.

"Fizeau made the first modern determination of the velocity of light in 1849, 315,300 kilometers per second. Then everybody took a shot at it. I've rounded up all the principal measures to date except Barker's at Johns Hopkins, which hasn't come out yet. Cast your eye down this column of figures and tell me how they strike you."

"How would I know? When my field is the English metaphysical poets—"

"I don't care whether your field is metaphysical poetry or ancient Etruscan pornography. Just tell me how they hit you."

Alyson dutifully examined the figures.

"Well, I'd say the velocity of light takes a slump every now and then."

"Right! Notice they follow a well-defined pattern. The velocity drops, levels out, then drops again." He rubbed his hands. "Now I'm convinced we're due for an *increase.*"

"Please, Zin, do we have to settle it tonight?"

"No, it'll wait." He rose reluctantly. "Just following up something occurred to me after the track meet."

"What's the velocity of light got to do with a track meet?"

"Nothing, probably. Still, time . . . distance . . . light, all tied up together, you know."

"I know we're going to catch it from our wives if we don't get a move on. Now get your coat and flash some speed in the direction of home."

Zinner caught the English professor a few days later as he was coming down the steps of the cafeteria. He wasted no time in polite chitchat.

"Seen the new JOSA?"

"The new which?"

"Journal of the Optical Society of America—what else?"

"Didn't know the Optical Society of America had a journal."

"It's got Barker's new value for the velocity of light. Know what he gets?"

Alyson raised a restraining hand. "Now don't tell me. Let me guess."

"He gets a weighted mean of 329,542.4 kilometers per second with a probable error of 0.2. It breaks the record for a new high."

"Please convey my heartiest congratulations."

"Best part is it fits right in with my track-meet hypothesis!"

"Don't tell me we're back on that again."

"This new value *looks* high," Zinner said, letting his voice fall. "Only it's not *really* high."

"Ah! I suspected there was something underhanded—"

"Measuring the speed of a light beam is not so different from timing a man in a race," Zinner hurried on. "Galileo was the first to try it. Here—you be Galileo." He seized Alyson

170

and backed him up against the wall. "I'm his assistant over here somewhere. We've both got lanterns. Galileo uncovers his lantern. Soon as I see his lantern I uncover *my* lantern. Galileo measures the time for the round trip. Say it's 300,000 kilometers per second."*

He paused for dramatic emphasis.

" 'Hmmmm. Looks kind of low,' Galileo says. 'I'll give it another try.' He doesn't know I'd gotten tired and started back home. Since we're closer now he gets 301,000 kilometers per second. 'The velocity of light has increased,' he announces. But, no, it wasn't that the speed of light *increased* —it was the distance that *decreased*."

Alyson had been showing signs of distress.

"D'you suppose I could be Galileo some other time? I'm already late for my seminar on Pope and his contemporaries."

Zinner stared in undisguised amazement.

"Are you fellows still muddling around with those old dopes? Honestly—"

"Some of those old dopes said some things that are very cogent to our present situation," Alyson informed him coldly.

Zinner continued staring after the man of letters until he was out of sight within the decrepit old Humanities Building.

When Alyson returned from his seminar late that afternoon he found Zinner with his feet on his desk, thumbing through a worn copy of *Pride and Prejudice*.

"This gal Jane Austen sure turned out some red-hot stuff," he commented, with a shake of his head.

"Was that what you came all the way over here to tell me?"

Zinner laid Jane Austen aside.

"Al, old man, I've decided you need a change."

"Thoughtful of you."

"You need to get away from this poisonous atmosphere

---

* In his classic experiment Galileo made no attempt to measure the time. He relates that he was unable to determine with certainty whether the appearance of the opposite light was instantaneous or not, but states that "if not instantaneous it was extraordinarily rapid." (*Dialogues Concerning the Two New Sciences* by Galileo Galelei, I, 1638.)

down here laden with coal-tar products . . . all this corruption and sordid lust."

"Corruption and lust always seemed like rather fascinating subjects for investigation."

Zinner shifted his feet to the floor.

"Seriously, how would you like to spend some nights on the mountain with me? I've got a big observation coming up. Pluto's going to occult a fifteenth-magnitude star. Nearly central this time."

The offer was tempting. Several times before he had kept the astronomer company while working at the big reflector, and had always enjoyed the experience. It was a welcome change from the routine of classwork. And as it happened, his wife was away, so there would be no conflict on the home front.

"What's more, not only is this the best occultation in years," said Zinner, "but it furnishes me with a splendid opportunity to test my shrinking solar system hypothesis."

It was Alyson's turn to stare with a wild surmise.

"First it was the hundred-yard dash in the Rose Bowl. Next it was the velocity of light. Now you've got us out to Pluto."

Zinner smiled with goodnatured tolerance.

"Living here as you do in the cloistered shelter of the Humanities, immersed in Jane Austen and her contemporaries, I dare say this sudden excursion to Pluto comes as a bit of shock. Actually it is a natural step, following logically upon the others."

He hesitated as if uncertain how to proceed.

"Pluto's the outermost planet but don't think I can't find it. I've got that little old planet nailed down tight.* The prediction of an occultation involves a correction for 'light time,' the time light takes to travel from Pluto to Earth. Planetary aberration's another name for it. Light time for the sun is

---

* Zinner was justified in referring to Pluto as a "little" planet. His work on the perturbations arising from the close approach of Uranus to Pluto late in 1967, yielded for the mass of Pluto the value $0.089 \times$ Earth. This gives 3.54 gm/cm^3 for the density of the planet, replacing the former ridiculous value of 50 gm/cm^3.

about eight minutes. For Jupiter at opposition about thirty-five minutes. But for Pluto the light time's around three hundred minutes—five hours.

"I'm assuming the solar system has shrunk by ten per cent. The distance from Pluto to Earth is then shorter by ten per cent. So the light time is correspondingly shorter. Which means the occultation should come early by about thirty minutes, an amount not easy to ignore."

"Well, that sounds reasonable," Alyson agreed. "Even I can understand it."

Zinner gave him a curious look.

"You know what would really cinch this thing? Some observations taken right here on the planet Earth."

"What kind of observations?"

"Observations of velocity in a race."

"Shouldn't think that would be difficult," said Alyson. "You've got the time . . . you know the distance . . ."

"But that's just what we *don't* know," Zinner said. "*Is* the distance a hundred yards? Or is it only ninety yards? The tape measure won't tell. We need a very special kind of velocities —*Doppler* velocities. Velocities derived from displacements of spectrum lines to the red or violet, the way we measure line-of-sight velocities in stars. We don't need a tape or stop watch for these measures. All we need is a photograph of the star's spectrum."

Alyson didn't seem to understand.

"Then why not pretend your boys are stars? You set up your spectroscope down the track . . . measure their violet shift . . . and *voilà!*"

"Wouldn't work. Lines in stellar spectra originate in glowing gases. Stars shine because they glow. A track star may shine but he never glows."

"Hang a lantern around their necks."

"Afraid that wouldn't work either," Zinner said.

They were silent for several minutes pondering this unhappy state of affairs. Finally Zinner got to his feet.

"Well, how about it? Coming?"

Alyson hesitated.

"Only thing . . . I was planning to run over to L.A. . . . pay that traffic fine."

"Thought you intended fighting that all the way to the supreme court?"

Alyson threw up his hands.

"What can you do? It's your word against the police. They've got their radar—"

"RADAR!"

It is doubtful if the word *radar* has ever been uttered with such vehemence since the U.S. Navy invented the acronym in 1942. Zinner seized Alyson by the hand and began pumping it up and down.

"My boy, that was no mere traffic violation. That was Fate in the form of a Los Angeles police officer intervening in behalf of Science. Is it possible that you fail to realize the enormous significance of that pinch? If radar can measure the velocity of that old car of yours, radar can also measure the velocity of a runner on the cinder path."

He began pacing up and down the narrow office.

"What's more, the radar set we want is here on the campus right now. Graduate student I know working on muscular reactions under extreme physical exertion for his thesis. Lactic acid in your body builds up. Fascinating subject."

He grabbed the telephone and dialed a number, but without response. "Probably left now. Catch him on the way home."

He resumed his pacing. "Trouble with our track data is we've been measuring the wrong thing. We've been measuring time instead of velocity. It's like trying to find which is the richest man in town by measuring how long they've been in business, instead of how fast they've been making money.

"Let's say a fellow runs the hundred in ten flat. That means his average velocity for the race was thirty feet per second. Now suppose he runs it in nine flat. Then his average velocity was . . . thirty-three point three feet per second.

"I maintain they don't run the hundred any faster today than in our time. Reason the time is nine seconds is because they're only running ninety yards."

"But can you prove that?"

"That's where science comes to the rescue. If radar shows the velocity of a nine-second hundred was thirty-three point three feet per second, then there's no getting around it—it was a full honest old-time hundred yards. But if radar shows the velocity for a nine-second hundred was thirty feet per second, it was a 'diminished' or 'spurious' present-day hundred."

"May I ask just one more question?" said Alyson.

"Go ahead."

"When do I leave for the mountain?"

Saturday evening.

Alyson wondered if he could ever get used to working on the Newtonian platform of the big reflector. The trouble with the Newtonian platform was that every time he moved, the platform moved. The sight of the concrete floor fifty feet below was not reassuring. Also, he wished Zinner wouldn't sit quite so close to the edge of the platform. You had no fail-safe guarantee. You just failed . . .

Zinner had come up the day before to attach his photometer to the telescope and make sure it was in readiness for the big event tonight. He was doing something at the guiding eyepiece now.

"Here's Pluto," he called over his shoulder. "Want to take a look?"

Alyson joined him at his precarious perch by the telescope.

"Here is a print of the star field," the astronomer said, showing him a photographic negative. "These dark spots are stars. This line I've drawn represents the path of Pluto. I've marked the planet's position at intervals of ten minutes. You'll find it right about here now."

Alyson found that identifying Pluto wasn't so easy even when the planet was staring him in the face.

"Pluto looks no different from the stars," he complained, feeling a little let down at his first sight of the distant world.

"It's not big enough to show a measurable disk," Zinner explained. "But it's got one all right. The stars haven't. They're just points."

Alyson didn't know the zero hour except that it was still quite a way off yet. He wandered around the platform while Zinner was checking some connections he had already checked a dozen times.

"When are we supposed to hear from your radar man?" Alyson inquired.

"Don't know," the astronomer said, frowning. "Thought I'd hear before this."

As if on cue the telephone rang at the control desk below. "Bet that's him now!"

They stood tense, straining to catch any words from below. After a minute the night assistant hung up.

"That wasn't for me, was it?" Zinner called down.

The night assistant returned to his mail-order catalogue. "Nope. Just another crossword-puzzle addict wants to know the name of an asteroid with four letters meaning 'god of love.' "

Zinner used several four-letter words. Alyson wandered over to the eyepiece again for another look at Pluto. He studied the star chart for a while, glanced at his wristwatch, then returned to the eyepiece.

"Looks to me as if Pluto's quite a ways ahead of your position on the chart."

Zinner made a quick check.

"It sure is—*way* ahead!" He looked troubled; checked again. "Battle stations, everybody!" he yelled. "Bill, get downstairs on that recorder. Al, we're going in."

There was a clatter from below as the night assistant headed for the lower depths. Alyson took up his position by the small auxiliary recorder on the platform. Zinner centered the image and touched the fine motion control. Now the telescope would track without further attention, held rigorously on target by the automatic guiding mechanism. With the touch of another button hours, minutes, and seconds of Universal Time began leaving their imprint on the record.

Alyson was intent on the wiggles in the tracing as the sensitive instrumentation responded to the signals from the photometer. There were so many irregularities due to atmospheric effects, it was not easy to determine the intensity of the light beam from the star and Pluto.

"Planet's awfully close," Zinner called from the telescope. "Getting anything over there yet?"

"Not yet," Zinner told him.

Now an unmistakable change was setting in. The trend of the curve was definitely downward.

"We're reading!" Alyson cried.

The tracing dropped rather sharply to approximately twenty-five per cent of its former value, after which it remained fairly constant. In about five minutes the curve began to rise and soon regained its pre-occultation value. Zinner continued operating for several minutes more before cutting out the photometer. Suddenly the dome lights came on, revealing two bedraggled but happy men grinning at each other.

"What I want to see is that time record," Zinner said, already on his way down the ladder.

Although Alyson followed as fast as he could, the astronomer already had several yards of Pluto spread around him by the time he reached the main recorder.

"Not much doubt immersion was here," Zinner said. "I'd put it at five hours fifteen minutes U.T. We can get the seconds later. Now when was immersion supposed to occur according to my very accurate calculations?"

He compared the times in his notebook with those imprinted on the record. For such a simple operation it required an extraordinarily long while.

"Immersion was an hour early," Zinner said.

Alyson gasped. "An hour! You're sure?"

"Can't be any doubt. I'd planned to start checking on Pluto at minus forty. Figured that was plenty. But *one hour!*"

The astronomer seemed dazed. He picked up the tracing and began running it through his fingers.

The dome was very still except for the ticking of some device connected with the telescope. Alyson had had no scientific training. Before tonight he had never given the stars more than casual attention. It would not have struck him as remarkable if the stars had gotten off schedule. They might as

177

well be one place as another. Now, for the first time, he was becoming aware of the awful majesty with which the heavenly bodies went through their motions, enacting a drama the minutest detail of which was inevitable from the beginning. Could there have been some slip in the performance? he asked himself. A line dropped or some cue missed?

"It can't be true," Zinner said.

It struck Alyson as ironic that the astronomer, far from being elated now that observation had confirmed his hypothesis, was behaving as if in deep shock. He decided he would never be able to understand the scientific mind.

"Why can't it be true?" Alyson asked.

"Oh, for all sorts of reasons," Zinner said impatiently. "It would ball up the whole solar system."

"But wasn't this what you wanted?"

"Why yes . . . sure, only I never really believed it. I was just . . . kidding. I never *meant* for it to happen!"

The telephone rang.

"Doctor Zinner, for you," the night assistant called from upstairs.

Zinner took it below. Most of the conversation was from the other end of the line. Occasionally the astronomer scribbled a number on the memo pad. When he finally hung up and turned from the phone, his face was blank.

"Well . . . how'd it go in the Rose Bowl?"

"Hundred was a shade under nine seconds."

"How'd the radar work?"

"All right."

"Get the velocity?"

Zinner consulted the memo pad. "Hit thirty-seven at the halfway mark. Average was around thirty-three."

"A full honest old-time hundred yards, then?"

Zinner didn't answer. He seemed preoccupied with the record. "How about a turn around the dome?" he said suddenly.

Alyson followed him through the door to the open balcony. There was a gentle breeze in the pines. Far below the lights of the valley shone faintly through the haze. After strolling around the dome, they stood in silence leaning against the railing, contemplating the red lights winking on the television towers.

Jupiter was the dominating object in the night sky. Gazing at it, Alyson wondered, is that a planet? another world up there? Or is it only part of a stage setting? A bright light shining through a hole in some canvas? Is it millions of miles away? Or so close I can almost reach out and touch it?

Zinner was the first to speak.

"Al, what's real and what isn't? How do we know when we've got something and when we haven't? You fellows in Humanities know all about philosophy. Where do I go for the answers? Tell me what to do."

"Tell you what to do?"

Alyson was thoughtful as he watched a meteor arch across the sky and fade away. After a moment he spoke.

> "Go and catch a falling star,
>   Get with child a mandrake root,
> Tell me where all past years are,
>   Or who cleft the Devil's foot."

Winston

by Kit Reed

Edna Waziki was beside herself by the time theirs came.
She talked about nothing else for months after they put in the
order and she sat by the window for hours, and when the
truck finally pulled in to the drive she screamed a scream that
brought the entire family on the run. The delivery man came
to the door with a little traveling case, with a handle on top
and holes poked in the end, and Edna giggled and the kids
laughed and danced and jumped around while Edna's husband Artie paid the driver and they jiggled uncontrollably
while Artie fumbled with the catch.

"It says here his name is Winston," Edna said, turning the
card so Margie and Little Art could read the name. "Now step
back, we don't want to scare him all at once."

Artie scowled into the suitcase. "Well where is the little
bastard?"

"Artie, *please*." Edna bent down, calling softly. "Tchum on,
Winston, tchum on."

Margie said, "Daddy, Daddy, I can see him."

Little Art was poking a stick into the opening. "Daddy,
Daddy, here he comes!"

"Damn foolishness," Artie said, but he crowded around with
his wife and children and they watched Winston come blinking into the light.

Margie gasped. "Oh Daddy, he's *teeny*."

"In he cute, oh, Artie, in he cute."

Artie snorted. "He sure don't look like much."

"You can't tell when they're little like this," Edna said. "But you just wait till he grows up!"

Margie was snickering. "Oh look, he made a puddle."

"Of course he has, he's nervous." Edna swept Winston to her bosom. "Poor thing, you poor little thing."

"Runt like that," Artie said, "he's never gonna come to anything."

"Honey, didn't you see his pedigree?"

"Oh Mama, he looks like a monkey."

"Shh, you'll hurt his feelings."

"Here Winston, here Winston." Little Art tried to make Winston take the stick.

"You leave him alone." Edna held Winston protectively; Winston was crying.

"He won't even take the stick."

"He'll take it," Artie said ominously. "He better take it. Lord knows I *paid* enough."

Edna hugged Winston protectively. "He's upset. He'll feel better when I clean him up."

Artie accused her: "You said he was guaranteed."

"He *is* guaranteed," Edna said, taking Winston to the bedroom; in the door she turned and said defensively, "You'll just have to wait, it all takes time."

She spent about an hour on him and when she came out he was calmer, much quieter, and he had stopped crying; he even sat up at the table with them, brought to adult height by a stack of city telephone books. He was about four, small-boned and blond, with a little blue romper suit buttoned fore and aft and large brown eyes which crackled with intelligence. He looked at them all in turn but he wouldn't touch his dish.

"See that," Artie said in exasperation. "Five thousand dollars and he won't even touch his dish."

"He'll eat," Edna said. "He just doesn't know us yet."

"Well he *better* get to know us. Five thousand dollars down the drain."

"It's *not* down the drain," Edna said; she was getting too upset to talk. "He'll make us proud, you just wait."

Freddy Kramer came in just then, to pick Artie up for

bowling. "So this is it," he said, giving Winston the once-over.

"First family on the block to have one," Artie said, with dawning pride. "I guess you might call it a kind of a status symbol."

"Don't look like much."

"You ought to see his pedigree." Looking at Freddy, who would never be able to afford one, Artie allowed himself to be expansive. "Lady writer and a college professor. Eye Q. a hundred and sixty, guaranteed."

Edna stroked Winston's fine blond hair. "Winston's going to college." It pleased her to see that Artie was smiling.

"Kid's gonna get his Ph.D."

Edna took Artie's hand under the table, saying in a low voice, "Oh Artie, you *are* glad. I knew you would be."

Freddy Kramer was looking at Winston with a look bordering on naked jealousy. "What gave you the idea?"

"Edna seen the ad." Artie went all squashy; Edna was massaging his knee. "And anything my baby wants . . ."

"You won't be sorry, Artie. Winston's gonna major in physics. He might even invent the next atomic bomb."

Freddy's lips were moving; he seemed to be figuring under his breath. "How big of a down payment would they want?"

"Depends on the product," Edna said.

"Now this one," Artie said, slapping Winston's shoulder, "this one's gonna support us in our old age. Ph.D. and one-letter man guaranteed. He might get our name in the papers, according to the ad."

Edna said vaguely, "There's something about a Guggenheim."

Winston started crying.

"Why Winston, what's the matter?"

"Little Art kicked him," Margie said.

"Well you kids keep off him until you learn to play with him nice."

"You can't get 'em like this no more," Artie was saying to

Freddy Kramer. "Parents had ten and retired to Europe on the take."

Freddy rubbed his nose. "Maybe if Flo and I sold the car . . ."

Artie proffered a piece of bread to Winston; Winston looked at it distastefully but he took it. "See, he likes me. Hey honey, he likes me."

"Of course he does," Edna said with pride. "He's our son."

Winston gave her a sudden sharp look which embarrassed her for no reason. Then he finished the bread and cleared his throat.

Artie was saying to Freddy, ". . . and if you can't get them into Exeter they're guaranteed for Culver at least."

"Shhh, honey, he's going to say something."

". . . It ain't every steamfitter that has a kid in Culver, ya know."

"Shh."

Winston spoke. "Wiwyiam Buckwey is a weactionary."

"Hey Freddy, did ya hear that?"

"I really gotta hand it to you," Freddy said.

They didn't go bowling that night after all; they all sat around the living room and first they had Winston read the daily papers to them, even the editorials, and when he was done they listened to him analyze the political situation and then Edna brought them all cake and they had Winston predict the season's batting averages while Artie wrote them down and then Winston wrote a poem about autumn and then Winston began to suck his thumb; Edna sent the other kids to bed and they went, complaining because Winston got to stay up and they knew he was going to end up with the rest of the cake; the grownups listened to Winston some more and then Winston and Artie got into a kind of political argument, Artie must have hurt his feelings a little, calling him a squirt and too young to know anything about *anything,* because Winston began to sniffle, and Edna said they were going to have to let her put him to bed now, he just looked tired to death.

She took him up to the front room, where they had laid in

the complete works of Bulwer-Lytton and the eleventh edition of the Britannica; she showed Winston the globe and the autoclave and the slide rule and the drafting board, thinking he would give little cries of delight and perhaps sit down at the desk at once and compose something on the silent keyboard they had bought him, but instead he clung to her shoulder and wouldn't even look. Finally she said, "Why honey, what's the matter?"

"I want my diddy," Winston said.

She found it finally, a tattered square of blanket jammed in the back of the traveling case, and once she had restored it to him Winston let her give him a bath and put him in his pajamas with the bunny feet; even in his pajamas he had that pedigreed look: his ankles and wrists were small and his fingers were long and she found herself wishing he looked just a *little* cuddlier, just a little more like one of her babies, but she suppressed the thought quickly.

In bed, she said to Artie, "Just imagine. Right here, our own little Ph.D." She hugged him. "Isn't it wonderful?"

"I don't know." Artie was looking at the ceiling. "I think he's kind of fresh."

The Wazikis were awakened by a hubbub in the back yard. Artie found Little Art and some of Little Art's friends grappling in the early-morning dirt and when he pried them off he found Winston, white and shaken and biting his lip so the other kids wouldn't see him cry. He extricated Winston and set him on the back stoop and then turned to Little Art and Margie; they sniggered and wouldn't look at him.

"What's the matter, Winston?"

But Winston wouldn't say anything, he only sat there wearing what Artie would learn to call his Hamlet look.

Little Art elbowed Artie, with a dirty snicker. "You got rooked."

"I *what*?"

"Dummy here can't even catch the ball."

Winston had stopped shaking. "My father couldn't catch a ball either," he said coldly, "and he was wunner-up for the Nobel Pwize."

There was something about Winston's attitude that Artie didn't like, but he cuffed Little Art all the same and said, "We didn't pay for him to catch the ball, dummy. You keep your hands off the merchandise."

"If he's so damn smart why can't he catch the ball?"

"Shut up and come on inside."

At breakfast Margie brought out her geography homework and Artie and Winston had a little set-to about what was the capital of the Cameroons; Winston was right of course and Edna made Artie apologize and then she had to smooth it over because it was obvious to everybody that the whole thing had put Artie on edge.

"Four-year-old kid. Four-year-old *kid*."

"I'm sowwy," said Winston, who in addition to the 160 I.Q. was nobody's fool, "they used to make me study all the time."

"Well they didn't teach ya manners."

"There there," Margie said, trying to smooth the frown from Artie's brow. "Just wait till you see the terrarium."

He pushed her fingers away. "What in hell is a terrarium?"

"I don't know, but Winston and I are going to make one."

"I don't want the kid playing with no explosives, and that's that."

Winston had on his Hamlet look. "Anything you say, Mr. Waziki."

Artie decided the kid *was* trying. "You can call me Pop."

"O.K., Mr. Waziki."

At work he found that Freddy Kramer had spread the word; he was something of a celebrity in the shop. By lunch time he was basking in the glow.

"Hundred and sixty," he said in the face of their doubt and envy, "and he calls me Pop."

All the same he was more gratified than he should have been when he came home from work to find Little Art and Winston at it again. Little Art had the Britannica on his lap and he was barking at Winston:

"Who was at the Diet of Worms."

185

Winston made a couple of stabs at it and subsided in embarrassment.

"Hey Pop, you been rooked."

Artie said weakly, "Lay off, kid."

"Hundred and sixty and he don't even know who was at the Diet of Worms."

Winston looked at his hands apologetically. "I'm bwand new."

"Well you just find out, kid. It's your business to know."

Edna swept Winston to her bosom, noting uncomfortably that he was all knees and elbows. "You just lay off him."

Winston dug his chin in her shoulder. "I want my diddy," Winston said.

Even Edna had to admit Winston was too intelligent to hang onto a silly piece of blanket, it didn't look good, and so she had Winston help her wrap up his diddy and put it away, and then they sent him up to his room to learn all he could about Weimeraner dogs and when he came out Artie got into a rage because he hadn't learned a thing about Weimeraners even though he had the whole V volume of the Britannica to look it up in because never mind what the wise kid kept trying to tell them, Artie knew it was spelled just like it sounds.

And as if he hadn't learned his lesson Winston had the nerve to dispute Artie over a point of steamfitting, the thing Artie knew best, and when they looked it up it turned out Winston was right. Then Little Artie wanted Winston to leg-wrestle, and expensive as Winston was, Artie let him because he, Artie, was the head of the family and if Winston was going to live with the Wazikis he was going to have to shape up.

The next day Edna had her bridge group and she dressed Winston in his pale tan romper suit, the one with the bunny-rabbit on the pocket, and she propped him up with his pocket Spinoza and the ladies all made a terrific fuss over him, chucking his chin and feeding him fudge and making him recite until finally he got nervous or something and he threw up right on the cretonne slipcover, Edna's favorite. She cleaned up the mess and brought him back in his *blue* romper suit but he wasn't so much of a hit after that.

"Isn't he kind of *sensitive?*" Maud Wilson said.

"He's bred for brains," Edna said patiently. "When they're bred for brains you've got to put up with a lot."

Melinda Patterson smiled a saccharine smile. "I just don't know whether it's worth it in the long run, putting up with all the mess."

"Winston is going to get his Ph.D." Edna saw she was losing them, and she went on quickly. "And next week he's going to win the Bonanza contest, just you wait and see."

She was sorry the minute she said it; the Bonanza contest was a kind of crossword puzzle and she didn't know whether Winston was trained for that kind of thing, but she had laid Winston on the line and he was just going to have to follow through; maybe he would win and the prize money would make up for all the trouble he had given them. If Winston won they would all get their pictures in the papers together, and it would be a lot easier to be *friends* with Winston after that. They might even let him have his diddy back. As soon as the ladies left she told Winston about the contest and when he cried she tried to cuddle him, but he wouldn't kiss her and she had to spank him. Then she got eight dictionaries, a thesaurus and that week's Bonanza puzzle and sent him to his room.

He tried, he tried for days, and when they came to check on him at the end of the week he said: "It's hopeless."

Artie glowered. "Don't you tell me what's hopeless."

"Look." He made them read one of last week's answers. THERE'S NO PLACE LIKE . . . and a four-letter word. "The answer is ROME because while there are many HOMES there is only one ROME." He said, "See? It's a hoked-up awbitwawy cheat."

"Do the puzzle, Winston."

"But it's all chance."

Artie shook him. "Don't you tell me what's chance."

Evelyn Cartwright was the first on the phone when Winston didn't win. "I just thought maybe he hadn't *entered,*" she said in honeyed tones. Edna was grim. "He entered five hundred and seventy-eight times."

187

"I.Q. one-sixty," Evelyn Cartwright said with a musical snigger. "All that money down the drain."

The guys in the shop laughed so hard that Artie came home early. "Kid just don't know his place. I'm gonna make him learn his place."

Edna thought maybe if she cut down on Winston's rations it would sharpen his brains, so she put him on bread and water and a little fish: brain food, according to the books. Could she help it if some part of her insisted that she serve rich stews to Artie and the kids at the same time? Could she help it if determination hardened her heart so that she didn't even watch Winston's tiny, tortured face as the others devoured ice cream and sugar cookies, and fell on meatloaves like twenty-one-inch shells and devoured coconut custard pies?

Artie decided a little outdoor work would put Winston in trim and build his character too so he turned him over to Margie and Little Art for a couple of hours every afternoon; they tried to make him catch the ball and they made him run foot races and practice broad-jumping and Artie always let it go on a little longer than it should have because after all, the kid had to turn out a one-letter man, it was in the guarantee.

What killed them was, after all they'd paid for him he sniveled all the time, even after Edna let him hang up the snapshot of his father the professor and his mother the lady writer sunning at Biarritz; they had sent it in a letter reminding the Wazikis that the true parents were entitled to half of Winston's future earnings, and it burned Artie so much that he tore it up and jumped up and down on the pieces and wouldn't let Winston see it at all, not even the part where they sent their love. All that money, and Winston could hardly keep his mind on the dumbest questions; Edna's next bridge gathering was a real washout, Winston cried the whole time, and all the ladies could talk about was how peaky he looked.

Artie thought maybe a Sane Mind in a Sound Body and from then on Winston slept on the screen porch for his health, they even let him have a blanket because it was kind of cold.

Artie's birthday was coming up and he had taken so much

guff from Freddy Kramer and the guys from the shop that he knew he had to show them, he would have a big beer party on his birthday, by that time Winston would be shaped up from the brain food and all that sleeping on the porch. He would have a big beer party on his birthday, he would get everybody greased and then he would have Winston come in and do his stuff. As it turned out they probably did drink too much, and maybe Artie did forget about Winston being outside for his constitutional, and maybe it was snowing by the time somebody remembered and they brought him in; maybe that's why all he did was stand there in his romper suit with his knees knocking and his jaw set in his Hamlet look.

Or maybe it was just plain stubbornness; whatever it was, Artie gave him a cuff and said, "Okay, Winston, tell the guys about the Diet of Worms."

"Yes, Mr. Waziki."

Artie gave him a belt. "And call me Pop."

"Yes, Mr. Waziki."

Artie gave him another belt and he started off on the Diet of Worms but he only got out a couple of lines before his mind wandered or something and he began staring at some spot in a corner and when Artie prodded him he turned to Artie with his face flaming and a look that bordered on apology and said, "I'm sowwy. I f-forget."

"What, forget." Artie poked him harder because all the guys were laughing. "What forget?"

Winston was shaking pretty hard, his knees were knocking; nerves, probably, Artie decided; Winston said, "I j-just."

"Awright, awright," Artie said, because the guys were pushing him and Winston had better hurry up and do *something*. He tried to steer him into familiar territory: "Tell the gang about the Weimeraner dog."

"Hell," Freddy Kramer said, egging the other guys on. "I bet he can't even add."

"Yeah," said somebody. "Big deal, Artie. What else did ya bring?"

Artie gripped Winston by the shoulders; the other guys were getting ugly and he had to do something quick. He shook

Winston, hard, hissing, "Times tables. Give 'em the times tables."

Winston just rolled up his eyes with an agonized, forgive-me look. His teeth were chattering so hard now that he couldn't even talk. Still he made a brave beginning: "W-wun."

"See," Artie said quickly, "he's about to give you the one-times."

"The hell he is, look at him."

Winston's face was flaming now, his eyes feverish, and when Artie pressed him he couldn't even talk. The guys were getting ugly and if Winston didn't do something in a minute they were all going to walk out on his birthday party and Artie would be finished down at the shop.

"He's going to give you the *times table*," Artie said doggedly, and he kept on shaking Winston.

"Forget it, Artie."

"Forget it *hell*." They were all milling and fuming and he had to act fast so he picked Winston up by the sailor collar. "Back in a minute. I'm gonna teach him, I'm gonna teach him for once and for all."

Then he took Winston upstairs and he got Edna's silver hairbrush and turned him over his knee, muttering, "Gonna teach him a *lesson*," and when he finally stopped spanking Winston he set him on his feet. Winston's legs buckled and his eyes rolled back so all Artie could see was the whites. He kept on for a couple of minutes, trying to make Winston stand up or answer or *something* and after a while he got scared and went down and called Edna, noting only in passing that the guys must have gotten depressed, hearing Winston yelling and all, everybody was gone.

"I guess I hurt him," he said as Edna rushed past him.

"You ruined him, you went and ruined him." Edna was crying over Winston's crumpled body.

"Five thousand dollars shot," Artie said.

Winston began to moan so they called the company doctor, after all, it was in the guarantee. Winston turned out to be in a coma or something, he was burning up with fever and they sat up with wet compresses and stuff for several days and when Winston began to come out of it they noticed something funny and they called the doctor in again. After he had been with Winston for several minutes he came out and Edna gripped him by the elbow saying: "All right? Is he going to be all right?"

The doctor looked weary beyond description. "With a lot of care he'll be all right."

Shrewdly, Artie followed up. "One-sixty and all?"

"He'll be all right, but he'll never think again."

"Then we get our money back."

"Read your contract," the doctor said, as if he had been through all this before. "You'll find your baby intellectuals are only guaranteed against failure."

"Failure, let me tell you about failure . . ."

But the doctor was moving toward the door. "Not against personal damage or acts of God."

Artie had the doctor by the shoulders now and they were in the doorway, wrangling, but Edna paid no attention; instead she took a bowl of chicken soup and crept up to Winston's room.

He was pale and diminished, lying there under the covers, but he looked more or less all right. He recognized her when she came in and he began to moan.

She stroked his forehead. "All right, baby, you're going to be all right."

"Sick." Winston was blubbering. "Sick."

"Mommy make you all right." Because he wouldn't stop crying she thought fast. "Diddy? Winston want his diddy?"

"Diddy," Winston said, and when she produced it, took it to his bosom with a look of bliss.

"That's a boy."

Winston stopped stroking his cheek with his diddy and looked around the room until his eyes rested on the globe. He tried to sit up. "Baw?"

"Ball, Winston. Ball."

"Baw."

"That's my baby. Ball. That's my baby, baby boy."

"Baw? Baw?"

"Him's a *sweet* boy." When he smiled like that he looked just like Margie or Little Artie. She swept him to her bosom. "Him can be my baby boy."

"Ba-by?"

She had an apple pie cooking; she would give the whole thing to him. "Baby, poor baby." She smoothed his hair back from his forehead. "All dat finking wadn't *dood* for him."

The History Makers

by James Sallis

In the morning (he wasn't sure which morning) he began
the letter . . .

Dear Jim,

The last time I saw you, you advised against my coming
here. You were quite insistent, and I don't believe the perfectly awful 3-2 beer we were drinking was wholly responsible
for said adamance. You virtually begged me not to come. And
I suppose you must have felt somewhat duty-bound to sway
me away. That since it was yourself who introduced me to
the Ephemera, you'd incurred some sort of liability for my
Fate. That you would be accountable.

I remember you said a man couldn't keep his sanity here;
that his mind would be whirled in a hundred directions at
once, and he would ravel to loose ends—that he would crimp
and crumble, swell and burst, along with this world. And
you held that there was nothing of value here. But the government and I, for our separate reasons, disagreed.

And can I refute you now by saying that I've found peace,
or purpose, or insight? No, of course not, not in or with this
letter. For all my whilom grandiloquence, and accustomed to
it as you are, such an effort would be fatuous and absurd.
What I *can* do: I can show you this world in what is possibly
the only way we can ever know it, I can show you where it
brims over to touch my own edges. I can let you look out my
window.

The Blue Twin. That was . . . three years ago? Close to that. ("Time is merely a device to keep everything from happening at once." Isn't that wonderful? I found it in one of the magazines I brought Out with me, in a review of some artist's work about which I remember only the name of one painting: A Romantic Longing To Be Scientific.) Three years . . . I miss Earth, dark Earth. I miss Vega.

(I remember that you were shortly to be reassigned to Ginh, and wonder if this letter will find you there among the towers.)

The Blue Twin, which we always insisted was the best bar in the Combine at least, probably the Union (and did I ever tell you that bars are the emblem of our civilization? A place to lean back in, to put your feet up, a place of silences and lurching conversations: still center, hub for a whirling universe. And pardon my euphuism, please).

And the two of us sitting there, talking of careers and things. Quietly, with the color-clustered walls of sky-bright Vega around us and the massive turning shut out. You dissuading. And bits of my land slaking into the sea. Talking, taking time to talk.

My work had soured, yours burgeoned, I envied you (though we always pretended it was the other way around). All my faces had run together like cheap watercolor. My classes had come to be for me nothing but abstract patterns, forming, breaking, reforming—while the faces around you were becoming distinct, defining themselves, giving you ways to go.

I envied you. So I took this sabbatical: "to do a book." And the sabbatical became an extended leave of absence, and that became a dismissal. And no book.

Things fall apart, the center cannot hold . . . Talking about dissent and revolution, the ways of change, things falling by the way and no Samaritan—and you mentioning something you'd seen in one of the Courier bulletins that crossed your desk: which was my introduction to it all, to Ephemera. (Ephemera. It was one of those pale poetic jokes, the sort that gave us Byzantium and Eldorado and Limbo and all the others, names for out-Union planets, for distant places. You wonder what kind of man is responsible.)

How many weeks then of reading, of requesting information, of clotted first drafts? How long before the night I collapsed into my bed and sat up again with the line "Hold hard these ancient minutes in a cuckoo's month" on my lips—days, weeks? It seemed years. Time, for me, had broken down. And I came to Ephemera . . .

The Ephemera. My window looks out now on one of their major cities, towered and splendid, the one I've come to call Siva. It is middle season, which means they are expanding: yesterday the city was miles away, a dark line on the horizon; tomorrow it will draw even closer and I'll have to move my squatter's hut back out of the way. The next day it will swell toward me again, then in the afternoon retreat—and the collapse will have begun. By the next morning I'll be able to see nothing of Siva, and the hut will have to be relocated, shuttled back in for the final moments.

They live in a separate time-plane from ours—is that too abrupt? I don't know another way to say it, or how I should prepare for saying it. Or even if it makes sense. They are but vaguely aware of my presence, and I can study them only with the extensive aid of machines, some I brought with me, a few I was able to requisition later (the government always hopes, always holds onto a chance for new resources). And all I've learned comes down to that one strange phrase. A separate time-plane.

When I first came here, I was constantly blundering into the edges of their city, or being blundered into by them; I was constantly making hasty retreats back into what I started calling the Deadlands. It took my first year just to plot the course of the cities. I've gotten little further.

It's a simple thing, once you have the key: the cities develop in dependence to the seasons. The problem comes with Ephemera's orbit, which is wildly eccentric (I'm tempted to say erratic), and with her queer climate. Seasons flash by, repeat themselves with subtle differences, linger and rush—all in apparent confusion. It takes a while to sort it all out in your mind, to resolve a year into particulars.

And now I've watched this city with its thousand names surge and subside a thousand times. I've watched its cycles repeat my charts, and I've thrown away the charts and been satisfied to call it Siva. All my social theories, my notes, my scribble-occluded papers, I've had to put away; I became a scientist, then simply an observer. Watching Siva.

It's always striking and beautiful. A few huts appear and before you can breathe a village is standing there. The huts sprawl out across the landscape and the whole thing begins to ripple with the changes that are going on, something as though the city were boiling. This visual undulation continues; the edges of the village move out away from it, catch the rippling, extend further: a continuous process. The further from center, the faster it moves. There's a time you recognize it as a town, a time when the undulation slows and almost stops—then, minutes later, endogeny begins again and its growth accelerates fantastically. It sprawls, it rises, it solidifies.

(A few days ago while I was watching, I got up to put some music—it was Bach—on the recorder. Then I came back and sat down. I must have become absorbed in the music, because later when the tape cut off, I looked up and the city was almost upon me. I keep thinking that someday I won't move back, that I'll be taken into the city, it will sprout and explode around me.)

Siva builds and swells, explodes upward, outward, blankets the landscape. Then, toward the end of the cycle, a strange peace inhabits it: a pause, a silence. Like Joshua's stopping the sun.

And then: what? I can't know what goes on in the city at these times. From photographs (rather incredible photographs) and inspection of the "ruins," I've gathered that something like this must occur: some psychic shakedown hits the people in full stride; most of them go catto, fold themselves into insensible knots—while the rest turn against the city and destroy it. Each time, it happens. Each time, I'm unable to discover the respective groups or even the overall reason. And each time, destruction is absolute. The momentary stasis breaks, and the city falls away. No wall or relic is left standing; even the rubble is somehow consumed. It happens so quickly, the cameras can't follow it; and I walk about for hours afterward, trying to read something in the scarred ground. . . . "All Pergamum is covered with thorn bushes; even its ruins have perished."

Three years. Amusing and frightening to think of all I've seen in that time, more than any other man. And what have I learned? One thing perhaps, one clear thing, and this by accident, poking about the "ruins." I found one of their devices for measuring time, which had inexplicably survived the relapse, a sort of recomplicated sundial—and I guessed from it that this race reckons time from conclusions rather than beginnings. (I leave it to you to decide whether this is a philosophical or psychological insight.) That is, their day—or year, or century, or whatever they might have termed it—seems to have been delimited by the sun's declension rather than its rise; and I assume this scheme, this perspective, would have become generalized (or itself simply expressed an already prevailing attitude). There's a part of the mechanism—a curious device, either rectifier or drive control, possibly both—that seems to work by the flux of the wind, I suppose bringing some sort of complex precision into their measurements: a kind of Aeolian clock.

And since that last sentence there's been a long pause as I sat here and tried to think: what can I say now . . . Hours ago, when I began this letter, I had some vague, instinctive notion of things I wanted to tell you. Now it's all fallen back out of reach again, and all I have for you and for myself are these pages of phatic gesturing: Look. See. That, and the first piece of an epiphany, an old song from the early years of Darkearth: "Time, time is winding up again."

And so I sit here and look out my window, watching this city build and fall. I stare at their clock, which no longer functions, and have no use for my own. I am backed to the sea, and tomorrow Siva will spread and extend out onto these waters. I'm left with the decision, the ancient decision: shall I move?

I put on my music—my Bach, my Mozart, my Telemann—and I beat out its rhythms on chrome tiles. For a while I lose myself in it, for a while I break out of the gather and issue of time . . .

And outside now, the sky fills with color like a bowl of strung ribbons, the ribbons fall, night billows about me. Twelve times I've begun this letter over a space of months, and each time faltered. Now at last, like the day, I've run through to a stammering end. I've filled hours and pages. Yet all I have to offer you is this: this record of my disability. Which I send with enduring love.

Your brother,
John

In the evening he finished the letter and set it aside and felt the drag of the sea against his chest.

He sat at the empty table he used for a desk, looking up at the opposite wall. On it, two reproductions and a mirror, forming a caret: mirror at the angle, below and left *The Persistence of Memory*, one of Monet's Notre Dame paintings across from that. Glass bolted in place, stiff paper tacked up—time arrested, time suspended, time recorded in passing. And about them depended the banks of shelves and instrumentation which covered the hut's walls like lines and symbols ranked on a page.

He rose, making a portrait of the mirror, seeing: this moment. Behind that, three years. Behind that, a lifetime. And behind that, nothing.

(Take for heraldry this image: the palimpsest, imperfectly erased.)

He ambled about his room, staring at the strange, three-dimensional objects which surrounded him, not understanding. He picked up the Ephemera chronometer, turned it over in his hands, put it back. Then (four steps) he stood by the tape deck. Making sound, shaping sound.

(All of this, all so . . . vivid, so clearly defined. Clear and sharp like an abstraction of plane intersecting plane, angle and obtrusion . . . hard, sharp on a flat ground.)

Bach churned out of the speakers, rose in volume as he spun controls, rose again till bass boomed and the walls rattled.

And then he was walking on the bare gray ground outside his hut . . .

(Feet killing quiet. No: because the silence hums like a live wire, sings like a thrown knife. Rather, my feet tick on the sands. Passing now a flat rock stood on its feet, leaning against the sky. A poem remembered . . . Time passes, you say. No. We go; time stays . . . And on Rhea there are a thousand vast molelike creatures burrowing away forever in heart-darkness, consuming a world.)

He stopped and stood on the beach in the baritone darkness, with the pale red sea ahead and the timed floodlights burning behind him. Three yards off, a fish broke water and sank back into a target of ripples.

Looked up. Four stars ticked in the sky, an orange moon shuttled up among them.

Looked down. The city, Siva, swept toward him.

(A simple truth. What denies time, dies. And that which accepts it, which places itself in time, lives again. Emblem of palimpsests. Vision of this palimpsest city.)

The Bach came to his ears then, urgent, exultant. The night was basso profundo, the moon boxed in stars. He sat watching a beetle scuttle across the sand, pushing a pebble before it, deep red on gray.

Later he looked up and the music was over. He turned and saw Siva at his penumbra's edge, turned back to still waters.

Turned back to silence . . .

Then the lights went off behind him and he was left alone with the fall and the surge of the sea.

The Big Flash

by Norman Spinrad

T minus 200 days . . . and counting . . .

They came on freaky for my taste—but that's the name of
the game: freaky means a draw in the rock business. And if
the Mandala was going to survive in LA, competing with a
network-owned joint like The American Dream, I'd just have
to hold my nose and out-freak the opposition. So after I had
dug the Four Horsemen for about an hour, I took them into
my office to talk turkey.

I sat down behind my Salvation Army desk (the Mandala
is the world's most expensive shoestring operation) and the
Horsemen sat down on the bridge chairs sequentially, estab-
lishing the group's pecking order.

First the head honcho, lead guitar and singer, Stony
Clarke—blond shoulder-length hair, eyes like something in a
morgue when he took off his steel-rimmed shades, a reputation as a heavy acid-head and the look of a speed-freak behind it. Then Hair, the drummer, dressed like a Hell's Angel,
swastikas and all, a junkie, with fanatic eyes that were a little
too close together, making me wonder whether he wore
swastikas because he grooved behind the Angel thing or made
like an Angel because it let him groove behind the swastika
in public. Number three was a cat who called himself Super
Spade and wasn't kidding—he wore earrings, natural hair, a
Stokeley Carmichael sweatshirt, and on a thong around his
neck a shrunken head that had been whitened with liquid
shoe polish. He was the utility infielder: sitar, base, organ,

flute, whatever. Number four, who called himself Mr. Jones, was about the creepiest cat I had ever seen in a rock group, and that is saying something. He was their visuals, synthesizer and electronics man. He was at least forty, wore Early Hippy clothes that looked like they had been made by Sy Devore, and was rumored to be some kind of Rand Corporation dropout. There's no business like show business.

"Okay, boys," I said, "you're strange, but you're my kind of strange. Where you worked before?"

"We ain't, baby," Clarke said. "We're the New Thing. I've been dealing crystal and acid in the Haight. Hair was drummer for some plastic group in New York. The Super Spade claims it's the reincarnation of Bird and it don't pay to argue. Mr. Jones, he don't talk too much. Maybe he's a Martian. We just started putting our thing together."

One thing about this business, the groups that don't have square managers, you can get cheap. They talk too much.

"Groovy," I said. "I'm happy to give you guys your start. Nobody knows you, but I think you got something going. So I'll take a chance and give you a week's booking. One A.M. to closing, which is two, Tuesday through Sunday, four hundred a week."

"Are you Jewish?" asked Hair.

"What?"

"Cool it," Clarke ordered. Hair cooled it. "What it means," Clarke told me, "is that four hundred sounds like pretty light bread."

"We don't sign if there's an option clause," Mr. Jones said.

"The Jones-thing has a good point," Clarke said. "We do the first week for four hundred, but after that it's a whole new scene, dig?"

I didn't feature that. If they hit it big, I could end up not being able to afford them. But on the other hand $400 was light bread, and I needed a cheap closing act pretty bad.

"Okay," I said. "But a verbal agreement that I get first crack at you when you finish the gig."

"Word of honor," said Stony Clarke.

That's this business—the word of honor of an ex-dealer and speed-freak.

T minus 199 days . . . and counting . . .

Being unconcerned with ends, the military mind can be easily manipulated, easily controlled, and easily confused. Ends are defined as those goals set by civilian authority. Ends are the conceded province of civilians; means are the province of the military, whose duty it is to achieve the ends set for it by the most advantageous application of the means at its command.

Thus the confusion over the war in Asia among my uniformed clients at the Pentagon. The end has been duly set: eradication of the guerillas. But the civilians have overstepped their bounds and meddled in means. The Generals regard this as unfair, a breach of contract, as it were. The Generals (or the faction among them most inclined to paranoia) are beginning to see the conduct of the war, the political limitation on means, as a ploy of the civilians for performing a putsch against their time-honored prerogatives.

This aspect of the situation would bode ill for the country, were it not for the fact that the growing paranoia among the Generals has enabled me to manipulate them into presenting both my scenarios to the President. The President has authorized implementation of the major scenario, provided that the minor scenario is successful in properly molding public opinion.

My major scenario is simple and direct. Knowing that the poor flying weather makes our conventional airpower, with its dependency on relative accuracy, ineffectual, the enemy has fallen into the pattern of grouping his forces into larger units and launching punishing annual offensives during the monsoon season. However, these larger units are highly vulnerable to tactical nuclear weapons, which do not depend upon accuracy for effect. Secure in the knowledge that domestic political considerations preclude the use of nuclear weapons, the enemy will once again form into division-sized units or larger during the next monsoon season. A parsimonious use of tactical nuclear weapons, even as few as twenty 100 kiloton bombs, employed simultaneously and in an advantageous pattern, will destroy a minimum of 200,000 enemy troops, or nearly two-thirds of his total force, in a twenty-four hour period. The blow will be crushing.

The minor scenario, upon whose success the implementation of the major scenario depends, is far more sophisticated, due to its subtler goal: public acceptance of, or, optimally, even public clamor for, the use of tactical nuclear weapons. The task is difficult, but my scenario is quite sound, if somewhat exotic, and with the full, if to-some-extent-clandestine support of the upper military hierarchy, certain civil government circles and the decision-makers in key aerospace corporations, the means now at my command would seem adequate. The risks, while statistically significant, do not exceed an acceptable level.

T minus 189 days . . . and counting . . .
The way I see it, the network deserved the shafting I gave them. They shafted me, didn't they? Four successful series I produce for those bastards, and two bomb out after thirteen weeks and they send me to the salt mines! A discotheque, can you imagine they make me producer at a lousy discotheque! A remittance man they make me, those schlockmeisters. Oh, those schnorrers made the American Dream sound like a kosher deal—20% of the net, they say. And you got access to all our sets and contract players, it'll make you a rich man, Herm. And like a yuk, I sign, being broke at the time, without reading the fine print. I should know they've set up the American Dream as a tax loss? I should know that I've *gotta* use their lousy sets and stiff contract players and have it written off against my gross? I should know their shtick is to run the American Dream at a loss and then do a network TV show out of the joint from which I don't see a penny? So I end up running the place for them at a paper loss, living on salary, while the network rakes it in off the TV show that I end up paying for out of my end.

Don't bums like that deserve to be shafted? It isn't enough

they use me as a tax loss patsy, they gotta tell me who to book! "Go sign the Four Horsemen, the group that's packing them in at the Mandala," they say. "We want them on *A Night With The American Dream*. They're hot."

"Yeah, they're hot," I say, "which means they'll cost a mint. I can't afford it."

They show me more fine print—next time I read the contract with a microscope. I *gotta* book whoever they tell me to and I gotta absorb the cost on my books! It's enough to make a Litvak turn anti-semit.

So I had to go to the Mandala to sign up these hippies. I made sure I didn't get there till 12:30 so I wouldn't have to stay in that nuthouse any longer than necessary. Such a dive! What Bernstein did was take a bankrupt Hollywood-Hollywood club on the Strip, knock down all the interior walls and put up this monster tent inside the shell. Just thin white screening over two-by-fours. Real shlock. Outside the tent, he's got projectors, lights, speakers, all the electronic mumbo-jumbo, and inside is like being surrounded by movie screens. Just the tent and the bare floor, not even a real stage, just a platform on wheels they shlepp in and out of the tent when they change groups.

So you can imagine he doesn't draw exactly a class crowd. Not with the American Dream up the street being run as a network tax loss. What they get is the smelly hard-core hippies I don't let in the door and the kind of j.d. high-school kids that think it's smart to hang around putzes like that. A lot of dope-pushing goes on. The cops don't like the place and the rousts draw professional troublemakers.

A real den of iniquity—I felt like I was walking onto a Cas-bah set. The last group had gone off and the Horsemen hadn't come on yet, so what you had was this crazy tent filled with hippies, half of them on acid or pot or amphetamine or for all I know Ajax, high-school would-be hippies, also mostly stoned and getting ugly, and a few crazy schwartzes looking to fight cops. All of them standing around waiting for something to happen, and about ready to make it happen. I stood

204

near the door, just in case. As they say, "the vibes were making me uptight."

All of a sudden the house lights go out and it's black as a network executive's heart. I hold my hand on my wallet—in this crowd, tell me there are no pickpockets. Just the pitch black and dead silence for what, ten beats, and then I start feeling something, I don't know, like something crawling along my bones, but I know it's some kind of subsonic effect and not my imagination, because all the hippies are standing still and you don't hear a sound.

Then from monster speakers so loud you feel it in your teeth, a heartbeat, but heavy, slow, half-time like maybe a whale's heart. The thing crawling along my bones seems to be synchronized with the heartbeat and I feel almost like I am that big dumb heart beating there in the darkness.

Then a dark red spot—so faint it's almost infrared—hits the stage which they have wheeled out. On the stage are four uglies in crazy black robes—you know, like the Grim Reaper wears—with that ugly red light all over them like blood. Creepy. Boom-ba-boom. Boom-ba-boom. The heartbeat still going, still that subsonic bone-crawl and the hippies are staring at the Four Horsemen like mesmerized chickens.

The bass player, a regular jungle-bunny, picks up the rhythm of the heartbeat. Dum-da-dum. Dum-da-dum. The drummer beats it out with earsplitting rim-shots. Then the electric guitar, tuned like a strangling cat, makes with horrible heavy chords. Whang-ka-whang. Whang-ka-whang.

It's just awful, I feel it in my guts, my bones; my eardrums are just like some great big throbbing vein. Everybody is swaying to it, I'm swaying to it. Boom-ba-boom. Boom-ba-boom.

Then the guitarist starts to chant in rhythm with the heartbeat, in a hoarse, shrill voice like somebody dying: *"The* big *flash . . . The* big *flash . . ."*

And the guy at the visuals console diddles around and rings of light start to climb the walls of the tent, blue at the bottom becoming green as they get higher, then yellow, orange and finally as they become a circle on the ceiling, eye-killing neon-red. Each circle takes exactly one heartbeat to climb the walls.

Boy, what an awful feeling! Like I was a tube of toothpaste being squeezed in rhythm till the top of my head felt like it was gonna squirt up with those circles of light through the ceiling.

And then they start to speed it up gradually. The same heartbeat, the same rim-shots, same chords, same circles of light, same *"The* big *flash* . . . *The* big *flash* . . ." same base, same subsonic bone-crawl, but just a little faster. . . . Then faster! Faster!

Thought I would die! Knew I would die! Heart beating like a lunatic. Rim-shots like a machine gun. Circles of light sucking me up the walls, into that red neon hole.

Oy, incredible! Over and over faster faster till the voice was a scream and the heartbeat a boom and the rim-shots a whine and the guitar howled feedback and my bones were jumping out of my body—

Every spot in the place came on and I went blind from the sudden light—

An awful explosion-sound came over every speaker, so loud it rocked me on my feet—

I felt myself squirting out of the top of my head and loved it.

Then:

The explosion became a rumble—

The light seemed to run together into a circle on the ceiling, leaving everything else black.

And the circle became a fireball.

The fireball became a slow-motion film of an atomic bomb cloud as the rumbling died away. Then the picture faded into a moment of total darkness and the house lights came on.

What a number!

Gevalt, what an act!

So after the show, when I got them alone and found out they had no manager, not even an option to the Mandala, I thought faster than I ever had in my life.

To make a long story short and sweet, I gave the network

the royal screw. I signed the Horsemen to a contract that made me their manager and gave me twenty percent of their take. Then I booked them into the American Dream at ten thousand a week, wrote a check as proprietor of the American Dream, handed the check to myself as manager of the Four Horsemen, then resigned as a network flunky, leaving them with a $10,000 bag and me with 20% of the hottest group since the Beatles.

What the hell, he who lives by the fine print shall perish by the fine print.

T minus 148 days . . . and counting . . .

"You haven't seen the tape yet, have you, B.D.?" Jake said. He was nervous as hell. When you reach my level in the network structure, you're used to making subordinates nervous, but Jake Pitkin was head of network continuity, not some office boy, and certainly should be used to dealing with executives at my level. Was the rumor really true?

We were alone in the screening room. It was doubtful that the projectionist could hear us.

"No, I haven't seen it yet," I said. "But I've heard some strange stories."

Jake looked positively deathly. "About the tape?" he said.

"About you, Jake," I said, deprecating the rumor with an easy smile. "That you don't want to air the show."

"It's true, B.D.," Jake said quietly.

"Do you realize what you're saying? Whatever our personal tastes—and I personally think there's something unhealthy about them—the Four Horsemen are the hottest thing in the country right now and that dirty little thief Herm Gellman held us up for a quarter of a million for an hour show. It cost another two hundred thousand to make it. We've spent another hundred thousand on promotion. We're getting top dollar from the sponsors. There's over a million dollars one way or the other riding on that show. That's how much we blow if we don't air it."

"I know that, B.D.," Jake said. "I also know this could cost me my job. Think about that. Because knowing all that, I'm

207

still against airing the tape. I'm going to run the closing segment for you. I'm sure enough that you'll agree with me to stake my job on it."

I had a terrible feeling in my stomach. I have superiors too and The Word was that *A Trip With The Four Horsemen* would be aired, period. No matter what. Something funny was going on. The price we were getting for commercial time was a precedent and the sponsor was a big aerospace company which had never bought network time before. What really bothered me was that Jake Pitkin had no reputation for courage; yet here he was laying his job on the line. He must be pretty sure I would come around to his way of thinking or he wouldn't dare. And though I couldn't tell Jake, I had no choice in the matter whatsoever.

"Okay, roll it," Jake said into the intercom mike. "What you're going to see," he said as the screening room lights went out, "is the last number."

On the screen:

A shot of empty blue sky, with soft, lazy electric guitar chords behind it. The camera pans across a few clouds to an extremely long shot on the sun. As the sun, no more than a tiny circle of light, moves into the center of the screen, a sitar-drone comes in behind the guitar.

Very slowly, the camera begins to zoom in on the sun. As the image of the sun expands, the sitar gets louder and the guitar begins to fade and a drum starts to give the sitar a beat. The sitar gets louder, the beat gets more pronounced and begins to speed up as the sun continues to expand. Finally, the whole screen is filled with unbearably bright light behind which the sitar and drum are in a frenzy.

Then over this, drowning out the sitar and drum, a voice like a sick thing in heat: *"Brighter . . . than a thousand suns . . ."*

The light dissolves into a closeup of a beautiful darkhaired girl with huge eyes and moist lips, and suddenly there is nothing on the sound track but soft guitar and voices crooning low: *"Brighter . . . Oh God, it's brighter . . . brighter . . . than a thousand suns . . ."*

The girl's face dissolves into a full shot of the Four Horsemen in their Grim Reaper robes and the same melody that had played behind the girl's face shifts into a minor key, picks up whining, reverberating electric guitar chords and a sitar-drone and becomes a dirge: *"Darker . . . the world grows darker . . ."*

And a series of cuts in time to the dirge:

A burning village in Asia strewn with bodies—

"Darker . . . the world grows darker . . ."

The corpse-heap at Auschwitz—

"Until it gets so dark . . ."

A gigantic auto graveyard with gaunt Negro children dwarfed in the foreground—

"I think I'll die . . ."

A Washington ghetto in flames with the Capitol misty in the background—

". . . before the daylight comes . . ."

A jump-cut to an extreme closeup on the lead singer of the Horsemen, his face twisted into a mask of desperation and ecstasy. And the sitar is playing double-time, the guitar is wailing and he is screaming at the top of his lungs: *"But before I die, let me make that trip before the nothing comes . . ."*

The girl's face again, but transparent, with a blinding yellow light shining through it. The sitar beat gets faster and faster with the guitar whining behind it and the voice is working itself up into a howling frenzy: *". . . the last big flash to light my sky . . ."*

Nothing but the blinding light now—

". . . and zap! the world is done . . ."

An utterly black screen for a beat that becomes black fading to blue at a horizon—

". . . but before we die let's dig that high that frees us from our binds . . . that blows all cool that ego-drool and burns us from our mind . . . the last big flash, mankind's last gas, the trip we can't take twice. . . ."

Suddenly, the music stops dead for half a beat. Then:

The screen is lit up by an enormous fireball—

A shattering rumble—

The fireball coalesces into a mushroom-pillar cloud as the roar goes on. As the roar begins to die out, fire is visible inside the monstrous nuclear cloud. And the girl's face is faintly visible superimposed over the cloud.

A soft voice, amplified over the roar, obscenely reverential now: *Brighter . . . great God, it's brighter . . . brighter than a thousand suns . . ."*

And the screen went blank and the lights came on.

I looked at Jake. Jake looked at me.

"That's sick," I said. "That's really sick."

"You don't want to run a thing like that, do you, B.D.?" Jake said softly.

I made some rapid mental calculations. The loathsome thing ran something under five minutes . . . it could be done. . . .

"You're right, Jake," I said. "We won't run a thing like that. We'll cut it out of the tape and squeeze in another commercial at each break. That should cover the time."

"You don't understand," Jake said. "The contract Herm rammed down our throats doesn't allow us to edit. The show's a package—all or nothing. Besides, the whole show's like that."

"All like that? What do you mean, all like that?"

Jake squirmed in his seat. "Those guys are . . . well, perverts, B.D.," he said.

"Perverts?"

"They're . . . well, they're in love with the atom bomb or something. Every number leads up to the same thing."

"You mean . . . they're *all* like that?"

"You got the picture, B.D.," Jake said. "We run an hour of *that* or we run nothing at all."

"Jesus."

I knew what I wanted to say. Burn the tape and write off the million dollars. But I also knew it would cost me my job. And I knew that five minutes after I was out the door, they would have someone in my job who would see things their way. Even my superiors seemed to be just handing down The Word from higher up. I had no choice. There was no choice.

"I'm sorry, Jake," I said. "We run it."

"I resign," said Jake Pitkin, who had no reputation for courage.

T minus 10 days . . . and counting . . .

"It's a clear violation of the Test-Ban Treaty," I said.

The Under Secretary looked as dazed as I felt. "We'll call it a peaceful use of atomic energy, and let the Russians scream," he said.

"It's insane."

"Perhaps," the Under Secretary said. "But you have your orders, General Carson, and I have mine. From higher up. At exactly eight fifty-eight P.M. local time on July fourth, you will drop a fifty kiloton atomic bomb on the designated ground zero at Yucca Flats."

"But the people . . . the television crews . . ."

"Will be at least two miles outside the danger zone. Surely, SAC can manage that kind of accuracy under 'laboratory conditions.'"

I stiffened. "I do not question the competence of any bomber crew under my command to perform this mission," I said. "I question the reason for the mission. I question the sanity of the orders."

The Under Secretary shrugged, smiled wanly. "Welcome to the club."

"You mean you don't know what this is all about either?"

"All I know is what was transmitted to me by the Secretary of Defense, and I got the feeling he doesn't know everything, either. You know that the Pentagon has been screaming for the use of tactical nuclear weapons to end the war in Asia —you SAC boys have been screaming the loudest. Well, several months ago, the President conditionally approved a plan for the use of tactical nuclear weapons during the next monsoon season."

211

I whistled. The civilians were finally coming to their senses. Or were they?

"But what does that have to do with—?"

"Public opinion," the Under Secretary said. "It was conditional upon a drastic change in public opinion. At the time the plan was approved, the polls showed that seventy-eight point eight percent of the population opposed the use of tactical nuclear weapons, nine point eight percent favored their use and the rest were undecided or had no opinion. The President agreed to authorize the use of tactical nuclear weapons by a date, several months from now, which is still top secret, provided that by that date at least sixty-five percent of the population approved their use and no more than twenty percent actively opposed it."

"I see . . . Just a ploy to keep the Joint Chiefs quiet."

"General Carson," the Under Secretary said, "apparently you are out of touch with the national mood. After the first Four Horsemen show, the polls showed that twenty-five percent of the population approved the use of nuclear weapons. After the second show, the figure was forty-one percent. It is now forty-eight percent. Only thirty-two percent are now actively opposed."

"You're trying to tell me that a rock group—"

"A rock group and the cult around it, General. It's become a national hysteria. There are imitators. Haven't you seen those buttons?"

"The ones with a mushroom cloud on them that say 'Do it'?"

The Under Secretary nodded. "Your guess is as good as mine whether the National Security Council just decided that the Horsemen hysteria could be used to mold public opinion, or whether the Four Horsemen were their creatures to begin with. But the results are the same either way—the Horsemen and the cult around them have won over precisely that element of the population which was most adamantly opposed to nuclear weapons: hippies, students, dropouts, draft-age youth. Demonstrations against the war and against nuclear weapons

212

have died down. We're pretty close to that sixty-five percent, Someone—perhaps the President himself—has decided that one more big Four Horsemen show will put us over the top."

"The President is behind this?"

"No one else can authorize the detonation of an atomic bomb, after all," the Under Secretary said. "We're letting them do the show live from Yucca Flats. It's being sponsored by an aerospace company heavily dependent on defense contracts. We're letting them truck in a live audience. Of course the government is behind it."

"And SAC drops an A-bomb as the show-stopper?"

"Exactly."

"I saw one of those shows," I said. "My kids were watching it. I got the strangest feeling . . . I almost wanted that red telephone to ring. . . ."

"I know what you mean," the Under Secretary said. "Sometimes I get the feeling that whoever's behind this has gotten caught up in the hysteria themselves . . . that the Horsemen are now using whoever was using them . . . a closed circle. But I've been tired lately. The war's making us all so tired. If only we could get it all over with . . ."

"We'd all like to get it over with one way or the other," I said.

T minus 60 minutes . . . and counting . . .

I had orders to muster *Backfish*'s crew for the live satellite relay of *The Four Horsemen's Fourth*. Superficially, it might seem strange to order the whole Polaris fleet to watch a television show, but the morale factor involved was quite significant.

Polaris subs are frustrating duty. Only top sailors are chosen and a good sailor craves action. Yet if we are ever called upon to act, our mission will have been a failure. We spend most of our time honing skills that must never be used. Deterrence is a sound strategy but a terrible drain on the men of the deterrent forces—a drain exacerbated in the past by the negative attitude of our countrymen toward our mission. Men who, in the service of their country, polish their skills to a razor edge and then must refrain from exercising them have a right to resent being treated as pariahs.

Therefore the positive change in the public attitude toward us that seems to be associated with the Four Horsemen has made them mascots of a kind to the Polaris fleet. In their strange way they seem to speak for us and to us.

I chose to watch the show in the missile control center, where a full crew must always be ready to launch the missiles on five-minute notice. I have always felt a sense of communion with the duty watch in the missile control center that I cannot share with the other men under my command. Here we are not Captain and crew but mind and hand. Should the order come, the will to fire the missiles will be mine and the act will be theirs. At such a moment, it will be good not to feel alone.

All eyes were on the television set mounted above the main console as the show came on and . . .

The screen was filled with a whirling spiral pattern, metallic yellow on metallic blue. There was a droning sound that seemed part sitar and part electronic and I had the feeling that the sound was somehow coming from inside my head and the spiral seemed etched directly on my retinas. It hurt mildly, yet nothing in the world could have made me turn away.

Then two voices, chanting against each other:

"Let it all come in. . . ."

"Let it all come out . . ."

"In . . . *out* . . . in . . . *out* . . . in . . . *out* . . ."

My head seemed to be pulsing—in-*out*, in-*out*, in-*out*—and the spiral pattern began to pulse color-changes with the words: yellow-on-blue (in) . . . green-on-red (*out*) . . . In-*out*-in-*out*-in-*out* . . .

In the screen . . . *out* my head . . . I seemed to be beating against some kind of invisible membrane between myself and the screen as if something were trying to embrace my mind and I were fighting it . . . But why was I fighting it?

The pulsing, the chanting, got faster and faster till in could not be told from *out* and negative spiral afterimages formed in my eyes faster than they could adjust to the changes, piled up on each other faster and faster till it seemed my head would explode—

The chanting and the droning broke and there were the Four Horsemen, in their robes, playing on some stage against a backdrop of clear blue sky. And a single voice, soothing now: "You are in . . ."

Then the view was directly above the Horsemen and I could see that they were on some kind of circular platform. The view moved slowly and smoothly up and away and I saw that the circular stage was atop a tall tower; around the tower and completely encircling it was a huge crowd seated on desert sands that stretched away to an empty infinity.

"And we are in and they are in . . ."

I was down among the crowd now; they seemed to melt and flow like plastic, pouring from the television screen to enfold me . . .

"And we are all in here together. . . ."

A strange and beautiful feeling . . . the music got faster and wilder, ecstatic . . . the hull of the *Backfish* seemed unreal . . . the crowd was swaying to it around me . . . the distance between myself and the crowd seemed to dissolve . . . I was there . . . they were here. . . . We were transfixed . . .

"Oh yeah, we are all in here together . . . together . . ."

T minus 45 minutes . . . and counting . . .

Jeremy and I sat staring at the television screen, ignoring each other and everything around us. Even with the short watches and the short tours of duty, you can get to feeling pretty strange down here in a hole in the ground under tons of concrete, just you and the guy with the other key, with nothing to do but think dark thoughts and get on each other's nerves. We're all supposed to be as stable as men can be, or so they tell us, and they must be right because the world's still here. I mean, it wouldn't take much—just two guys on the same

215

watch over the same three Minutemen flipping out at the same time, turning their keys in the dual lock, pressing the three buttons . . . Pow! World War III!

A bad thought, the kind we're not supposed to think or I'll start watching Jeremy and he'll start watching me and we'll get a paranoia feedback going. . . . But that can't happen; we're too stable, too responsible. As long as we remember that it's healthy to feel a little spooky down here, we'll be all right.

But the television set is a good idea. It keeps us in contact with the outside world, keeps it real. It'd be too easy to start thinking that the missile control center down here is the only real world and that nothing that happens up there really matters. . . . Bad thought!

The Four Horsemen . . . somehow these guys help you get it all out. I mean that feeling that it might be better to release all that tension, get it all over with. Watching The Four Horsemen, you're able to go with it without doing any harm, let it wash over you and then through you. I suppose they are crazy; they're all the human craziness in ourselves that we've got to keep very careful watch over down here. Letting it all come out watching the Horsemen makes it surer that none of it will come out down here. I guess that's why a lot of us have taken to wearing those "Do It" buttons off duty. The brass doesn't mind; they seem to understand that it's the kind of inside sick joke we need to keep us functioning.

Now that spiral thing they had started the show with—and the droning—came back on. Zap! I was right back in the screen again, as if the commercial hadn't happened.

"We are all in here together . . ."

And then a closeup of the lead singer, looking straight at me, as close as Jeremy and somehow more real. A mean-looking guy with something behind his eyes that told me he knew where everything lousy and rotten was at.

A bass began to thrum behind him and some kind of electronic hum that set my teeth on edge. He began playing his guitar, mean and low-down. And singing in that kind of drop-dead tone of voice that starts brawls in bars:

"I stabbed my mother and I mugged my paw . . ."

A riff of heavy guitar-chords echoed the words mockingly as a huge swastika (red-on-black, black-on-red) pulsed like a naked vein on the screen—

The face of the Horseman, leering—

"Nailed my sister to the toilet door . . ."

Guitar behind the pulsing swastika—

"Drowned a puppy in a ce-ment machine. . . . Burned a kitten just to hear it scream. . . ."

On the screen, just a big fire burning in slow-motion, and the voice became a slow, shrill, agonized wail:

"Oh God, I've got this red-hot fire burning in the marrow of my brain. . . .

"Oh yes, I got this fire burning . . . in the stinking marrow of my brain. . . .

"Gotta get me a blowtorch . . . and set some naked flesh on flame. . . ."

The fire dissolved into the face of a screaming Oriental woman, who ran through a burning village clawing at the napalm on her back.

"I got this message. . . . boiling in the bubbles of my blood . . . A man ain't nothing but a fire burning . . . in a dirty glob of mud. . . ."

A film-clip of a Nuremburg rally: a revolving swastika of marching men waving torches—

Then the leader of the Horsemen superimposed over the twisted flaming cross:

"Don't you hate me, baby, can't you feel somethin' screaming in your mind?

"Don't you hate me, baby, feel me drowning you in slime!"

Just the face of the Horseman howling hate—

"Oh yes, I'm a monster, mother. . . ."

A long view of the crowd around the platform, on their feet, waving arms, screaming soundlessly. Then a quick zoom in and a kaleidoscope of faces, eyes feverish, mouths open and howling—

"Just call me—"

The face of the Horseman superimposed over the crazed faces of the crowd—

"Mankind!"

I looked at Jeremy. He was toying with the key on the chain around his neck. He was sweating. I suddenly realized that I was sweating too and that my own key was throbbing in my hand alive. . . .

T minus 13 minutes . . . and counting . . .

A funny feeling, the Captain watching the Four Horsemen here in the *Backfish*'s missile control center with us. Sitting in front of my console watching the television set with the Captain kind of breathing down my neck . . . I got the feeling he knew what was going through me and I couldn't know what was going through him . . . and it gave the fire inside me a kind of greasy feel I didn't like. . . .

Then the commercial was over and that spiral-thing came on again and whoosh! it sucked me right back into the television set and I stopped worrying about the Captain or anything like that. . . .

Just the spiral going yellow-blue, red-green, and then starting to whirl and whirl, faster and faster, changing colors and whirling, whirling, whirling. . . . And the sound of a kind of Coney Island carousel tinkling behind it, faster and faster and faster, whirling and whirling and whirling, flashing red-green, yellow-blue, and whirling, whirling, whirling . . .

And this big hum filling my body and whirling, whirling, whirling . . . My muscles relaxing, going limp, whirling, whirling, whirling, all limp, whirling, whirling, whirling, oh so nice, just whirling, whirling . . .

And in the center of the flashing spiraling colors, a bright dot of colorless light, right at the center, not moving, not changing, while the whole world went whirling and whirling in colors around it, and the humming was coming from the dot the way the carousel-music was coming from the spinning colors and the dot was humming its song to me. . . .

The dot was a light way down at the end of a long, whirling, whirling tunnel. The humming started to get a little louder.

The bright dot started to get a little bigger. I was drifting down the tunnel toward it, whirling, whirling, whirling . . .

T minus 11 minutes . . . and counting . . .

Whirling, whirling, whirling down a long, long tunnel of pulsing colors, whirling, whirling, toward the circle of light way down at the end of the tunnel . . . How nice it would be to finally get there and soak up the beautiful hum filling my body and then I could forget that I was down here in this hole in the ground with a hard brass key in my hand, just Duke and me, down here in a cave under the ground that was a spiral of flashing colors, whirling, whirling toward the friendly light at the end of the tunnel, whirling, whirling . . .

T minus 10 minutes . . . and counting . . .

The circle of light at the end of the whirling tunnel was getting bigger and bigger and the humming was getting louder and louder and I was feeling better and better and the *Backfish*'s missile control center was getting dimmer and dimmer as the awful weight of command got lighter and lighter, whirling, whirling, and I felt so good I wanted to cry, whirling, whirling . . .

T minus 9 minutes . . . and counting . . .

Whirling, whirling . . . I was whirling, Jeremy was whirling, the hole in the ground was whirling, and the circle of light at the end of the tunnel whirled closer and closer and— I was through! A place filled with yellow light. Pale metal-yellow light. Then pale metallic blue. Yellow. Blue. Yellow. Blue. Yellow-blue-yellow-blue-yellow-blue-yellow . . .

Pure light pulsing . . . and pure sound droning. And just the *feeling* of letters I couldn't read between the pulses—not-yellow and not-blue—too quick and too faint to be visible, but important, very important . . .

And then a voice that seemed to be singing from inside my head, almost as if it were my own:

"Oh, oh, oh . . . don't I really wanna know . . . Oh, oh, oh . . . don't I really wanna know . . ."

The world pulsing, flashing around those words I couldn't read, couldn't quite read, had to read, could *almost* read . . .

"Oh, oh, oh . . . great God I really wanna know. . . ."

Strange amorphous shapes clouding the blue-yellow-blue flickering universe, hiding the words I had to read . . . Dammit, why wouldn't they get out of the way so I could find out what I had to know!

"Tell me tell me tell me tell me tell me . . . Gotta know gotta know gotta know gotta know . . ."

T minus 7 minutes . . . and counting . . .

Couldn't read the words! Why wouldn't the Captain let me read the words?

And that voice inside me: *"Gotta know . . . gotta know . . . gotta know why it hurts me so. . . ."* Why wouldn't it shut up and let me read the words? Why wouldn't the words hold still? Or just slow down a little? If they'd slow down a little, I could read them and then I'd know what I had to do. . . .

T minus 6 minutes . . . and counting . . .

I felt the sweaty key in the palm of my hand . . . I saw Duke stroking his own key. Had to know! Now—through the pulsing blue-yellow-blue light and the unreadable words that were building up an awful pressure in the back of my brain—I could see the Four Horsemen. They were on their knees, crying, looking up at something and begging: *"Tell me tell me tell me tell me . . ."*

Then soft billows of rich red-and-orange fire filled the world and a huge voice was trying to speak. But it couldn't form the words. It stuttered and moaned—

The yellow-blue-yellow flashing around the words I couldn't read—the same words, I suddenly sensed, that the voice of the fire was trying so hard to form—and the Four Horsemen on their knees begging: *"Tell me tell me tell me . . ."*

The friendly warm fire trying so hard to speak—

"Tell me tell me tell me tell me. . . ."

220

T minus 4 minutes . . . and counting . . .

What were the words? What was the order? I could sense my men silently imploring me to tell them. After all, I was their Captain, it was my duty to tell them. It was my duty to find out!

"Tell me tell me tell me . . ." the robed figures on their knees implored through the flickering pulse in my brain and I could almost make out the words . . . almost . . .

"Tell me tell me tell me . . ." I whispered to the warm orange fire that was trying so hard but couldn't quite form the words. The men were whispering it too: "Tell me tell me . . ."

T minus 3 minutes . . . and counting . . .

The question burning blue and yellow in my brain: WHAT WAS THE FIRE TRYING TO TELL ME? WHAT WERE THE WORDS I COULDN'T READ?

Had to unlock the words! Had to find the key!

A key . . . *The* key? THE KEY! And there was the lock that imprisoned the words, right in front of me! Put the key in the lock . . . I looked at Jeremy. Wasn't there some reason, long ago and far away, why Jeremy might try to stop me from putting the key in the lock?

But Jeremy didn't move as I fitted the key into the lock. . . .

T minus 2 minutes . . . and counting . . .

Why wouldn't the Captain tell me what the order was? The fire knew, but it couldn't tell. My head ached from the pulsing, but I couldn't read the words.

"Tell me tell me tell me . . ." I begged.

Then I realized that the Captain was asking too.

T minus 90 seconds . . . and counting . . .

"Tell me tell me tell me . . ." the Horsemen begged. And the words I couldn't read were a fire in my brain.

Duke's key was in the lock in front of us. From very far away, he said: "We have to do it together."

221

Of course . . . our keys . . . our keys would unlock the words!

I put my key into the lock. One, two, three, we turned our keys together. A lid on the console popped open. Under the lid were three red buttons. Three signs on the console lit up in red letters: "ARMED."

T minus 60 seconds . . . and counting . . .

The men were waiting for me to give some order. I didn't know what the order was. A magnificent orange fire was trying to tell me but it couldn't get the words out. . . . Robed figures were praying to the fire. . . .

Then, through the yellow-blue flicker that hid the words I had to read, I saw a vast crowd encircling a tower. The crowd was on its feet begging silently—

The tower in the center of the crowd became the orange fire that was trying to tell me what the words were—

Became a great mushroom of billowing smoke and blinding orange-red glare. . . .

T minus 30 seconds . . . and counting . . .

The huge pillar of fire was trying to tell Jeremy and me what the words were, what we had to do. The crowd was screaming at the cloud of flame. The yellow-blue flicker was getting faster and faster behind the mushroom cloud. I could almost read the words! I could see that there were two of them!

T minus 20 seconds . . . and counting . . .

Why didn't the Captain tell us? I could almost see the words!

Then I heard the crowd around the beautiful mushroom cloud shouting: "DO IT! DO IT! DO IT! DO IT! DO IT!"

T minus 10 seconds . . . and counting . . .

"DO IT! DO IT! DO IT! DO IT! DO IT! DO IT! DO IT!"

What did they want me to do? Did Duke know?

222

9

The men were waiting! What was the order? They hunched over the firing controls, waiting. . . . The firing controls . . . ?

"DO IT! DO IT! DO IT! DO IT! DO IT!"

8

"DO IT! DO IT! DO IT! DO IT! DO IT!": the crowd screaming.

"Jeremy!" I shouted. "I can read the words!"

7

My hands hovered over my bank of firing buttons. . . .

"DO IT! DO IT! DO IT! DO IT!" the words said.

Didn't the Captain understand?

6

"What do they want us to do, Jeremy?"

5

Why didn't the mushroom cloud give the order? My men were waiting! A good sailor craves action.

Then a great voice spoke from the pillar of fire: "DO IT . . . DO IT . . . DO IT. . . ."

4

"There's only one thing we can do down here, Duke."

3

"The order, men! Action! Fire!"

2

Yes, yes, yes! Jeremy—

1

I reached for my bank of firing buttons. Along the console, the men reached for their buttons. But I was too fast for them! I would be first!

0

THE BIG FLASH